What others have said about MISSING STICKS:

"What a great task you have attacked!....I had my eyes opened by your novel....If I were ever to be a hero I would like you to tell my story."

> Bud Berry, D-Day C-47 copilot in the 6th Serial, carrying elements of the 506th Parachute Infantry Regiment into Normandy.

"John Taylor has written an action–packed book as if he were imbedded with the Paratroopers and Glider troopers on D-Day!"

> Pat Macri, 101st Paratrooper who jumped with the 506th Parachute Infantry Regiment and fought all the way to Bechtesgarten.

"Amazing story." Matthew Kress, military historian.

Also by J. M. Taylor

Flash of Emerald

Behind the Green Water

Gulf Winds (due for release in 2009)

MISSING STICKS

J. M. TAYLOR

SCREAMING EAGLE PRESS
LUTZ, FLORIDA

Printed in the United States of America
First Edition

ISBN: 1879043009

EAN-13: 9781879043008

PREFACE

Faces streaked with soot or burnt cork, over six thousand paratroopers and glidermen of the 101st Airborne Division Screaming Eagles jumped or crashed into the swamps, canals, hedgerows and villages of the Cotentin Peninsular of France sometime after midnight on D-Day, the Sixth day of June 1944.

The Facts: Over four hundred C-47 Dakotas carried the Screaming Eagles through the darkness and into a thick cloud bank that night. One load of pathfinders crashed into the English Channel. Planes were seen to explode in midair. Others crashed and burned past all recognition, probably due to ground fire. Just before dawn, the initial glider serials slammed between the hedgerows, into trees and each other. Come dawn, eighteen planes, each carrying a stick of fifteen to twenty paratroopers, were missing.

I have listened to and read accounts written by and about the paratroopers and glidermen, and their aircrews, and wondered who the missing men were. What could, what would the missing men have done if they had made it safely to the ground? This is a novel about those missing men, their buddies and the friends and enemies they met on the ground, and dedicated to all of our Servicemen and Women who have sacrificed for our Nation.

Each and every character is a figment of my imagination, but represent those men who in reality secured the beach approaches for those who followed across Utah Beach on D-Day.

At the end of the day, remember this is a work of fiction. Please do not mistake any of the characters or incidents for the real men who were there, the actions they took, and the sacrifices they made.

God Bless Them All.

J. M. Taylor

ACKNOWLEDGMENTS

The stories in this book have their roots in events I have read or been told about, and a few personal experiences as a paratrooper, although with no combat jumps unless you count the jumps into an oxen-occupied rice paddy outside of An Khe or into a mountainous pile of briars at Phan Rang circa 1965-1966.

My thanks and gratitude to those troopers and air crews who are the basis for this story. In particular, I thank the two men who were there and who have provided me their insights into what really happened:

Patrick (Pat) S. Macri, 101st Airborne Division Signal Company: Pat participated in the Normandy and Market Garden assaults, the battle of Bastogne and was with the Division all the way to Berchtesgaden. On D-Day Pat jumped soon after midnight, intermingled with members of the 506th Parachute Infantry Regiment. He, with the other Screaming Eagles on the ground, initially fought as Infantry for their place in France and history.

Gerald (Bud) Berry: Bud was copilot to Major Howard U. Morton, Squadron Commander of the 91st Squadron, 439th Troop Carrier Group in the 6th Serial carrying the 506th PIR under Col. Robert Sink. His aircraft and passengers were designated as Stick #64, carrying elements of Dog Company, 506th PIR. The aircraft was identified by Tail Number 43-15213.

Captain Harold A. Capelluto was flying Bud's left wing in Aircraft 42-93095, Stick #66, with paratroopers from Headquarters Company of the 506th PIR on board. That aircraft, carrying the 506th HQ Company Commander, Capt. Meehan, was shot down with all aboard lost, one of the real Missing Sticks.

The photo above shows stick #56 of the 2nd Battalion of the 506th PIR receiving a final briefing by Lieutenant Bobuck. This aircraft and stick flew in the "V" formation just ahead of Bud and Stick #64. Note the Screaming Eagle patch and unit helmet designations were censored out of this Army photograph.

In addition, thanks to **John Witt, Matthew Kress** and **Tom Houlihan** for their sage advice on military matters and other stray facts.

This novel exists because my old friend and mentor, **Ann Turner Cook**, continued to correct my editorial mistakes and literary leaps of faith.

And finally, my dear wife **Peggy**, to whom I owe all.

Any remaining technical and editorial errors are mine alone.

J. M. Taylor

CONTENTS

SUPREME HEADQUARTERS
ALLIED EXPEDITIONARY FORCE

Soldiers, Sailors and Airmen of the Allied Expeditionary Force!

You are about to embark upon the Great Crusade, toward which we have striven these many months. The eyes of the world are upon you. The hopes and prayers of liberty-loving people everywhere march with you. In company with our brave Allies and brothers-in-arms on other Fronts, you will bring about the destruction of the German war machine, the elimination of Nazi tyranny over the oppressed peoples of Europe, and security for ourselves in a free world.

Your task will not be an easy one. Your enemy is well trained, well equipped and battle-hardened. He will fight savagely.

But this is the year 1944! Much has happened since the Nazi triumphs of 1940-41. The United Nations have inflicted upon the Germans great defeats, in open battle, man-to-man. Our air offensive has seriously reduced their strength in the air and their capacity to wage war on the ground. Our Home Fronts have given us an overwhelming superiority in weapons and munitions of war, and placed at our disposal great reserves of trained fighting men. The tide has turned! The free men of the world are marching together to Victory!

I have full confidence in your courage, devotion to duty and skill in battle. We will accept nothing less than full Victory!

Good Luck! And let us all beseech the blessing of Almighty God upon this great and noble undertaking.

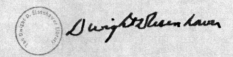

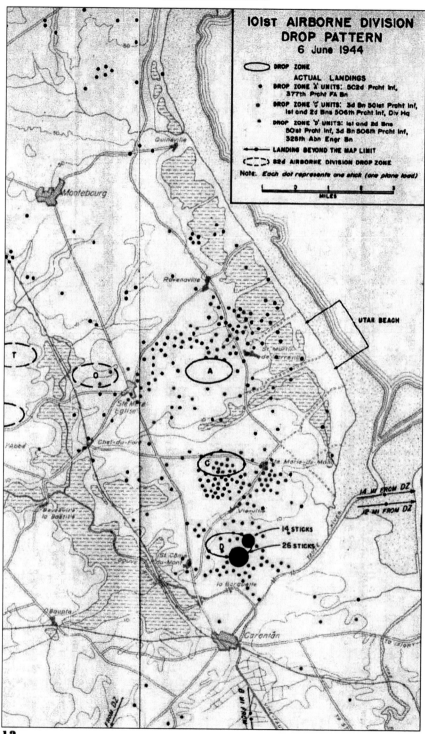

101st AIRBORNE DIVISION
DROP PATTERN
6 June 1944

DROP ZONE

ACTUAL LANDINGS
- DROP ZONE 'A' UNITS: 502d Prcht Inf,
  377th Prcht FA Bn
- DROP ZONE 'C' UNITS: 3d Bn 501st Prcht Inf,
  1st and 2d Bns 506th Prcht Inf, Div Hq
- DROP ZONE 'D' UNITS: 1st and 2d Bns
  501st Prcht Inf, 3d Bn 506th Prcht Inf,
  326th Abn Engr Bn

→ LANDING BEYOND THE MAP LIMIT

82d AIRBORNE DIVISION DROP ZONE

Note: Each dot represents one stick (one plane load)

MILES

UTAH BEACH

14 MI FROM DZ

12 MI FROM DZ

14 STICKS

26 STICKS

CHAPTER 1 - 101ST PATHFINDERS

Tech Sergeant Alex Pfister slammed back against the bulkhead as the C-47 tipped up on its right wing. Engines screaming, the plane banked back to the left, flinging him in the opposite direction. His helmet cracked against the bulkhead separating the jumpers from the radio operator's compartment. Whirling lights spinning inside his head joined the blinding flak explosions outside the fuselage. Dazed, Pfister's knees buckled and he slumped back down onto his seat as the plane jolted from side to side, violent explosions splitting the night sky. Lines of multicolored tracers reached up in slow, majestic arcs to race past the windows. He shook his head, trying to distinguish which lights were inside and which were outside his eyeballs.

Flames trailed from both engines. One engine coughed, backfired. The plane slewed, righted. The emergency bell added its shrill trilling to the screams of the engines. The crew chief jerked his intercom headset off and started shucking his parachute. "We're going down," he shouted. "Get ready to ditch."

The pathfinders followed his lead, ripped away their chutes and inflated their Mae Wests, ghostly yellow in the fire storm spewing from the dying engines. Pfister climbed clear, up on the metal seat as the navigator tossed the plane's life raft bundle toward the door. He hung onto the corner of the cockpit door and stripped off his parachute, leg bag, gas mask, everything he could rip loose with one hand as he clung to the bouncing plane with the other.

A red flare bloomed in the night, lighting the waves, close enough to touch.

Seconds after the crew chief's warning, the Dakota slapped a wave and bounced across the rough Channel waters, flinging men and cargo around the cabin. Pfister, last man in the stick, found himself jammed between an errant door bundle and the radio operator.

"I gotta get out," the kid screamed, still in his ungainly flak suit.

Pfister helped him unbuckle the suit, shoved the kid toward the door and checked the cockpit. Top hatch was open. Cockpit was empty. The cockpit instrument lights flickered, went dark. Pfister turned and splashed through the rushing water toward the rear door. Everyone else was gone. Engines were silent, no flak, just the sloshing of water. He climbed over a bundle abandoned in the aisle. At the door, sea water surged in, pushing him back into the plane. Sparks shot out from the red light by the door. It went coal mine dark inside the fuselage.

"Alex, come on," someone yelled.

Pfister grabbed a door bundle, pulled himself toward the door. A cord came loose in his hand. His heart stopped. In case of an emergency, the Eureka radar could be destroyed with an attached bundle of C-2. The cord he held in his hand was the pull for the friction igniter. The damp fuse sizzled at his feet.

Pfister leaped over the bundle, splashed through the knee-deep surge, grabbed the door frame and dived into the open water. Behind him a dim flash lit the water, followed by a muffled boom that vibrated through his body. Pfister held his breath as he sank, the pressure pounding at his ears. Too busy with the kid, he hadn't inflated his own Mae West. He ran his hands along the vest. Don't panic, he reminded himself. Shit. He was drowning in the English Channel. If ever, this was the time to panic, scream, shout. He finally found the tiny wooden toggle and yanked. The toggle slipped from his fingers. He felt the pressure growing as he dropped toward the bottom. Desperate, he started kicking, so disoriented in the cold, black water he didn't know if he was going toward the surface or down to his sure death. He frantically searched, found the toggle again. This time he squeezed the bit of wood with an iron grip and yanked again, harder.

The vest inflated with a gush of carbon dioxide and spun him around. Pfister felt the vest straps pull at his crotch. He slowly floated upward. His gut cramped as he fought the urge to suck in a great breath, knowing all he would get was a lung full of water. He kicked, praying this time the vest had him upright.

Was this what it had come to, after all he had endured, given up?

His head broke the surface and he gasped in a great, long gulp of salty air. He fumbled at his helmet strap, then realized he still had on his gloves. No wonder he had such a hard time with the toggle. He stripped the gloves off and slipped his chin strap free. His face dropped back under the surface, choked as his nose filled with water. He flung his helmet into the sea, wiggled clear of his web gear. With a gasp, he bobbed to the surface and almost as quickly sank back under. His carbine was already gone with the leg bag, so he emptied the extra ammo from his pockets as he floated back up, anything that would get him closer to another breath of air.

Finally he burst back through the surface. At the top of a swell he spotted heads bobbing in the raft, twisting in the choppy sea. Another wave topped with froth broke in his face, salt stinging his eyes. He blinked and the heads swirled away, swept out in the Channel by a gust of wind. The next wave washed over his head, and he slid back under the surface, gagging on the salt water filling his stomach. He ran his hand along the Mae West, found the inflation tube. When his head broke the surface he took in a big breath and blew into the tube, swelling the vest tight. The strap cut even deeper into his crotch, but at least his nose didn't dip under water with each swell.

Salt spray stung his eyes as he tried to kick up higher and find the raft. There, a glimpse, then the raft and his fellow paratroopers vanished into the inky darkness. On his own, Pfister started to swim. Awkward in the vest, he stopped, panting, coughing as he again sucked in more water than air. Which direction? Pfister flung his head side-to-side, clearing his eyes, trying to make sure he was headed toward shore. He swallowed his panic and paddled around in a circle. Over his left shoulder a stream of tracers ran up into the clouds. Land must be that way, somewhere under the tracers, in the darkness. An unexpected wave slapped his face. He coughed, hacked out the froth that splashed up his nose and spat it back into the Channel. The dying storm had left the Channel choppy, even close in to the Cotentin Peninsular. He churned the water until his arms and legs ached and his desperate strokes began to drain his strength.

Assigned to Division G2 as a translator and interrogator, Pfister's latest argument with his OIC had resulted in his final fall from grace. Tonight he was detailed to protect the pathfinders, his initial mission to keep the pathfinders safe as they set up the Eureka radar and lights to guide the rest of the Second Battalion of the 506th Parachute Infantry Regiment to a secure landing. Then he was to scout the lay of the land and report back to headquarters as the rest of the Division assembled. Those plans had gone to hell when the plane entered a cloud bank and emerged into concentrated antiaircraft fire.

Now he floated, alone, struggling to stay alive, likely within sight of the German beach defenses. The night around him was dark as

15

pitch as a squall pushed him around. He timed the swells, tried not to breathe when he slid down in a trough, his face dipping deep into the water. Through the salt mists he caught a glimpse of a distant light. The current twisted him around, and the light swirled out of his vision, his one tie with land—and life.

The tide must be pushing him. Where, he had no idea, other than he must be close to shore and the German positions.

Shivering, he sensed the current accelerate, as if he were in a narrow channel. In the glow of sporadic flak bursts he could see massive gun emplacements flowing past, quicker and quicker, then a low bank, spiny reeds silhouetted by a distant flare, low marshes. The tidal flow at the mouth of the Douve River had swept him away from the raft and the pathfinders, through the tidal marsh, then sucked him into the mouth of the river and up into the narrow channel.

He fought the urge to scream for help. Anyone who heard him would more likely shoot first. He stopped stroking and scanned the sky. A distant plane droned somewhere in the clouds. He peered though the thin mist over the water that surrounded him. Now quiet, only a whisper of chill water swirling around his body penetrated the silence. No gulls, not even the screech of a cricket. The water slowed, stilled. High tide. Soon it would turn, sweeping him out into the English Channel and in the midst of the oncoming fleet, the greatest armada since Spain had visions of grandeur. His heavy clothes pulled at him, fighting the life vest's buoyancy and his fading strength.

Unexpectedly, his foot hit bottom. Pfister stood, legs quivering with exhaustion. Chin deep, he felt around with his toes, numb as they were, searching for the slope that would lead him to dry land. He began to shiver. The cold had soaked though his impregnated jump suit, soaking him through his underwear to his bare skin. Now that he had stopped swimming, the chill cut through him like a razor-sharp trench knife. Still too dark to distinguish sea from sand except when a string of tracers reflected from the low clouds. No sounds of tidal flow, only his own feeble splashes.

Sensing a slight upslope, he struggled though the water, one slow step at the time. Hip deep, the tide began to pull at his body. Panting with exertion, he plunged against the outgoing tide until his outstretched fingers encountered a clump of cord grass. He had grown up hunting ducks in the Delaware marshes, swum the frigid waters off Lewes. Never had he been this cold. Never had he been alone in such a silent, forbidding sea. He pushed his dark hair back out of his eyes and searched the shoreline for the few feet he could see around him. Hair long, not cut short like his buddies, the overbearing G2 officer had ordered him to let it grow long in case he had the opportunity to question captured Germans. Friendly association, the officer had said with scarce hidden disdain toward Pfister's German Jew origins.

Teeth chattering, Pfister pulled himself up onto the marsh and slid forward into the grass. Voices floated across the marsh. He clamped his jaw tight, clenching his teeth. The voices came closer. Pfister burrowed down into the marsh grass, crawling away from the sound. Suddenly he dropped off into a shallow slew. The splash seemed to boom across the marsh.

The voices stopped. A crunch. A second, a cautious footstep, closer. A third. A yellow flashlight beam sliced the fog and swept across the top of the reeds.

Pfister let the cold water wash over him as he struggled to stay as low as possible and still hold his face out of the water. He felt himself sliding, pulled by the outgoing tide toward the voices. He reached up and rammed his numb fingers into a clump of marsh grass.

"Whoooo!" a man shouted.

Pfister braced for the bullet, instead felt the beat of wings as a grey heron burst from the marsh, inches from his fingers, splattering mud and bits of grass into his face as it cut through the light beam waving overhead. It took all of Pfister's willpower not to cry out. He wormed his free hand up to the collar of his jump suit and slowly unzipped the slit pocket. Afraid his fingers were too cold to hold on to the picked bone handle; he eased his jump knife out and wound the lanyard around his hand. He willed his hand to stop shaking, slid his thumb up and flicked off the safety, then down to the brass button release.

A man laughed. "So what is the matter. Are you afraid of the dark?" the man said in accented German. "I wager you pissed in your pants."

"So, Ruslan, the bird didn't scare you? Was that a mouse in your pocket that yelped?" answered a second voice. They both sounded like eastern Europeans, not native speaking Germans, probably Georgian if the order of battle reports were correct, part of the German 709th or 352nd Divisions, a mixture of Russians and Georgians.

Accents so thick, Pfister had trouble understanding their conversation. He lay still, listening. After all these years, he always suspected the atrocious accents of his students had tainted his ear, that he had lost touch with the idioms. Or, he thought, maybe these idiots just couldn't speak good German.

"I'm going back to the command post," the one called Ruslan said. "Look in the sky. See all the flak along the railroad track. Something big is happening tonight."

"I'll be there after I take a piss," the other said.

A single set of footsteps trooped toward him across the marsh. Closer, the marsh grass crunched. Suddenly a stream sizzled into the water beside Pfister's face. He pressed the release and the knife blade flicked out with a "swick," locking the razor sharp blade open.

The sentry turned at the noise. "What—?" he muttered.

Pfister gathered his legs under him and lunged up out of the water. He grabbed the surprised sentry by the collar of his long coat. The sentry gasped, fumbled for his rifle. He turned, twisted, tried to escape Pfister's tenuous grip; the sentry's attempt to yell muffled in the high collar. Pfister shook his head, blinded for an instant as the sentry's helmet cracked him across the nose and spun off into the marsh. The rifle dropped into the grass as the German clawed at Pfister's hand. Pfister dragged the sentry down, into the water, gripped the knife tight in his numb fingers and slashed with his fading strength.

The sentry jerked back as the blade sliced across his cheek. He flailed his arms, kicked. A shout started deep in the sentry's throat, but before it was more than a gurgle in the shallow water, the knife rasped across bone. Warm blood gushed over Pfister's fingers and the sentry slowly stopped struggling.

Pfister climbed up on to the marsh grass, squatted and looked around, shivering. No one else in sight. He scuttled along the path toward a darker mound. Rising up, he made out the glow of a light, faint behind a curtained entrance. He eased off the path to the right and stopped, shivering with cold. A triangular sign dangled from a single strand of barbed wire. He held the sign close to his face. "*Minen.*" He didn't need a degree in languages to figure that one out.

The intelligence reports warned the coastal defenses would be heavily mined. Pfister took advantage of a break in the clouds to stretch up and quickly scan the area, stark in the dim moonlight.

A rounded bunker stood atop the sand dune ahead. Triangular signs marked minefields on each side of the path that led to a wall, then on into the bunker.

"Shota." A head rose out of the trench. "Where are you?" the soldier called out in bastardized low German.

Pfister slowly lowered himself into the marsh grass as the soldier came down the path, rifle still slung over his shoulder. Heavy rain drops began to patter down, driven by the swirling wind into a wall of rain.

Pfister held his breath as the sentry stopped and stared across the marsh. He suddenly realized his jump knife was gone. Damn. He'd just have to kill this son of a bitch with his hands.

"Shota, you dumb peasant. It is raining too hard to stand out here. Besides, the Captain doesn't believe we will have trouble tonight, just more air raids. You stay if you like. I will go back." The sentry shook his head and turned back to the bunker, muttering into the mists.

Pfister took a deep breath, savoring the rain beating on his bare head. It had been raining outside Heilbronn the night the Nazis came and took his parents. Aunt Hilda had told him to run, stay in the fields. He had hid in a muddy field of ripe wheat, shivering in the driving rain until dawn. He never saw his mother, father or Aunt Hilda again. That's why he was a paratrooper, not some ass-kissing desk clerk. He had a score to settle, with all the Nazis—Germans, Russians or Georgians.

He stumbled back to the edge of the water, trembling with the cold and exhaustion. The dead sentry's body was gone, probably washed out to sea. His rifle lay half-hidden in the marsh grass. Pfister slid back the bolt and shook his head at the stupidity. The chamber was empty. No bullets in the well. He slipped the bayonet off the end of the rifle, felt its blade. To his surprise, the edge was sharp. Not razor sharp like his lost jump knife, but good enough. Rifle over his shoulder, Pfister trotted back to the wire marking the minefield, hacking the Mae West into strips as he ran. He stopped to grab the sentry's helmet and plop it on his head. Too large, it bobbed around on the wet webbing. He twisted the marker wire around the bayonet haft, snapping off a length of wire about a yard long. He snapped the bayonet back on the end of the rifle and wrapped the wire around his hands, padded with the remnants of the rubberized vest.

A concrete walled trench, sunk parallel to the water, guarded the entrance. He paused on the steps that led down into the trench. At the far end a curtain wavered in the wind, letting flecks of light flicker through, along with the smell of cigarette smoke. He edged up to the curtain, shivering as water dripped down from the awkward German helmet and ran down his neck.

He eased the curtain open. A single dim light bulb gave off just enough light to see two men standing inside. One leaned over a desk, talking over a telephone in muffled tones. The other soldier stood back against a wall, cigarette glowing in the shadows. Pfister backed away from the curtain and down the trench until he was back out in the driving rain.

"Ruslan," he called out. No response. He tried again, louder. "Ruslan." Ruslan was an old Georgian name. Had he heard it right? Was the son of bitch's name Joe?

The curtain fluttered and a glowing cigarette announced the man's exit, pausing to pull on a greatcoat. No ready weapon, poor light discipline, ungrammatical German, these soldiers must be some of the foreign deserters brought over from the Eastern Front to bolster the coastal defenses.

Pfister turned his back to the bunker and stood facing out to sea, rifle casually slung over his shoulder. He was taller than the man he had killed; always had thought of himself as tough kid considering the way he had grown up, an adopted German Jew in a strange neighborhood. He had played college football, topped off with the rigors of airborne school and months of training all across England. For Papa, he ready for this, and more. The improvised garrote stretched between his hands, Pfister ignored the oncoming man behind him. Pfister bent his knees and slouched, trying to mimic the dead man's appearance. Another gust of driving rain helped in the farce.

"Shota? Do you see something?" Ruslan stopped beside Pfister and blew a stream of cigarette smoke into the damp air.

MISSING STICKS

Just as the instructor had taught, Pfister whirled behind Ruslan and flipped the stiff wire over the sentry's helmet. The wire barbs grabbed on the sentry's collar, but Pfister spun on his heel, jerked the wire taut, arched his back and levered the struggling man up into the air. Pfister staggered as Ruslan's heels kicked against his calves, his rough hands clawed at Pfister's grip on the wire garrotte. A final frantic spasm, a tremor and the man stopped thrashing his arms and legs.

Pfister let the body drop and stood, hands on knees as he caught his breath. Killing was getting harder, not easier. He pulled off the sentry's greatcoat and rolled the still body over to work the dead man's arms out of the coat sleeves. The coat was thin and threadbare, probably scrounged from some other long dead soldier. He rifled the pockets and came up with a cartridge pouch and a pack of cigarettes. With a hurried glance back at the bunker Pfister slid the body into the water and watched it bob and twist in the current, then slowly drift out to join his companion.

Pfister slipped on the coat, loaded a stripper clip of bullets into the rifle and walked back toward the bunker. He stopped just before the curtain, stuck one of the German cigarettes in his mouth and shook the water out of his Zippo, blew on the wick until it took a spark. The flame, cupped in his trembling hands, wavered as he bent to shelter from the wind. He dipped the cigarette to the flame, drew in a lung full of smoke and coughed. Tasted like shit. He looked at the pack. "*Sonder Mischung.*" Special mixture was right, right out of a Turkish barnyard. He bent his head down, cupped his hand over the cigarette to hide his face and pushed the curtain aside.

The man at the table barely glanced up. Closer, Pfister could see he was dressed in riding breeches. A peaked hat sat on the table. He carried a Walther P-38 pistol holstered at his belt.

Now what? Pfister stifled his first impulse to shoot the Nazi in the back. Who knew what waited on the other side of the door set into the side wall—an exit, a room packed with real solders? He should have kept the garrote. He shivered as water ran down his legs and puddled around his feet, wondering if he could run the German through with the bayonet before he screamed for help. Pfister stifled a flinch when exploding ack-ack boomed outside, closer than before, so close the curtain quivered. The first waves of paratroopers were coming in.

"You. Come over here," ordered the German officer. And he was an officer, no doubt, with his sharp face and a distinct Austro-Bavarian dialect, probably Viennese. With a superior attitude to match.

Too late for the bayonet. Pfister ground out his cigarette in an overflowing ash tray and marched over to the table in his best mock-*Wehrmacht Heer* style. Halfway across the room he remembered the sloppy appearance of the Georgians floating out to sea, slowed his pace and slumped his shoulders, letting the German helmet slide down his forehead until the iron rim all but covered his eyes.

The officer handed Pfister the phone, hardly looking at him. "Here. Take any reports called in." He bent and listened to the speakers mounted on top of a radio in the middle of the table. Garbled voices distorted with the distinctive single-sideband tones muttered from the speaker. "Alert me if there is any reported activity in our sector." He pulled a long leather coat off a hook. "I will be out with the patrol. Fools are reporting parachutists inland. I think they have all had too much schnapps. Who would attack in this storm? But I will see." He spun on his heel and snatched opened the door.

Pfister held his breath when two men playing cards in the next room snapped to their feet. These were real German soldiers, combat awards dangling from their uniforms. The officer waved toward a door behind them. "Franz. Come with me." He pointed to the other man. "Willie. Check the generator. I want to make sure our radio does not fail us tonight." Both men grabbed their long coats. When one of the men opened the outer door, the muted sound of a generator rolled in with the chill draft. The captain looked back and Pfister involuntarily stiffened, then relaxed when the captain shut the door.

Pfister closed his eyes for a moment. He was still alive. He shed the oversized German helmet and ran his fingers through his wet hair, still shivering. He slid the rifle off his shoulder, propped it against the wall and let out his breath. A map lay on the table by the radio, corners curling in the damp. He unsnapped the bayonet and slid it over the map, as if the blade were to keep the paper flat. As he scanned the hand-drawn map annotations marking the trench lines and emplacements, he realized they detailed the entire German defensive line. He had been right in his thoughts about location. The bunker was at the far end of the 101st Airborne Division's objectives, on the south side of the mouth of the Douve River. He grinned. The planning map back in England, made mostly from aerial photos, was probably more accurate, except for the hidden tunnels. Lots of those. He stepped closer to see if there was anything of value on the map, debating his options. He never got a chance to exercise them before the door opened behind him. Pfister glanced over his shoulder and recognized the burly soldier, Willie, the one sent to check the generator, field cap cocked up on the back of his head.

"You fall in the water, Ruslan the Russian?" Willie asked with obvious contempt. From his appearance and dialect, he was neither an officer nor Viennese. More likely from around Stuttgart by his Swabian accent. And didn't know a Georgian from a Russian.

Pfister glanced down. Water dripped off the greatcoat and his pants, down over his jump boots, thankfully covered with mud. Were there more men on the other side of the door? He shivered again, suddenly remembering how cold he was. How alone he was.

"Hey. Ruslan. Got water in your ears?" Willie stepped up behind him and roughly thumped Pfister on his shoulder.

In his mind Pfister had scoffed at all those months of hand-to-hand combat training, thinking it a waste of time, especially for an ex-college grad student language instructor. He slid his hand to the map and grasped the cold bayonet handle, remembering how sharp the blade had felt. No ammo in the rifle, but a sharp blade. The Georgians had come from a strange stock.

"Ruslan?" The German roughly shook his shoulder.

Pfister whirled and slashed the bayonet like a saber. The soldier jumped back, but not quick enough. The blade whipped through the air, made contact, then spun out of Pfister's chilled fingers, through the curtain and into the night. The soldier screamed and clutched at his cheek. A heavy line of blood seeped through the skin.

Pfister charged, a good old fashion bull rush. By the time Pfister had snapped the soldier's neck, he had stopped scoffing at the hand-to-hand instructors' credentials. He quickly stepped to the door. The other room was empty. The only sounds were distant rapid fire guns, antiaircraft.

He took off the greatcoat and his own jump jacket, stinking with the CC-2 impregnating compound that was supposed to keep them safe from poison gases, then stripped off the soldier's tunic. He removed the awards and rank epaulettes and slipped the German's tunic over his wet undershirt until he was a damp imitation of a Georgian "volunteer" private. He hung his dripping jump jacket in the back of a dark alcove on the far side of the greatcoat, reluctant to give up his identity completely. He grinned when he spotted an open box of stick grenades in the alcove, all ready to stem the invasion. He would have to see they were put to good use. A distant light glimmered, hinting the alcove hid the entrance to a dark tunnel leading to the defense line. No time to go exploring now. Maybe he would get a chance to investigate later.

He grabbed the dead soldier by the arms, dragged the body out and rolled it into the marsh grass. Pfister figured when morning and the invasion came, one more dead soldier in the weeds would hardly count.

He stood for a moment in the swirling rain and looked toward the sounds of the sea. He could only imagine the thousands of boats and men churning through the dissipating storm toward Normandy. A noise back in the bunker startled him. Shit. He had left the rifle standing against the wall. He crept down to the curtain, searched the room. The tinny bell-like noise was the phone ringing. He slipped through the curtain, picked up the handset and answered in German.

"Hey kraut. I got a stick of dynamite to stick up your ass," boomed out of the earpiece.

Pfister looked at the phone and started laughing. "This is Kangaroo Two Charlie," he finally answered in English. "Where are you?"

Silence for a moment. Then, "Who the dickens is this?"

"I told your dumb ass, this is Kangaroo Two Charlie. I came down off the coast and I'm in a German bunker. Where—?"

Before he could finish an excited German voice broke in. "Sector three, we have paratroopers all around us. We are surrounded. What are our orders?"

Without thinking, Pfister responded in his best German. "Put down your weapons and surrender immediately. We are outnumbered. It is no use to fight any longer." He heard gunshots, then silence.

"Hey, Kangaroo, what was that all about?"

Pfister heard voices in the next room. "Got to go. You take care. Stay alive, trooper." He snapped to attention when the German officer strode in, reached up and snatched off his cap and smoothed his long wet hair. But not a shiver, the obnoxious Nazi bastard.

Pfister held his breath when the German took of his leather coat and hung it over the greatcoat. His own jump jacket hung not too far back in the darkness, festooned with a full color Screaming Eagle patch in all its glory.

The officer turned and caught Pfister staring at him. He frowned at the puddled floor, then at Pfister, shivering in his wet clothes. "Where are Willie and the other soldier?" the officer asked. A captain from the embroidered epaulettes, and one who had seen combat if that was really an Iron Cross that dangled from his jacket pocket. Not a man to be trifled with. Pfister prayed his transformation from helmet and greatcoat to stripped tunic and bare head was enough to suggest he was someone different.

Pfister looked the captain in the eye. "The transport dropped me off up the road, sir. I had to walk in the rain." He wiggled his toes in his water soaked boots, mind racing. "No one was here when I arrived, sir. The phone rang and I answered. Sector three is reporting paratroopers all around."

"Yes. Something is happening. Give me the phone." The captain snatched the handset away from Pfister and cranked the bell. "What is your name?"

Pfister stood straighter, as he imagined a soldier of the German army would do, even one of the "volunteer" Georgians, as he visualized the intelligence order of battle for the Axis troops. He snapped out an answer, not too sharp, he hoped, dredging up the name of a Georgian author from his academic days. "Private Zurab, sir. 795th Battalion, sir." Then he wondered if they had crashed in the German 352nd Division sector, or if the author was a woman. Was Zurab her given name or her surname? Ah, lying. Never leads to any good, he had always preached to his students. But the officer continued, not disturbed by the lie. Probably below the Nazi to read in Georgian.

"What is your specialty?"

Pfister gestured toward the phone. "Telephone operator, sir." That he had done before, something he knew how to do. Except before it had been in an American headquarters.

"Ah. Did you know Generalleutnant Hellmich?"

Pfister let a confused look cloud his face, not hard since he was trying to remember who commanded which German division, then took a stab. "No sir. Our division commander is Generalleutnant von Schlieben." He shook his head. "I was never in his presence, only heard his name spoken in the command center, sir." Pfister hoped the German captain attributed his shivering to the cold, and, if he was wrong about the generals, his ignorance.

This time it was the captain who stared into Pfister's eyes.

Pfister began to wonder if he had left some sign of being an American paratrooper show.

"Well, Zurab. You must have made a great enemy to be sent here. Now that you are here, do not make any mistakes. I think the Americans are coming. Soon. Understand?"

"Yes, sir."

The captain slowly nodded his head, turned away and spoke into the phone. "Yes. We are under attack by paratroopers. Not little toy men as some have reported, these are real paratroopers." The captain stiffened. "Yes, Major. We will hold our positions until relieved by the armored forces." Even in the dim light from the single bulb Pfister could see the man's mouth tighten to a grim line. He turned to Pfister and handed him the phone. "Write down any important reports. I will be above checking the gun positions. Do not be concerned. We will crush any invasion. The Furher himself has released the panzers. Soon the tanks will smash the invaders back into the sea."

Pfister's heart sank. Panzers. After the officer left, Pfister retrieved the oil cloth wrapped around his briar and his last pouch of Bond Street pipe tobacco from his jump jacket. Might as well enjoy himself before it was over. He wanted a smoke and couldn't take another of those Nazi turds. He cranked the phone once he had the pipe going and a pleasant billow of smoke surrounding the table. No one answered. That had to be good. But the officer had said the panzers were coming. What could he do to stop them. Damn little, stuck in here.

Now what? He ran his finger through his hair, squeezing out the water. What seeds of discontent could he sow before he had to fight his way to the American positions, where ever they might be?

An ornate alarm clock next to the radio, probably pilfered from a French home, ticked away, just past two o'clock in the morning.

MISSING STICKS

The shore bombardment was scheduled to begin at dawn, 0600 hours. Four hours of mischief left before he had to haul ass out of the target zone. First thing, find the radio antenna lead and cut it, far enough from the radio that the smart-ass captain wouldn't figure it out. Then, rig a few of the grenades and blow the place up. What else could he do? He might just wait here and make sure that Nazi son of a bitch didn't live through the night.

Papa would approve.

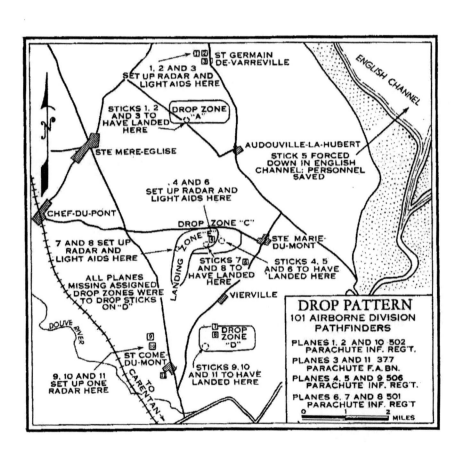

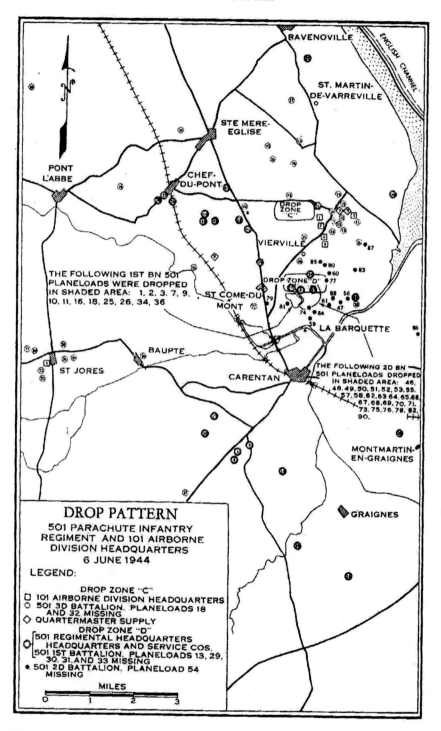

DROP PATTERN
501 PARACHUTE INFANTRY REGIMENT AND 101 AIRBORNE DIVISION HEADQUARTERS
6 JUNE 1944

LEGEND:

DROP ZONE "C"
- ☐ 101 AIRBORNE DIVISION HEADQUARTERS
- ○ 501 3D BATTALION. PLANELOADS 18 AND 32 MISSING
- ◇ QUARTERMASTER SUPPLY

DROP ZONE "D"
- ◎ 501 REGIMENTAL HEADQUARTERS HEADQUARTERS AND SERVICE COS.
- 501 1ST BATTALION. PLANELOADS 13, 29, 30, 31, AND 33 MISSING
- • 501 2D BATTALION. PLANELOAD 54 MISSING

MILES
0   1   2   3

THE FOLLOWING 1ST BN 501 PLANELOADS WERE DROPPED IN SHADED AREA: 1, 2, 3, 7, 9, 10, 11, 16, 18, 25, 26, 34, 36

THE FOLLOWING 2D BN 501 PLANELOADS DROPPED IN SHADED AREA: 46, 48, 49, 50, 51, 52, 53, 55, 57, 58, 62, 63, 64, 65, 66, 67, 68, 69, 70, 71, 73, 75, 76, 78, 82, 90.

CHAPTER 2 - 1/501ST PRCHT INF

Packed tight in the lumbering C-47, Corporal William Meade tapped his static line hook against the reserve chute strapped to his chest, keeping time with his foot on the cabin floor. Next to him, his buddy Larson puffed on a Lucky Strike, eyes squeezed shut. Meade tapped Larson's helmet with the metal static line hook. Larson started, coughed, as the smoke swirled and whisked down the aisle and out into the darkness.

"When'd you start smoking?" Meade yelled over the wind and the synchronized roaring of the big Pratt & Whitney engines. "You never smoked before, not even at Toccoa or Camp Mackall."

Larson ground the butt under his boot. "Tonight. Good a time as ever. Free cigs, so why not?"

"Why now?"

"Might be my last chance. I forgot to call Betty before we left Carolina, but at least I get to smoke at least once more."

Meade shook his head. "Betty who?"

"Betty Grable, dummy." Larson pulled a wrinkled photograph from his shirt, barely visible in the moonlight glinting in through the C-47's windshield. "Soon's I get back, gonna call her."

Meade laughed. "You and a million other GIs."

Out the side window the tiny blobs of the ships crossing the Channel and their silvery wakes gradually disappeared. The Channel faded into a dull grey mantle marked by bits of white, the moon reflected from white caps whipped up by the gusts left by the dying storm that had delayed their jump for a day. Meade spotted a flicker of light though the small window. Likely one of the cow islands, Jersey or Guernsey, or one of the signal ships the G2 briefer told them the armada would fly past.

"No use staring. We'll be there soon enough, Will." Larson tucked the photo back in his jacket, buttoned the top button and tightened his chin strap.

The leather chin cup scrubbed the stubble into Meade's chin when he followed suit and buckled his strap. Should have shaved closer. Should have gotten a job as a welder and stayed in the Savannah shipyard like his brothers. He ran his tongue around his mouth. It tasted like it was stuffed with moldy rags. He couldn't work up a bit of spit. Must be the air sickness pills the medic had given him, or just plain fear. No, not fear. Ike had told them "...he had full confidence in our courage." Meade had the sheet of paper from Ike in his pocket that said so. Still, his stomach churned.

Synchronized leaners, all in a row the paratroopers tilted toward the back of the plane as the pilots pulled up, climbing away from the water.

Hope Ike knows what the hell he's talking about.

The radio operator leaned though the cockpit door. He held up ten fingers, closed his fists and flashed them again. A cigarette stuck in the corner of his mouth danced as he shouted down the aisle, "Twenty minutes." Below, the glitter of the moon reflecting from the Atlantic slid beneath a thick mantle of clouds.

Meade pulled every strap tight once again, working down from his chin strap to the weapons bag lashed to his leg. The air whistling through the plane chilled the sweat running down his neck. His stomach climbed up toward his throat. The empty ice cream carton the crew chief had given each paratrooper to be sick in was somewhere under his butt, probably crushed in the metal seat, too late to fish out.

Swallow and sweat.

A distant line of tracers arced up, joined by another. The light show slowly disappeared into a bank of clouds. The C-47 and its load of paratroopers had climbed to around fifteen hundred feet and leveled out, finally, after all these years of training, somewhere over France.

Lieutenant Verona stood in the back of the plane, feet wide astraddle a bundle of machine guns, ammo and C-2 explosive, holding on to the static line anchor cable stretched down the length of the troop compartment. He screamed out over the bedlam, "Stand up and hook up." Verona had skipped "Get Ready." No worry. Meade had been ready from the moment Verona had led them to the crowded Merryfield Airport taxiway and found the Goony Bird with their number chalked on the side. Least their platoon leader could muster up enough spit to yell out the jump commands.

Meade and the rest of first and second squad lurched to their feet like one giant person, all squeezed together, loaded with guns and grenades and entrenching tools and ammunition and French money,

K-rations, canteens; all hung under and around the T-7 main parachute and reserve and the flapping Mae West life vests. And not to forget, Larson's wrinkled photo of Betty Grable. Meade pointed at Larson's chest with his static line hook. "Keep Betty safe, Lars," he shouted over the screaming wind.

Larson nodded, patted his jacket and grinned, his teeth glinting in the bright moonlight shining down through the astrodome.

Meade wished he had a picture to button by his heart. Too late. He had let the love of his life slip away back in L. A. Ironically, she was in movies. And he was a paratrooper about to jump into combat.

They staggered upright, Meade pushing the stick, the seventeenth man in line, one of many paratroopers of the 101st Airborne Division's 501st Parachute Infantry Regiment flying toward an unknown destiny. A Screaming Eagle. One who wanted to fly, out the door, out of the airplane threading between the wavering streams of tracers floating up around them, every hue of the rainbow as the festive looking tracers accelerated past.

Verona pointed at the jumpers. Every trooper leaned forward, eyes focused on Verona. One hand cupped, he yelled over the roar of the engines, "Hook up."

Meade snapped his static line hook over the anchor cable and ran his gloved thumb over the release button. Seated. He fumbled with the safety pin, awkward through the thick horsehide gloves.

"Check your equipment."

Meade gave up trying to insert the pin, pulled a bight in the static line and grabbed the loop. He rattled his static line hook on the cable, then slid his hands over his equipment and tugged on Larson's static line. Everything felt right. They were squeezed together too tight to tell for sure.

Larson twisted around to check Meade's static line, a big shit-eating grin on his face. Always fun and games.

"Sound off for equipment check."

Meade screamed, "Seventeen O.K.," and slapped Larson on the butt, followed by each man in front of him yelling out his O.K.

The engine noise changed pitch and they slid down, down into thick clouds. The glow from the moon evaporated. Meade's heart beat faster as they dropped into the inky blackness, unbroken except for the faint glow of the red light back by the jump door and the cockpit instruments up front. He took a deep breath, tried to relax.

The slip stream screamed past the open door as the plane nosed over into a shallow dive that was supposed to take them down to five hundred feet above the hedgerows of Normandy. Basketball sized balls of fire shot past the windows. The plane trembled, then shook harder, a vibration working up from the floor to rattle Meade's teeth.

He slammed into the bulkhead, and then bounced back against Larson as the plane lurched through the sky. They burst through the cloud bank to a circus spectacle of search lights probing the sky and lines of tracers flashing past.

Briefers had told them the plane would slow to jump speed. Somebody lied. The engines strained as the revs built to a scream, and the C-47 raced through the sky.

The light by the open jump door blinked red. Four minutes to the jump. Where had the twenty minute warning gone?

A rattle of machine gun fire raked through the thin skin, stitching an irregular row of ragged holes above the windows, more holes than tracers. A break in the clouds and the moon shined through the bullet holes, an array of tiny silver overhead lights. The plane lurched from side to side. Tracers wove around them, ripping into the wings. A thunderous explosion tore a flaming hole in the black sky just off to the side, sending a blinding flash back though the windshield. The plane shuddered. Then everything steadied, wings level. Meade thought for a moment they were clear.

He blinked furiously, trying to regain his night vision. Had they sounded off for equipment check? Meade's mind was a blur.

"Jump, jump," someone was yelling. The plane drilled on through the night; steady on course through all the ground fire. Meade twisted to peer into the cockpit, lit with the glow of tracer fire reflected from the low clouds. The radio operator lay sprawled on his back across the throttles, gigantic in his flak suit. Smoke whipped from the cigarette still pursed between his lips, the glowing tip fed by the wind whistling though jagged holes in the windshield. Meade stepped past the empty radio compartment and leaned into the cockpit as far as his static line would reach. The pilot lay slumped against the left side of the cockpit. Meade pulled against his static line, moved closer to the pilot, the wind screaming through the windshield whipping tears from Meade's eyes. He reached out, touched the pilot. The pilot's head fell forward, helmet askew, arms hanging by his sides.

On the other side of the cockpit—Meade shook his head, blinked away his tears, unwilling to believe what he had found—the copilot had no face. The Dakota's engines strained, throttles held forward by the weight of the radioman. The plane slowly rolled in a gentle bank, the tilt of the low clouds above hinting at the angle of the turn. Ahead a solid wall of tracers filled the windshield. The engines' synchronized roar picked up an odd tone, the beat of the engines going up and down.

Got to get out. Meade reached across the pilot and toggled the green light on the overhead control panel.

Meade pulled himself back to his feet and turned to see the line of paratroopers pouring out the door. Meade waddled after them, half hanging from the anchor cable as he stumbled over a crumpled body. A static line, stretched taut between the anchor cable and a motionless trooper on the floor, blocked his exit. Meade pulled his trench knife from the sheath strapped to his boot and hacked through the thick line in one frantic slash. Free, he staggered as another burst of flak shook the plane.

One man waited at the door. "Come on, you jerk. Can't stall all night. Betty's awaiting," Larson screamed, turned and dove out into the night.

Meade followed, all his training taking over as he instinctively locked his body, knees together, chin down, arms in tight. Out the door and a giant hammer slammed him against the side of the plane. His helmet thumped down the aluminum fuselage as he spun in the slipstream and past the tail wheel. The harness straps bit into his body and, with a tremendous jerk, his chute snatched him free of his static line, his last connection with the Dakota and its dead crew. He fell, floating for a moment. A blur of tracers flashed past. Overhead his white canopy billowed, lit by a high flak burst. He looked toward his feet, through the blackness, wondering how high he was. Then he hit with a splash and the numbing shock of cold water.

His feet slammed into a soft bottom. The cold water slapped him in the face, stinging like a terribly bad belly flop in the pond back home. His face went under water as he fell forward, his mouth and nose full of water. He struggled upright in the muck, spat out the nasty water. His feet slithered, slipped in the muddy bottom. His head went back under. Waving his arms, he struggled to get his balance, finally getting his head out of the water long enough to take a deep breath. He staggered in the neck deep water and gasped for air, trying to stay upright. He sputtered and yanked at the straps and buckles as his risers pulled at his shoulders, the white canopy now a dirty grey in the water.

His chute caught in the current, pulled him forward, trying to drag him under. Surprised his trench knife was still in his hand, Meade sliced through the risers. He hacked away as the current sucked at him, the razor-sharp blade shedding the Mae West, weapons container, belly and leg straps. Almost floating with all the extra weight gone, he stopped slashing at his gear and concentrated on breathing. He felt several stings where the cold water washed over cuts on his arms and legs. A wonder he hadn't cut his own throat.

His pop had warned him, told him not to join the Army, don't volunteer for the paratroopers, for God's sake, be anything but an infantryman, pop had repeated over and over between coughing fits, wracked by the scars left by the poison gas that had wafted into the

AEF's trenches. Meade spit out a mouthful of muddy water, tainted with a hint of gasoline. At least it wasn't poison.

He hoped.

Meade shook his head to clear his eyes. Oily black water, dark banks on each side, maybe thirty feet across, marked what back home they would call a big creek. Rain drops pattered down, speckling the water's surface. He wasn't in the Atlantic or the Channel, thank God. Water ran down out of his helmet liner as he struggled through the mud and slithered up the bank. He flinched as tracers rose to the sky, an antiaircraft gun position so close he could hear the men shouting, in German.

What now? Rush them with his trench knife? Meade started to shiver. Whatever he did, he wasn't going to get it done lying on a muddy bank in the rain. He crawled into a thicket of brush and searched the black night around him. Nothing. He climbed to his knees and unfastened his chin strap. Thick trees broke the uneven horizon, spiked with flowing lines of tracers rising up all around. The racket beat on his ears. Overhead dark blurs, airplanes, some streaming fire, roared past. One screamed just feet over his head going the opposite direction from the others, some of them barely skimming the tree tops.

Meade wondered where he was. His battalion was supposed to capture and hold the bridges north of Carentan, hold any armor threat back away from the beaches. With the air crew dead, they had surely flown far from the planned drop zone. But where?

He climbed to his feet and edged away from the incessant roar of the antiaircraft gun, turned and crept along the edge of the narrow waterway. A shadow moved to his front. He stopped. Meade held the knife ready, honed blade twinkling as it reflected tracers rising from the far side of the trees.

"'Bout time you found me. Some damn squad leader you are, for Christ's sake," a voice whispered from the trees.

Meade dropped to a crouch.

"Up here, dammit."

Meade stared at the dripping trees until he could see a shadowy form swaying back and forth. "Jeeze, Lars. Scare me half to death."

"I'll kick your ass half to death if you don't cut me down."

Meade sheathed his knife, grabbed a dangling leg and hauled Larson down, tree limbs creaking, smaller branches snapping, until the chute broke free and the two men crashed to the ground. Larson's chute gently settled down over their heads, shutting out the fleeting bits of moonlight.

Footsteps. "Be still." Meade whispered. They lay entangled under the canopy as the steps approached, then passed. Meade froze, listening to his heart pound. Several more men marched past, muttering in German. Thank God, Larson had the luck of the draw to have a brown canopy.

They lay for another minute, ears straining. No more footsteps.

"They gone?" Larson finally asked.

"Hope the hell so," Meade whispered back and pulled the canopy clear. "Got your gear?"

"Sure," Larson replied. He jerked the end of his waist band free and unstrapped his Thompson, then worked at the remaining snaps and straps. He undid his crotch straps and stretched back with a groan. "Got a Thompson and a pistol and a bunch of .45 mags for them." He picked up a bag that had dropped from the loosened crotch straps. "Plus a bag of Gammon grenades."

Meade inspected his arms and legs in the faint light. Nicks, no more than scratches. Damn lucky, the way he was flailing around with the knife. "Landed in the water. Had to drop all my stuff to get out." He took the bag of grenades and draped the strap over his shoulder. "Give me the pistol. Got a round in the chamber?"

"Damn straight." Larson handed him the pistol and a pair of magazines.

Meade dropped the magazines in his pocket and thumbed back the hammer on the .45 pistol. "The antiaircraft gun crew must have seen us come down. Let's get away from here, find the rest of the outfit." He started along the side of the waterway, away from the gun emplacement.

With a clack Larson chambered a round in his Thompson and followed. "Are we close to Carentan?" he asked.

"Not likely. Air crew was all dead in the cockpit. I'm pretty sure we overflew the DZ by a ways." Meade stopped. Ahead a road rose up from the marshy ground, leading to a cluster of houses. He eased forward until he was at the base of a signpost. A flash of gunfire from a quad-barreled AA gun on the far side of a hedgerow lit the letters on the sign. "Baupte," he spelled off. Meade sniffed, sulfur and tobacco smoke. He turned to see that Larson had crept up beside him, cigarette glowing under his cupped hand. "Where the hell is Baupte? You remember it from the briefings? Reckon it's close to Carentan and the bridges?"

Before Larson could answer, a door opened, spilling out a splash of light and low guttural voices. Meade dropped to the ground with Larson close on his heels. Two men filed out, leaving the house dark.

"I got not a clue where we are," whispered Larson. He ground the cigarette into the packed dirt. "And I ain't going to ask them for directions."

An engine started. A thin light glowed between two buildings and a vehicle nosed out. Tiny cat eye lights turned toward them.

Meade rolled off the road and into the ditch, sliding down a muddy bank to the bottom and bumped against Larson, already burrowed down in the thin damp grass.

The vehicle stopped, motor rumbling.

"Looks kind of like a halftrack." Larson whispered as he crawled back up to the edge of the ditch. "I can see helmets sticking over the top. Come on. Let's haul ass."

Meade's heart throbbed in his chest. The aircrew in the cockpit, the trooper in the aisle, all dead. Time for someone to pay the price.

"Hold it. Thompson ready?"

Larson stared at him. "Yeah. What? We going to take on that tin car? That's probably a machine gun on top." He nodded with his head as the armored halftrack lurched forward. "See, the gun, toward the front."

The halftrack stopped and another German ran out of the house, pulling on a long coat against the sporadic drizzle.

"Yeah, I see the damn gun, but nobody's manning it. Must be too much rain for them." Meade dug one of the Gammon grenades out of the musette bag and unscrewed the cap. "Let's see if these sacks of shit really work." He looked at Larson. "Ready to start this damn war?"

Larson scrambled over to a low wall and brought his Thompson up. He looked back and nodded. This time he forgot to grin.

On his knees, Meade lobbed the grenade high in the air, underhand like a softball, and dropped flat to the ground, pistol in his left hand. For a moment he thought he had tossed the grenade too far. A thump, then a scream started, cut short as the grenade exploded with a muted roar. Pieces of metal whistled over his head. One man staggered from around the side of the car. An ear-rattling burst from Larson's Thompson knocked the German down.

For a moment it was quiet except for the crackle of burning papers and a low moan. On the other side of the trees the antiaircraft gun opened back up as a plane approached, low, engines straining.

Meade stood, trotted over to the armored car. He stuffed the pistol in his waist band and snatched up a bolt action rifle similar to the old American '03 from the dead man's hand, then pulled off a leather cartridge belt heavy with stripper clips.

Overhead the plane crossed under the moon, heading against the flow of the other planes and into the teeth of the ground fire. Tracers raked the plane and it staggered, seemed to hang in the sky. Flames streamed from one engine.

A burst of submachine gun fire rattled off the cobbles from the alley between the houses, sending sparks and ricochets toward them. "I'm getting out of here," Larson shouted. He turned and ran down the shoulder of the road and into the ditch.

"Lars. Come back." Meade dropped to a knee and returned fire with the rifle, aiming toward the muzzle flash. He was rewarded by a short scream. "They're shooting our guys out of the sky. Let's go get those guns. Come on. We can do it. Betty will wait for you, man. Kill every son of a bitching German between here and Berlin." He worked the bolt as he ran toward the armored car, jerked the rear door open and dragged out a body hanging off the machine gun. "Get in here and hot wire this buggy, Lars. You told me there was nothing in Phoenix City, Alabama you couldn't start, key or no key. Come on. Get it going."

A rifle fired from down the road. Meade found the pistol grip on the machine gun and triggered a burst, startled at the rate of fire, sound like ripping a heavy piece of canvas, twice as fast as their machine guns. Another explosion—no, the halftrack engine backfired, caught. Meade held on to the machine gun as Larson drove hell-bent through the small town, careening between the houses and past a church, treads grinding away at the cobbled streets of the town. A machine gun opened up when they came up to a railroad crossing. Meade swung the gun around and fired a long burst in return. The machine gun went quiet. The halftrack veered off the road and lurched over a set of tracks. Larson had chosen the rail bed. So be it.

Their war had started.

CHAPTER 3 - 2/506TH PRCHT INF

Corporal Lou Keller sprawled on the cabin floor, surrounded by the rest of his stick. They lay all in a tumble, tossed around inside the Dakota like a pile of wet rags. Everything had been going fine until the jump light flicked from red to green in the jinking aircraft. Then everything that could went wrong. An explosion outside the door flung Lieutenant Bartlett, their jumpmaster, and the crew chief standing behind him back against the rear bulkhead and scattered the rest of the stick around the cabin, mostly on the floor with Keller.

Keller struggled to his feet. The Lieutenant didn't move. Splattered blood shimmered in the glow of the warning light. The crew chief struggled to untangle his safety line from the Lieutenant, finally unsnapping the line from his harness. The next man in line, Sterling, their medic, grappled with a bundle jammed in the door.

Bullets rattled against the plane like hail. The jump light exploded into fragments. A lurch and Keller went down on all fours, grabbed the edge of a seat and struggled back up.

Someone screamed, "Go, go, go."

Sterling finally freed the bundle, kicked it into the night and leaped through the door.

The remaining bundle blocked the narrow space between the seats. The next man in line shoved at the bundle, a compact package of bags packed with a mortar tube and base plate and parachute. The bag's static line looped across the aisle, apparently snagged on the seat supports.

The crew chief climbed to his feet shaking his head, blood streaming down his face, screaming into the intercom. The plane steadied. The crew chief grabbed the overhead cable to steady himself and faced the paratroopers. "We missed the drop zone. Pilot's dead. Copilot's going back around. Go when I give you the word." The crew chief disconnected the bundle's static line, kicked it out the door and leaned out into the airstream. He turned toward the paratroopers, mouth open to shout. The plane lurched, hard up on one wing. The plane snapped back on the other wing in a steep, diving turn, flinging the crew chief out the door.

Keller slammed back onto his butt, clawing at the vomit-slick seat, finally used his static line to haul himself upright. A stream of orange-red exhaust flashed past the window—an airplane going in the opposite direction. Keller's plane reared back, climbing.

"Get out, jump," a voice screamed in his ear.

Keller, the biggest man on board by a head, heaved the two men between him and the door forward. They both stumbled over Lieutenant Bartlett, motionless on the floor. Keller scrambled over the pile of bodies, dove through the door and out into the dark night. A familiar jerk and he was dangling from his risers, spinning around and around. He looked up, relieved to see his canopy swirling overhead, when a roar passed under him. He glanced down to see a dark blur, another plane with white invasion stripes clearly marked on its body and wings, flash under his feet. The turbulence sent him up, up, until he thought he was going to flip all the way over the apex of his canopy. His stomach flipped at the top of his swing. Weightless for an instant, he fell, bottomed, then rose up again like he was on a giant swing set. At the top of his swing he stared down to see a black monster coming at him, another plane. He squeezed his eyes shut, felt a rush of air, then slammed into the ground. Perfect three point PLF—feet, butt, head.

Keller took a deep breath and opened his eyes. He lay on his back as a low-flying Dakota passed over him, for an instant blotting out the faint outline of the moon glowing through the clouds.

Overhead another plane screamed past in a steep turn away from converging streams of tracers, then exploded. A black blur tumbled out of the wreckage. A parachute blossomed and quickly dropped down on the far side of a hedgerow. As his senses returned Keller could hear something pattering down all around him. One of the somethings clanked against his helmet and bounced away. Another lump thumped down on his leg. Expecting, for some reason, a cold piece of hail, he picked it up, then quickly tossed it aside as the sharp fragment burned through his leather gloves and seared his fingers. Most likely from the exploding German flak rounds. His ears finally registered the cacophony of fire rising up all around him. The slow bark of an 88, the snarl of a light machine gun, the roar of a quad 20mm. In the occasional pauses, an irregular crackle of rifle fire punctured the night. Then the smells registered. Burning horsehide from his gloves that reminded him of branding ponies, and an unidentifiable smell, maybe the impregnated suit smoldering. Vomit. And something else. Once a cowboy, Keller recognized the other. Cow shit. He had landed in a pasture, once again in a pile of shit, the story of his life.

The crack and whiz of a bullet over his head reminded him he wasn't in Texas. He yanked his belly band out of the buckle, unsnapped the left side of the reserve from the D-ring and dug at the leg straps, untangling the Mae West, weapons container, musette bag and the rest of his gear from the parachute harness. He rolled to his stomach and contemplated the pile of gear. Before he could decide what to take and what to leave, a second burst of fire cut through the heavy night air. He snatched up the weapons container, quickly assembled his M1 rifle and draped the musette bag around his neck. Ammunition? Back at the departure airfield he had stashed two clips in the container, but they were nowhere to be found. He patted his sides, relieved to locate the two cloth bandoleers of .30-06 draped around his neck, the cartridge belt with its pockets stuffed with ammo and a canteen of water around his waist. He slipped a clip out of the cartridge belt, loaded the rifle and thumbed the safety off.

Voices, German, yelled across the pasture. He unfastened his chin strap and pushed his helmet back. A herd of dark figures slipped along the trees. Beyond them a carbine spat out a welcome with a rapid burst of fire, the distinctive pops softer than the sharp cracks from the German rifles. The Germans answered the carbine with a ragged volley of bolt action rifles, the click of the bolts clear in the night, then yelling, again in German.

Keller dug his elbows deep into the soft ground and picked out one of the blobs. He fired. A scream pierced the night. He swung the rifle, fired again, swung, fired again. Like a herd of deer running up McKittrick Canyon, the Germans broke for the far end of the pasture. He fired again, not sure if he had hit anything. He hugged the ground as they shot back. Rounds snapped overhead, all too close.

Hell fire. Deer never shot back. Not even Texas deer. He crawled away from the Germans, the night blacker than an abandoned silver mine. Reaching a dark mass, he slid into a shallow ditch alongside one of the hedgerows the briefers had talked about, except the hedgerow was thicker and higher than they had said. He rose to a crouch and hurried alongside the impenetrable thicket, away from the Germans. A few steps down the row he came to a break in the hedge blocked by a wooden gate. He vaulted over the gate, keeping close to the hedgerow, and crept forward. A limb crackled in the inky blackness. Keller stopped, tried to slow his breathing before he hyperventilated and passed out. Air was too thick. He never thought he'd miss the high desert. Take it easy, like a stalk, he reminded himself.

Flak bursting in the sky lit rows of men standing stock still. He blinked, let his eyes flow over the scene until he realized he was crouched in the edge of an orchard, surrounded by rows of low trees. He slowly stood. The trees were maybe only a year or two old, newly planted and only three or four feet tall. Not very dangerous.

He looked over the tops of the trees, pretending he was far up on a mountain, letting his eyes sweep across the trees to the hedgerow where the trees towered in comparison to the orchard. The dark folds of a parachute canopy emerged from the shadows, draped down from the upper limbs of a tree. He slipped down the orchard row and moved closer. An empty harness dangled about ten feet off the ground. He stopped, looked out of the sides of his eyes. There. A round shape in the midst of the hedge. He slowly slid his hand down to the cartridge belt where he had stashed his cricket. Dumb fool thing, he had thought when they passed them out. A toy. Now he wished he could find it before the fellow with the carbine decided Keller was one of the Germans. He shook his glove off and wiggled his fingers into the first aid pouch where he had stashed the toy with his extra plug of Beechnut. He pulled out the clicker and snapped it once, released it for the return click. He took a deep breath, waiting.

He was answered by a crash of breaking tree limbs. The round shape resolved into a helmet moving toward him with a one-sided gimp.

"Flash," a hoarse voice whispered.

Keller's mind went blank for a moment. Then he remembered the reply. "Thunder."

Footsteps crunched through the edge of the trees toward him, Keller slid the rifle around and up as the figure approached.

"Damn glad to see you, soldier," the man said with an unmistakable Georgia drawl. "With that eagle on your shoulder and that play-toy you're clicking, I'm guessing you're 101st."

Keller leaned closer. The man facing him was a Lieutenant. "Yes sir. Corporal Keller, sir. Second of the 506th. What unit you with?"

"My name's O'Shey. Headquarters, third battalion, 505th. Eighty-second." The Lieutenant slapped a fresh magazine in his carbine. "Where'd those German's go?"

Keller motioned back across the fence. "I shot at them and they took off across that pasture."

"Did they have an American with them?"

"Couldn't tell, sir."

"I heard an American voice and a Thompson firing. They came across the fence about the time I got out of my chute. I was hung up in the damn tree so I opened up on them. Somebody, you I guess, started shooting behind them and they took off. Did you hear what they said?"

"Heard them, but I don't speak German. I just shot at them."

"Well, let's go back and check. We need to get as many people together as we can, then start raising some Cain. You with me?"

"Sure, sir. I'll cut across the field and get the rest of my equipment." Keller followed O'Shey to the gate, back over the fence and along the hedgerow. Searching for his gear Keller ran across the empty field toward a dark pile. The pile turned out to be a dead German, his flesh already chilled and wrinkled with the morning dew. A few steps away a second pile moaned when Keller touched it. Keller held his rifle on the German and rolled him over with the toe of his boot.

The German yelped and grabbed Keller's leg, jerking it out from under him. Keller's rifle flew out of his hand when he hit the ground. He rolled up, pulled his bayonet from the scabbard at his belt as the German kicked his arm. The bayonet flew off into the darkness. Time to be done with this. Keller grabbed the German's head and gave it a sharp twist, a quick snap like wringing a chicken's neck before Sunday dinner. The German collapsed to the ground.

Keller took a deep breath, his heart pounding in his chest. Tracers streaming overhead reflected in the dead man's eyes, almost a friendly twinkle. Keller shuddered, found his rifle in the dew-damp grass. To hell with the rest of his gear. Maybe he'd find it later. He wiped his hands on the German's tunic, stood and trotted after O'Shey. Germans, not deer. They shot back.

When Keller reached O'Shey, the Lieutenant stopped, held up his hand. Ahead loud voices argued in German.

The Lieutenant crept forward and knelt on a knee.

Keller wiped the dew from his recovered M1 as he followed O'Shey and knelt beside him. Through a narrow opening Keller saw three figures standing by a low wall. One spoke German, and then switched to English. "What is your unit? Where do you come from? Are you many?"

"I come from kiss-my-ass, kraut, along with ten fucking thousand of my buddies."

The interrogator swung a rifle and the man went down.

"Can you take the one on the left from here?" whispered O'Shey. He raised his carbine to his shoulder.

Keller followed suit, settled his elbow on his knee and found the German in his sight. "Easy."

"Do it."

Keller fired an instant after O'Shey's carbine coughed. The two Germans went down. Keller's target stayed down, but the one on the right struggled back to his feet. Before Keller could shoot, the third man rose up and the two went back to the ground.

Keller scrambled to his feet and followed the Lieutenant's tortured gait to the three men on the ground.

"Freeze," O'Shey barked.

The man they assumed was an American struggled to his knees despite the command.

"What's your name, soldier?"

"Stimson, O' Duce, commo platoon. God dammit, don't shoot me," the man answered.

"Krauts dead?" O'Shey asked.

Stimson held up a trench knife. "One, I know for sure." He nudged the second body with his boot. "Dead like a doornail." He pulled a Thompson out from under one of the bodies and held it up like a trophy. "Son of a bitches thought they were going to get my Tommy. Got the jump on me when I was changing magazines. Tough shit on them." Stimson stopped, sniffed. "Speaking of, which one of you been rolling around in the barn lot?"

Keller spoke up. "Just me. I landed in a cow pie." He knelt by the Germans and took a pair of stick grenades out of one boot. "How do these things work?" he asked. "All I could grab was a musette bag stuffed with K-rats, francs, socks and extra Beechnut. Grenades, rest of my gear is somewhere yonder in the pasture."

O'Shey leaned closer in the dark. "Potato masher? Unscrew the cap on the end of the handle. Supposed to be a string you pull, and then throw."

Keller stuck the stick grenades under his belt.

"Stimson, what you got?" the Lieutenant asked.

"Tommy and magazines." Stimson draped a magazine pouch around his neck and over one shoulder. "And this." He wiped his trench knife on one of the German's tunics and stuck it back into a sheath lashed to his boot. "Got a reel of field wire and a EE-8 field phone in my backpack. Kraut took it, but it's probably around here somewhere."

"Take it if you can find it, but we got to get a move on, fighting to do." The lieutenant took a step back and looked around them. "Stimson, you watch our back. Keller, take the lead and find out where the path along the wall takes us. We got to get some more people together."

Stimson shook his head. "Whoa. Sir. I ain't with your unit. I got to find my own."

The lieutenant stared at Stimson for a moment. "I'm Lieutenant O'Shey, soldier. These may be butter bars on my shoulders, but I jumped into Sicily as a buck sergeant, and earned my commission the hard way. I lived through the shittiest jump you could ever dream of, and then marched across Sicily. I know what paratroopers are supposed to do. That's kill krauts. If you really are airborne, quit your bitching and follow me."

Stimson grinned at him. "Thought you looked too mean to be a fuzzy faced L. T. Airborne, sir."

"Damn right." O'Shey motioned toward a cow path alongside the low wall. "Head out, Keller."

The path led Keller to a farm road marked with wagon ruts. Another hundred yards and he ran into hard pack wide enough to be called a real road, marked with a signpost.

"Keller," the Lieutenant called out. "Hold up."

Keller heard the distinctive click of a Zippo. He glanced back. Stimson stood watch at the edge of the road while the Lieutenant crouched against the wall, the flame of his lighter reflecting off a map sheet. A snap and the flame disappeared.

O'Shea motioned the two men over. He pointed to the post. "We're not even close to Ste. Mere-Eglise, my unit's objective. Sign says Baupte one direction and Carentan the other. Let's head toward Carentan. We should find some more of our guys along the way. I've seen a couple of planes dropping around us. But be careful, Keller. Don't walk us into an ambush. And don't start shooting until you have to save Stimson's butt again," he said with a grin. "Ready?"

"I'm ready. Let's go," Stimson said, tucking his canteen back in its pouch.

Keller suddenly realized how tired and thirsty he was. The jump, the Germans, the twinkle in the dead man's eyes; he felt like he needed to find a barn and get a good nap. The odor of ripe manure wafted around him. And a bath would be great. He had worked for days on the ranch with just a splash of water on his face in the morning, but the Army routine of a shower a day had got him out of the notion of living caked in trail dust and cow shit. Up side, maybe the Germans would mistake him for a cow if he walked into an ambush.

Keller shook the odd thoughts out of his head and focused on the road ahead as they walked toward through the night. Planes buzzed across the sky, seemingly coming and going in random patterns. Tracers and an occasional flare silhouetted distant parachutes, some white, some dark, spilling from the planes. He hurried his steps, moving toward the tiny dots dropping out of the sky, distant troopers, his buddies and friends. He held up his hand when he came to a slight rise. Across another orchard a railroad track, twin ribbons glinting in the moonlight, paralleled the road. O'Shey and Stimson moved up on each side of him.

"See any krauts?" asked O'Shey.

"No, sir. But I think we ought to move off the road and follow the tracks." He pointed across the tracks at the tree line. "That would be a perfect place for a machine gun. It's damned dark back in the trees. I can't tell if there is anything there or not. Sure as crap don't want to blunder into an ambush."

"You're right. Move on down the tracks a ways, then we'll cut over and back to the road if we don't see anything. Stimson, you lead. Keller, you tail end Charlie this leg."

Stimson started down the railroad tracks, cinders crunching under his jump boots, followed by O'Shey.

Keller let them get a few steps ahead when he spotted something big in the darkness ahead. "Pssst," he hissed at them. "Stop."

The two men eased to the ground and Keller crawled up to them, unburned coal and cinders cutting into his elbows and knees.

"What's up there?" asked O'Shey, peering into the night. "I don't see squat."

Before Keller could answer, a light flickered, illuminating a gun mounted on a rail car. Four barrels swung around, pointed toward the sky, and heads bobbed along the car, shouting in German.

Keller flinched when the gun opened up, first just two barrels, then all four, tracers streaking up into the sky. He rolled back and looked up. A C-47 flew directly over them, paratroopers tumbling out the door. The line of tracers chewed down the airframe, then through the line of opening parachutes.

Up in the sky screams split the air. Then, as quickly as it started, the gun stopped firing. On the far side of the tracks something crashed through the trees and hit the ground with such a thump Keller felt it through the muddy ground.

A machine gun on the other side of the tree line spewed out a series of short bursts toward where any surviving paratroopers would have landed.

"They ain't going to do that again," muttered O'Shey. "Keller, give Stimson one of those potato mashers. I'm going to cross the tracks to the other side. When I open up, you two toss the grenades as close to the AA gun as you can, then start shooting." He dug through a musette bag. "I got a frag grenade I'll toss and one C-2 bundle. After we put down the crew, I'll blow that son of a bitchin' gun. Get ready." O'Shey scuttled across the tracks and disappeared into the darkness.

"You sign up for this shit?" Stimson whispered back to Keller.

"I never volunteered for jack." The scream from the falling trooper, the sickening thump still echoed in Keller's head. "But it sounds like a plan to me." Keller handed Stimson one of the stick grenades and led Stimson down the side of the rail bed until he was just yards short of the railcar. His steps crunched in the mixture of cinders, gravel and coal fragments, so loud he realized he was tiptoeing in his jump boots like a cartoon character at the Saturday movie. He moved away from the track until he could feel soft mud under his boots. When he glanced back Stimson had vanished in the shadows along the edge of another orchard, this one with trees taller than a man. A soft squish of boots in mud signaled Stimson was still there.

Indistinct forms moved around the rail car. Containers rattled and men grunted. A dropped shell casing thumped on the ground, clanged against a steel rail.

A loud voice yelled out.

Keller froze. Germans' have ass-chewing NCOs, too, he guessed.

Someone on the gun mount laughed. Heads moved around the gun barrels and shield.

Keller dropped to his knees in the mud and laid his rifle on the ground. How many rounds did he fire in the pasture? Five, six, out of eight. He pulled a full clip from his cartridge belt and snagged it handy on the rifle sling, then a second. He unscrewed the cap from the wooden grenade handle, already slick with his sweat. Shook it until the string dangled from the hollowed out end, a thumb-sized porcelain ball threaded to the end of the string like a button.

He held the grenade ready to throw, and waited for O'Shey's signal. Sweat dripped into his eyes. Cow stench floated around him, mixed with the smell of damp grass, mud and the slight sulfur smell of railroad coal.

Behind him the roar of an approaching plane grew louder. Again the gun barrels swiveled around so they pointed directly over his head. And as before, two barrels opened up, the gunner finding the range, then all four, deafening as they spat pure fire and brimstone up toward the plane.

Had O'Shey told them to wait for some signal? Bullshit. Signal enough. Keller yanked the lanyard and threw the grenade in an overhand loop, hoping it exploded somewhere near the gun crew and not at the Lieutenant's feet. He plopped down to his belly in the mud and snatched up his rifle. One tick, two ticks, and the grenade exploded, a measly little pop, followed by a second.

Must be Stimson's. Then another, louder, maybe O'Shey's frag.

The gun stopped firing. A man roared, a terrible noise like a wounded grizzly. A rifle barked out into the night.

Oh, goodness. They had stirred up a wasp's nest. Muddy M1 to his cheek, he started shooting, only a couple of rounds before the empty clip clanged out of his rifle. Mud spattered in his face and bullets cracked overhead. He shoved a full clip down the well and resumed firing. He spotted fleeting targets, legs, arms, around the shield, bodies darting to the ammo bins; but mostly he just fired, aiming below where he thought the gun's armor shield ended.

Down the tracks Stimson's Thompson stuttered, short, deep bursts. O'Shey's carbine popped on the far side. Good. At least he hadn't killed the Lieutenant with the damned potato masher.

The gun mount swiveled. The barrels depressed and started firing, swinging down toward him. Giant tracers snarled over his head, deafening, crashing through the orchard. Keller raked the car with rifle fire, trying to keep his fire low, hoping he could slow the crew from reloading before the damn gun chewed him up. Each tracer seemed to race toward him like ball lightning, then cracked over his head, half blinding him. Two ready clips gone, he clawed across the cinders toward the rail car, trying to stay under the line of fire. Desperate, he flopped over the near side iron rail and rolled underneath the rail car. He lay on his back, dug out another clip from a bandoleer and slammed it in his rifle. He rolled toward O'Shey's side of the rail car, away from the tracer fire pounding into the trees.

Before he reached the far rail an explosion slammed his helmet against the railroad tie, jammed his nose into the cinders. He lay there for a moment, head buzzing from the explosion, nose stinging. He shook the buzz from his head and rolled out from beneath the rail car, now nothing but a dead silence in his ears. A soldier wearing a distinctive German helmet ran across the flat bed, stopped and turned, submachine gun at his shoulder, moving like an actor in one of the old 16mm silent movies the farm extension agent showed on balmy summer nights. A silent stutter of rapid muzzle flashes reached out toward where Keller imagined Stimson was. Keller suddenly realized he was deaf from the explosion. The German and his gun were silent, but he wasn't an actor. He was for damn real.

MISSING STICKS

Keller stood, snapped his rifle up to his check and pulled the trigger, once, twice. Mud and bits of cinders dug into his cheek with the recoil. The German fell back, then stood back up, screaming. Keller fired again as the flame from the German's gun reached out toward him and Keller's M1 exploded out of his hand. The muddy stock slapped him in the cheek, spinning him around, rifle lost.

He dropped to his knees and felt across the ground until he located his rifle, smothered in dirt and cinder bits.

Another explosion rocked the railcar.

The blast slammed him flat to the ground. Head on a swivel, he staggered back to his feet. The German was gone. He looked back toward the trees. No sign of O'Shey. Keller found a ladder and clambered up on to the rail car. A lantern swayed at the near end, glass globe missing, but somehow the wick still flickered enough to see the carnage. Broken men lay sprawled across the wrecked gun carriage and ammo containers. The Lieutenant's C-2 had done its job. Bits and pieces of bodies testified to the terrible explosion that had finally destroyed the gun.

The rail car floor swayed. Keller dropped to a crouch.

Stimson ran down the car toward him, poking at the dead bodies as he came. Stimson stopped over one of the bodies, shaking his head. He looked up at Keller. His lips moved, but Keller had trouble understanding. Finally, though the buzzing in his head, Keller made out his words.

"L.T.'s in the middle of all that mess." Stimson handed Keller a single dog tag. "He won't be marching across France."

Keller dropped O'Shey's tag in his pocket and sighed. He pulled the bag of Beechnut out of his first aid kit, stuffed a wad in his cheek and dropped the rest of the tobacco into his musette bag. With O'Shey dead up on the rail car, he might need to get to his first aid pouch in a hurry, the way things were going. Damn. "Hope you ain't carrying mine before this is over."

Stimson clicked a full magazine into his Thompson. "Can't, man. You're the boss, now."

"Right." Keller hopped down from the rail car. "O.K. Let's get out of here. Ready to go?"

"Airborne, Corporal."

CHAPTER 4 - 435TH TP CARRIER GP

The line of tracers rose ever so slowly up from the ground. Accelerating as they came closer, brilliant colored balls raced across the sky, filling the windshield from side to side. The plane yawed, staggered with a hit. The *Havana Express* wallowed like a fat pig in mud, then suddenly dropped like a lead bucket. Felt like some of the aileron and rudder control cables had been shot away. Captain Frank Howell looked across the C-47's cockpit and out the starboard window. That was the least of their troubles. Flames shot out of number two engine. "Feather your engine, Joey, then shut it down. I'll try and keep us in the sky."

Howell had been flying DC-3s for years, so an engine failure wasn't a completely new thing. But this time he didn't have Pan Am Ops to call and to declare an emergency. Not a runway for miles that he knew about. He shoved the port engine throttle to max revs and simultaneously sawed at the steering wheel and worked the yoke, fighting to keep them level and stop the nose from yawing around. Despite his efforts and the sweat dropping off his nose, the plane continued sinking. The altimeter wound down through four hundred feet and kept dropping, fast. He kept the yoke pulled back as far as he dared, balancing between maintaining altitude and stalling. He reached up and slapped the toggle switch that released the belly bundles. A lurch, and the altimeter needle jumped up back to indicate three hundred and fifty feet for an instant before it began swinging back down.

"Lou," he yelled into the intercom. "Tell the jumpers we're not high enough for a safe jump. Everybody hang on and I'll land us in Paris." An unintelligible reply came back from the crew chief.

Well, maybe not Paris. If only he could gain altitude. A little higher and he could get enough air under them to give the paratroopers in the back, Joey and the rest of the crew a chance.

The control yoke shuddered as a burst of machine gun bullets raked into the plane. Wind whistled though a pair of holes in the side Plexiglas. He hauled back on the wheel until it was tight against his gut. The entire plane staggered. Controls mushy, *Havana Express* felt on the edge of a stall. Howell glanced over his shoulder. Kenny, the radio operator, stood in the doorway, hanging on to the sides of the bulkhead. He looked like he was scared to death. Smart man.

"Got the prop feathered, ignition off on number two," Joey yelled.

Howell glanced over at his copilot. Blood streamed down the young Lieutenant's face. "Make sure the fuel to number two is shut off. Check the cross valve. By some miracle, we might want to save enough gas in the tanks to fly us home."

The miracle didn't happen. Number one began streaming orange flames streaked with black smoke. "Joey, lower the flaps to half." He turned to shout back in the cabin. Kenny had disappeared. "Everybody, prepare to crash land," he yelled over his shoulder to anyone who cared. Howell leaned forward against his seat belt and peered through the windshield, searching for a clearing. Dead ahead a building burned, flames reaching up into the sky. Tracers boiled the air over an open field lit by the fire. Parachutes littered the ground and draped the trees surrounding the field like discarded handkerchiefs.

To his left a sparkle of explosions glittered and danced across the ground. He fought the controls and managed to turn the plane away from the raging battle, more with the throttles than anything else. The plane jounced in the turbulence, fighting the turn.

Another glint of light—the moon reflecting from a ribbon of water off to his right. Water he could do. That's how he got the nickname—Captain Splash—he never repeated to his Troop Carrier friends, for the many water landings he had made in the old Sikorsky S-38 flying between Key West and Havana running rum. He had bragged about flying DC-3s to get in the Army Air Corps, but kept his Sikorsky time under his hat. Even to this day he still didn't want anything to do with the Coast Guard, his old nemesis on his Cuban runs during Prohibition, and, by extension, the Navy.

The C-47 flew about the same as the Sikorsky, both powered by two Pratt & Whitneys, slow and reliable. Except a bunch of damn Nazis had poked this Dakota full of holes. Nothing new, he had been shot at before. A bullet from a revenue cutter had thumped right through the sides of the old Sikorsky before he could roll away in a fog bank off Key Largo, smashing open a crate of rum. Stunk to high heaven. But this time the sky was a solid wall of bullets and old

Havana Express wasn't going to make it back to the clouds. Right now, with both engines flaming, the water looked pretty good.

A thump jarred his butt and an involuntary pucker raised him up off his ass. Likely a bullet had smacked through the bottom of the thin seat bottom and embedded itself in the parachute seat pack. At least he hoped it had stopped there, but was too busy to check. Wouldn't need the chute, anyway. Too low to jump. For the first time since he volunteered to fly for the Army Air Force, Howell wished he was wearing one of those silly flak helmets instead of his oh-so-jaunty billed cap

"Gear down?" screamed Joey.

"No, no. Keep the gear up. I'm going to belly land her in the water." A line of tracers sliced across in front of the windshield, then raked through the side of the airplane. "Ring the crash bell, kid."

No answer. Howell glanced over. Joey's head was slumped down. His arms hung limp. When Howell looked back up, moon-lit water filled the windshield. He hauled back on the yoke with his left hand and desperately rolled the trim wheel with his right, fighting to bring the nose up. He eased the throttles back and forth, trying to balance between keeping control and falling out of the sky. The plane began to jiggle. Air speed down around seventy knots. If he stalled it, they'd plummet like a rock. Too low to drop the nose for speed. Just hang on.

A sudden jerk snatched him tight against his seat belt. Tail dragging in the water.

He began to feel they might just make it. A water-level stall would be perfect. Instead, his teeth clicked together as the Dakota's nose crashed down, dove for the bottom, driving his butt into the hard seat and slamming him forward against his seat belt. He tasted blood as he bit his tongue.

Water shot thorough the holes in the Plexiglas, stinging his eyes. Vague darkness rushed past on each side of the plane. Howell felt as if he were spinning, flung first back against the seat, then slammed to one side and then the other, then hard again against the seat belt. His neck popped as his head snapped back and forth.

For a moment Howell thought the *Havana Express* was still flying as he swayed in his seat. The plane rocked from side to side, then stilled. Howell ripped off his headset. A familiar voice yelled in the back; Lou urging people out.

Howell snapped his harness free and climbed out of his seat to check Joey. Thank God, a pulse throbbed in the kid's neck. Howell unfastened Joey's chin strap, his hand sliding over a deep crease in one side of the helmet. He gently removed the helmet. A thin line of blood ran down the side of Joey's head, a sickly orange in the faint glow from the gauges. Howell looked back into the cabin for help. The jumpers, Kenny and Lou were long gone. Dim forms silently bobbed in the water. Howell prayed they were all discarded parachute packs. Water sloshed around his ankles, soaking his socks over his brogans. "You hang tight, kid," he whispered to his unconscious copilot. Howell reached over and unsnapped Joey's seat belt and parachute pack. His own breath rasped in his throat with the exertion. The smell of burning insulation tickled his nose. He slapped the master electrical switches off. Time to get the hell out.

Howell stood on his empty seat, rotated the release levers and flung open the escape hatch in the top of the cockpit. He stuck his head into the cool air. A patter of light rain splattered on his face as he looked up. A C-47 limped overhead streaming orange flames, tracers reaching up from the ground and sparkling against the wounded plane. "Hold her steady," he muttered, willing the plane safe flight home.

Around him water shimmered as far as he could see, fore and aft and off to the left. Dark trees marked the near channel side. He dropped back down and grabbed Joey by the collar. "Come on, son. Got to get you out of here." He stripped off the bulky flak suit he had insisted his copilot wear and pushed Joey's limp body up through the hatch. Thank God the kid had worn his helmet. And thank God he was such a skinny kid. With a final grunt, he shoved Joey atop the fuselage.

He squinted at the indistinct outline of the tree tops. Too far to swim, especially towing Joey.

Howell dropped back down and dragged one of the A-2 life raft bags out of the side compartment. He hurriedly scrabbled behind his seat in the dim light, sloshing through the water until he came up with the Remington shotgun and his map case. One last look around to make sure everyone was out, and he dragged the raft to the hatch.

Cussing, fumbling with the awkward raft bag, he shoved the bag into the hatch. The floppy bag jammed in the narrow opening. Cold water climbed up his legs as the shotgun barrel snagged on the bulkhead and he tumbled back into the cockpit. Damn. He and Joey were going to drown in the middle of France while he shoved a friggin' life raft around. Both feet on the center console, he balanced a foot on the throttle levers and put his shoulder to the bag. One last shove, an extra grunt, and he finally wiggled the bag through the hatch.

Howell clambered out into a thin mist, dragging the Remington and map case behind him. Flying into Havana he had learned the rack and clack of a twelve-gauge pump was a mighty deterrent to trouble, and if you were already in it, a quick way out. And, from the sounds of gunshots echoing off the trees, they were in plenty of trouble tonight.

Outside, water slapped against the skin of the plane. The vertical stabilizer rose up out of the water where the ass-end ought to be, already sunk under the surface. To port an oil slick glistened, surrounding a splotch that Howell supposed was a propeller tip. He pulled the raft out and yanked the lanyard. With a whoosh the rubber-coated fabric tubes inflated. He slid Joey into the raft as the tubes swelled to form the walls of a minuscule boat. He clambered over the side as the C-47 settled out from under his feet. A great bubble stinking of hydralic fluid belched from the open hatch as they floated free. The tail rocked as the plane settled, then steadied as the fuselage sank out from under them.

The near silence was eerie, broken only by the lapping of the water around the edge of the raft and occasional distant gunfire. As his night vision improved, the darkness resolved around him. An irregular line of vegetation lined the horizon, outlined by tracers arcing up into a cloud bank that momentarily parted for quick glimpse of the moon. Most of the ground fire had come from the left side of the aircraft, probably the north. The wounded C-47 was long gone; back to England, Howell hoped.

Envisioning the briefing photos and maps, he figured they were in the Douve River. Where he wasn't exactly sure, maybe where it flowed south, but more likely where it turned west and emptied into the English Channel. Not more than a narrow stream on the maps, and all but invisible on the photos. But the briefers had warned that the Germans could flood the marshes.

So, he was in a big swamp, like the Everglades he was familiar with. He hoped this one didn't have any gators.

Working a paddle Howell assembled from the accessory pack, the awkward raft swirled around more in circles that in a straight line. He paddled toward what he thought was the south and the closest tree line, wondering if he would find a medic close by. Sweat ran down his face as he dug the paddle into the water.

He jerked back as an object bobbed up in front of him. "Hey," he hollered out in surprise, his cry echoing back to him. Rifle fire barked toward him from the bank. Further along a machine gun opened up, stray rounds snapping overhead.

"Thunder." He whispered the challenge this time. Or was he supposed to say "Flash?" Whichever, the bobbing object didn't answer. A chute streamed out from the flotsam and washed past. Just a cargo container.

Howell reached out, grabbed a handful of shroud lines and hauled on them. The flotsam thrashed around, resolved into a paratrooper spluttering water as his head sank back below the surface. Howell grabbed a riser and pulled the half-drowned soldier closer. Another grunt and Howell rolled him over the side and into the bottom of the raft.

Out of the murky darkness a hoarse voice called out, more a gurgle than a shout. Howell buried his face in Joey's wet shirt as another rifle shot cracked overhead.

Howell looked up, squinted across the faint starlight glimmering off the steel black water. A bareheaded soldier bobbed in the dark water, his Mae West inflated up to his ears, but barely keeping him afloat. Howell paddled to the man, fighting against the pull of the first man's chute dragging behind like a giant sea anchor. The raft took on water, but stayed afloat as the second man slithered over the side.

"Hey. Don't leaf me," another voice suddenly whispered out of the darkness.

Damn river was full of people. Shit. He had put them there, he reminded himself.

Howell grabbed a handful of slick nylon cloth and hauled until he finally reached the shroud lines. The man lunged up out of the water, grabbed the line strung along the top of the raft and pulled himself in. The raft bobbed and bounced, sloshing more water in over the sides. Howell felt the cold water soak through his pants and suck the heat from his legs as he knelt beside Joey. He lifted Joey's head up out of the cold water, untangling him from the shroud lines that lay draped across the raft in a tangle. The chutes swirled out behind the raft in the current, tugging the raft around in dizzying circles.

Howell pushed away the lines and bent to check on Joey. Still a pulse, but not a sign of consciousness. "Any of you guys a medic?" Howell asked the other three. The first man he had pulled out didn't answer, just lay in the bottom of the raft, shivering and coughing water.

The last man in finished shedding his parachute harness and Mae West, tossed the tangled harness into the water with a splash and whispered, "I'm a mess sergeant," The tiny raft shifted, almost swamped as the cook pulled out a long knife and sliced away the parachute risers, freeing the incoherent man on the bottom of the raft from his canopy.

The other man in the boat struggled out of his undeployed parachute harness. "Infantry, BAR man, till I lost the damn thing in the swamp." He finally slipped all his buckles, shrugged and let the chute fall into the water.

The cook turned to Howell, sliding his knife back into a sheath. "I know a little first aid. What's your problem?"

"The kid, here. He took a lick to his head. Shrapnel, something caved in his helmet."

The raft lurched as the cook crawled forward, threatening to topple them all into the black water. "Can't see dick shit out here. Best we just let him be until we get off this raft."

Howell left Joey cradled in the man's arms, turned to the BAR man and handed him a second paddle. "Let's get this damn rubber duck to the bank." Sweating like a drunk pig, he pulled at the water, trying to match the soldier's strokes, until his arms ached.

When they reached the trees, Howell, the cook and the infantry-man climbed over the sides and sloshed through the shallow water, pulling the raft through a shoulder-high stand of bulrushes. Gasping with effort, Howell finally stumbled onto a grassy bank. He and the other men slid the raft with Joey and the remaining man up onto an embankment under the trees.

The infantryman stood there, panting, as he pulled out a pistol from a shoulder holster, racked the slide back and shook the water from the pistol. "Damn. Didn't fink I'd be in a boat tonight," he lisped. "You our pilot?" he asked.

"Yeah. Didn't do a very good job, did I?"

The infantryman spit, ran his fingers across his lips. "I think I lost a couple of teef, but I can get new ones. But, by God, 'spite what my pop warned me, I didn't drown. How 'bout you, Sergeant Barkley?"

The cook, still bent over Joey, chuckled. "Alive is good. Tonight, I'll take it."

"Did everybody get out the back?" Howell asked.

Barkley nodded. "I think everybody got their vests inflated and out the door." He pointed at the man still lying in the bottom of the boat. "That guy went out into the water with his static line still hooked up. Deployed his chute. Crew chief had to cut him loose before I could clear the door. Then my damn reserve handle snagged, chute deployed and damn near pulled me to the bottom." He stood and took a deep breath. "Your buddy's alive, and not bleeding anywhere bad. I put a dressing over that lick on his head, but I can't do anything more for him. If he's lucky, he'll wake up with nothing more than a hell of a headache. But he could have a concussion."

All three ducked as a ragged volley of small arms fire rattled through the trees.

The infantryman slapped a magazine in the butt of his pistol and let the slide rack forward. A grenade exploded, closer than the previous gunfire. "Captain, sorry to leave you, but I got things to do. Why don't you hunker down and stay with these two. We should have the area cleared soon after dawn."

"You think so?" asked Howell.

"I sure as hell hope so." The infantryman held out his hand. "Name's Rudy. Rudy Livingston, with the 501st. Don't worry, Cap. You got us out of the water. We'll take care of the krauts." He grinned, his missing teeth a dark gap in the moonlight. Without another word the infantryman started across the field toward the sound of gunfire, the mess sergeant hard on his heels.

Howell pulled Joey back under a tree limb, thick with damp leaves. He went back to the raft and dragged the third man over to join Joey.

"What now?" he muttered to the trees. He knew the answer. Keep Joey safe, hide from the Germans and stay alive.

A cough broke the quiet. The remaining soldier heaved, spat out a gout of water. He shook his head and rolled over on his knees. "Where are we?" he asked.

"Don't really know for sure," Howell answered. "We landed in water, probably a river basin flooded by the Germans."

The soldier started pawing at his gear. "I got to get out of here. Help me." He unbuckled his reserve and started randomly jerking at his harness.

"Easy. You damn near drowned out there. Hell, I thought you had drowned. You all right?"

The soldier hacked and spit, then let Howell help him strip off his harness. His hand was icy cold, skin wrinkled, when he grabbed Howell's wrist. "Do you know exactly where we are?"

Howell thought for a moment. "No, not exactly. Somewhere on the Douve most likely, close to Carentan."

"How far to the rail line?" The soldier sounded desperate.

Howell frowned, picturing the maps in his mind. "Well, a couple of tracks on the map lead into Carentan. If we are where I think, we're probably less than a mile from the southernmost line."

The soldier patted his waist. "Thank God," he muttered.

"That you're alive?" asked Howell.

"Nope." The soldier stripped a long package from around his waist. "Well, yeah, that, too. But mostly that I've still got the C-2 bundles. Got to have them." He patted around his pockets, started frantically searching through his pockets. "Damn. Can't find the fuses."

Howell chuckled. "Personally, I think that's a good thing. Jumping with C-2 and fuses all together doesn't sound too damn smart to me." He knelt down to check on Joey. "Look. I got a wounded guy here. Can you help?"

The soldier shook his head. "Sorry. They didn't even give me a first aid course before they stuck me in this uniform and wrapped the C-2 around me. Did you say you were hurt?" He stopped for a spasm of coughing, bent sideways to thump water from his ear. "Sorry. I think I swallowed half that river." He kept patting his pockets, apparently still searching for the fuses.

60

"No, not me," replied Howell. "My copilot took a lick to the head. He's still—"

At that moment Joey groaned, pushed himself up on an elbow. He opened his eyes, blinked at Howell. "Did we land? Everybody O.K.?"

Howell took a great breath of relief. "Yep. We landed. I think Lou got everyone out the back." He held Joey down when he tried to sit up. "You take it easy. We need to find a medic."

"I'm O.K. Let me up."

Howell finally let Joey stagger to his feet. Joey swayed for a moment, looking around. "Where are we?"

Howell leaned closer. Joey's eyes had a glazed look to them. "Take it easy. I need to get you checked out before you start running around. That thunk on the noggin left you more addled than usual." He looked over at the other soldier, hands on knees, still hacking up water. "You want to come with us?"

The soldier straightened, stretching his back. "I need to get going. Got to get rid of this stuff." He patted the fat belt of C-2 bundles he had draped over his shoulders. He looked around, fished a pair of thick glasses from a pocket, put them on and blinked his eyes like maybe he could finally see. "Which way's the railroad?"

Howell pointed in the direction he thought was south. "The other two troopers that I picked up took off in that direction. You might be able to catch up with them. If you see a medic, ask him to come find us."

The soldier stuck out his hand. "Stan Levine. Thanks for hauling my ass out of the drink. I hope you and your copilot make it back to fly again. But I gotta get going."

A shot rang out, the bullet zinging over their heads. Levine dropped to the ground.

He looked up at Howell. "Sorry. I'm not used to all the shooting," he whispered, brushing mud and leaves from his hands as he climbed back to his feet.

Howell looked closer at Levine's collar. He had a major's leaf on one side and upside-down signal flags on the other, reversed so both were on the wrong side. Who the hell was this guy? Howell slid his shotgun up and clicked off the safety. Not too gently he shoved the barrel under Levine's chin, pressed the muzzle into his throat. "Why don't we just hold up a minute, buddy, and you tell me who you really are and what you're doing." He eased the barrel down far enough that Levine could speak.

Levine started back into Howell's eyes for a moment and blinked behind the glasses, hands wide out to the sides. "I'm not really Army."

"I figured that out," answered Howell.

"I work at Camp Evans for Western Electric, back in Jersey. New Jersey, the one outside of New York. I know about radars. The Army heard the Germans had a new model *Wurzburg* radar somewhere along the rail line outside of Carentan. They wanted me to find it, collect a couple of choice parts for our guys back in the labs. Apparently the Brits did something like that last year. Our guys wanted to see if this one had any new improvements."

"You going to take this radar all by yourself?"

"Of course not. But I have no idea where the soldiers are who were to escort me to the radar site. I was only supposed to identify and take the correct tubes and any other parts I thought important. The lieutenant—he thought it was a grand joke—gave me the C-2 to carry. I figured 'why not' since everyone else on the plane was a walking bomb with all their grenades and mines stowed in every pocket and pouch. So now, I'm going to try to find the radar myself."

"And get your ass killed trying." Howell lowered the shotgun.

"Why don't you wait until we can link up with some more troops?" asked Joey. He gingerly touched his head.

He seemed to be more lucid, Howell noticed, relieved. But they still needed to find a medic.

Levine shook his head. "My grandfather, my aunt, all my family lived in Berlin. One cousin wrote that they were loaded into boxcars and taken to a *Vernichtungslager*."

"What's that?" asked Joey.

"Look. I don't want to be here, much less jump out of an airplane. A bunch of intelligence guys sat me down, told me about a bunch of camps, mostly over in Poland. Where the fucking Nazis exterminate Jews. Extermination camps where the prisoners are burned—dead or alive. Nobody has heard from my family since they were taken." He looked up toward the sound of an approaching plane. "Look, I'm not one of those hotshot scientists designing new radar systems. As far as my department is concerned, I'm just a technician who understands a little bit about radars. So, I volunteered and got to be a paratrooper for a day. No, not even a day. Just this one night. But this is my chance. For my family."

"I'm ready to go with you," Joey announced. He pulled out his Smith & Wesson .38 revolver and took a step.

Howell reached out and grabbed him by the arm as he staggered for a moment. "Hold on, hotshot," he cautioned Joey. "You're going to get yourself killed." Howell shook his head in exasperation. "First, you're heading in the direction the most shooting's coming from. Second, that's the wrong way that Mister Fireworks, here, needs to go if he's going to find the railroad." He pointed toward an orderly row of low trees, indistinct in the ghostly moonlit mists rolling in off the river. "The railroad should be a couple hundred yards that way. If we get separated, head across that orchard and toward the next opening in the tree line. If that's not the right direction, we're so far lost we'll have to ask the next kraut we see." He turned Joey and shoved him toward the trees. "Now, come on." Water squishing out of his brogans, Howell led his crew through an ancient orchard to a hedgerow. There he followed a cow path to a house beside the road, then on to a set of railroad tracks.

They stopped between the tracks, silver ribbons in the moonlight. "Now which way?" Howell asked Levine. "East or west?"

Levine looked up and down the railway, shaking his head. "Let's try—" His suggestion was cut off by the thundering of an antiaircraft gun as it raked an oncoming aircraft. The tracers rose from the direction Levine had first turned. The firing stopped as the plane passed overhead.

"You go where you want," said Levine. "But first, I'm going to knock out that damned gun." He pulled a pistol from a shoulder holster and started toward the antiaircraft gun. He jumped, a tiny hop, when the gun resumed firing.

Before he could take another step several small explosions and gunfire erupted down the track. Suddenly, a sharp blast shook the ground, followed by several reports, then silence.

"Son of a bitch," exclaimed Howell. "Somebody else took care of that gun."

"Good. That means some of our guys are over there." Levine turned and started along the tracks, cinders crunching under his feet. "Coming with me? I got a radar to find and blow the hell up."

CHAPTER 5 - B/377TH PRCHT FA

First Sergeant Juan Salazar couldn't believe he had found the one person he had sincerely hoped had been shot by the Germans. Surrounded by people itching to kill them, Private Jacob Rankin sat like a fool on the edge of a muddy ditch, chowing down on the contents of a K-Ration box.

"Come on Jake, we got to find the rest of the battery before light."

Rankin grinned up at him like a idiot.

"Just got to finish these meat and eggs—"

Before Rankin could finish anything, Salazar jerked him up by the collar and shook him. "You little shit. Do what I say or I'll shoot you myself." Salazar shoved Rankin up to the path. "Now move out and stay alert." Somebody once said they should pick Boy Scouts, farmers and small town boys to be paratroopers. Jake Rankin apparently was none of those, nothing but a troublemaker, what ever rock he came out from under. Probably grow up to be a small time gangster, if he had any sense, which apparently he also lacked. "Where's your helmet?"

Rankin ran his finger through his silver hair, an odd, prematurely grey thatch, disheveled like the rest of the man. "Jeez, Top. My pot came loose when I went out the door. Darn'd if I know where it lit. Probably out there somewhere." He looked around in the inky darkness. "I left my liner back at the last crossroads where I got a drink of water. Durn thing hurts my head. And anyway, that old fiber liner wouldn't stop no bullet, no ways. It just keeps me from seeing good."

Hopeless. Salazar thought for a moment about just leaving the little jerk sitting in the ditch. He peered through the darkness to check their rear.

His ear itched, the part he had left in Spain in his first fight with the Nazis. He had no idea where he was now, other than somewhere in France. Worse, he had no idea where the puny little pack seventy-five bundles had landed. The 377th Parachute Artillery Regiment had trained months with a bunch of clerks and infantrymen to get them proficient with the 105mm brutes he loved. Then, at the last minute Headquarters, in their almighty wisdom, had swapped out the 105s for those piss ant seventy-fives. The better to parachute with, they said. Well, here he was with his carbine, a shit-heavy satchel of Brit high explosive antitank rounds, and Rankin. Not a seventy-five gun tube in sight. Shit again. He needed to find a big stick. He'd be better off.

His silver hair glinting in the moonlight, Rankin shuffled up the narrow road like a hobo looking for a handout. Well, at least Salazar could keep tabs on him. The last time Rankin had been out of his sight for more than to take a piss, the dumb ass had ended up AWOL in a pub off base, drunk as a skunk and telling anyone who would listen wild stories about the upcoming invasion. The fact that the unit was sequestered in Membury for the impending drop was the only thing that kept Rankin out of a court martial, and even that had been a close thing. Salazar had been more worried that Rankin's fellow squad members would throw him into the Channel on the trip over. As it was, the dumb kid sported a black eye and a swollen lip. His fellow troopers hadn't taken too well to the reports. So here they were, Top and his favorite trooper.

Rankin stopped between the muddy ruts, clenched fist up in the air.

Salazar froze. What in hell was the fool playing at? His ear tingled. Whenever danger seemed near, the missing ear lobe seemed to come alive. It was humming tonight.

Rankin slowly eased down to a crouch.

Salazar swallowed the impulse to yell at Rankin to get on with it. Instead, he bent low, rushed across the road, slid through the mud to a stone wall and worked his way up until he was even with Rankin.

Rankin motioned ahead with his chin toward a cluster of small houses. The farm road funneled between the first two houses, then opened up to a small square. A lantern perched on top of a knee-high wall lit the square with a flickering yellow light, a scene out of a Saturday matinee scary movie. The wall surrounded a grassy plot. In the center of the square the wings of a marble angel reached up toward the black sky.

On the far side of the statue a crew of Germans rolled a gun into the square, scurrying around like a bed of ants.

Salazar paused, touched the silver medallion dangling between his dog tags. "St. Michael, defend us in our hour of conflict," he muttered. He counted ten men, one of them the gun chief with a pointing baton, hollering instructions. It was a big damn gun mounted on wheels. The long barrel poked out from an armored shield, a real weapon, not one of those play-toy seventy-five millimeter pack howitzers. On the far side of the square several Germans darted back and forth unloading ammo boxes from an open troop carrier. From the size and heft of the rounds, an eighty-eight. Big damn gun!

Salazar edged closer to the corner of the house.

The sound of a bell cut the night air. The gun chief snatched up a field phone and held it to his ear. He barked into the phone and pointed up with his baton, barking even louder at his crew. Following the line of the baton, Salazar made out the dim outlines of planes slipping in and out of the clouds, an irregular formation, most coming in their direction. In the planes' path twenty millimeter and machine gun tracers reached up and wove terrible patterns across the sky. The formation broke, individual planes diving and twisting. One turned away from the fires. The rest stayed the course, kept coming.

"Oh, Lord almighty," Salazar whispered as the stray plane turned directly into converging lines of tracers. The plane snapped up on one wing, then straightened, heading directly toward the eighty-eight.

As the plane approached, the gun crew's activity grew more frantic. The chief's commands elevated from barks to screams. He pounded the baton against the gun's armor shield, urging his men on. Several of the men scrambled to form a line from the gun to a stack of ammo boxes, slipping and sliding on the mud-coated stones, lining up ready rounds by the breech as fast as they could pass them forward. One of the crew at the carriage frantically whirled a wheel and the tube elevated from the trail position to near vertical. With a clang, the loader slammed a cartridge into the chamber. The breech slammed and the loader picked up a fresh round, poised, ready. The Germans grew silent, focused on the approaching plane.

Salazar glanced across the road, swept his eyes along the dark shadows, peered into the empty doorways. Mary take mercy on us! Rankin had pulled off his usual vanishing act. Salazar was on his own. Now what? Orders were not to engage the Germans until effective units had assembled, then to attack assigned objectives. Made sense. But Salazar had been up there on the receiving end of the flak. If he let this antiaircraft gun crew fire, how many planes, how many men would come flaming down? He flinched when the first round exploded out of the muzzle. The automatic loader flipped the brass case out with a clang and the next round slammed home.

Salazar breathed a sigh of relief as the single plane veered away. "Oh, no. Follow the other guy, dummies," he muttered, when the trailing formation began a sweeping turn away from a wall of tracers and onto a path that would bring them directly overhead.

The gun chief pointed his baton in the direction of the oncoming serial, a formation of three that had recovered their staggered "V" after passing through the tracers, followed by a second formation of three. The chief shouted, even louder. The aimer whirled the wheel, the gun traversed over and an instant later the gun spat a second projectile toward the oncoming planes. The dirty orange explosion bloomed at what appeared to be the same altitude as the formation, directly in their path. The kill was set up.

Salazar bit his tongue with the next report. Flak rocked the lead plane. Enough. Before the next projectile left the tube he brought his carbine up and dropped the man at the end of the ammo line, then the next, snapping two more quick .30 caliber rounds into the startled German crew, the report of his carbine smothered by the roar of the eighty-eight. A third, then a fourth man went down before the crew chief turned and shouted the alarm just before the next round blasted from the eight-eight's muzzle. Salazar triggered off the rest of his magazine, spraying the area as the gun crew dove for cover.

Salazar fumbled a new magazine out of his cartridge belt. Christ! He was supposed to be directing a howitzer, not playing infantry.

The gun chief spun and pointed his baton directly at him, screaming as Salazar jammed the magazine in the carbine. A flash of gunfire registered in the corner of Salazar's eye as a rifle spat from the roof of the house across the street. The chief paused, arm still raised, then spun away in a graceful pirouette. The baton fell to the grass and the chief tumbled to the ground clutching his throat.

A flurry of wild German gunfire pinged off the cobblestones around the square and plopped into the muddy road behind him. Fragments of stone chipped from the corner of the house sang over his head. Bullets whined and cracked past Salazar's ear. Across the road, up on the roof an arm went up and a blur whizzed through the air. Salazar dropped flat to the ground, arms crossed over his head. The fool kid had thrown a grenade, right at the ammo boxes. Dummy was trying his damndest to get them both killed.

The grenade explosion rocked the square. Fragments whined and ricocheted past him. He looked up to see dust drifting in the air, sparkling in the lantern light. Shielded by the angel, the lantern tottered, but somehow managed to stay lit and in one piece on the low wall. The house beside him shifted, timbers groaned. Salazar glanced up at the eve over his head. Much to his surprise the roof didn't cave in on him like he expected. He rolled to his feet, ran toward the eighty-eight and crouched behind the stone base supporting the angel.

A rifle muzzle poked around the stack of ammo crates. A wild shot whined across the square. In response a bullet cracked past his head from behind and splintered an ammo crate. A blur scrambled from behind the crate, over the cobblestones and fled behind the jumbled pile of empty shell cases. Salazar charged to find a German crawling on his hands and knees toward a dropped rifle. Still on the run, Salazar cracked the carbine butt across the German's head to make sure he didn't make it.

Panting, he spun around. Bodies lay scattered across the square, but no one else reached for a weapon. "Jake," he yelled. "Anybody else?"

"Nobody moving, Top," was the answer from the roof.

"Then off that roof. Get down here and help me with this gun."

"Top, Top!"

Salazar looked up.

A brief glimmer of the moon exposed Rankin standing on the top of the roof, arm extended. "Down the road. I can hear a tank." He paused. "See the lights?"

Salazar hopped on the gun mount, stretched up on his toes so he could see over the armor shield and past the houses. A small village, the four houses and tiny square gave way to a road that led out into the late night, or was it early morning, mists rolling in from the pastures. He had jumped at 0105 hours. The amphibious landings wouldn't start until dawn. He glanced at his watch. Broken. Didn't matter, night or morning. Orders were hold until the Infantry got across the beaches.

A weak beam of light danced across the mist rising up from the fields, maybe eight hundred yards out. The light angled in their direction, probing through the night. He slung his carbine over his back, dropped into a seat on the right side of the tube and spun one of the wheels. Well greased, the gun tube depressed. "Rankin. Get your ass over here." He kept working the wheel until the barrel lay almost horizontal. Salazar jumped when the field phone bell rang.

Rankin appeared at his elbow. "Want me to answer the phone?"

Salazar stared at Rankin. Jesus have mercy.

Rankin stood there, grinning his stupid grin back at him.

"No, don't answer the damn phone. Grab one of those cartridges and push it in the chamber. Stick the pointy end in the breech till it seats. Just be careful the breech doesn't chop off your fingers." Salazar reached across and spun the second wheel. The gun smoothly traversed to the left. Salazar put his eye to the telescopic sight. The tank jumped out of the darkness. About a 6x scope, enough magnification, but the side light was too dim to use for range finding.

"Can you shoot this thing?" asked Rankin as he slid a round onto the tray, caressing the nose as if to confirm he had the pointy end forward.

"I been an artilleryman for fifteen years, son. I can shoot anything that will throw a projectile down range."

A movement in the mists and Salazar spotted the tank lurching across the field. He took his eye off the unfamiliar scope and squinted at the distant headlight pointing first up, then down as the tank climbed out of the field and onto the road. Maybe six hundred yards out now. Hard to tell in the dark. Anyway, a dead flat shot for the eighty-eight.

He stared down at the gun mount. Too dark to figure out how it worked by looking. Sure as hell didn't have a technical manual to study. He ran his hands over the mechanism, searching for a lanyard. Either for real or in his mind, he could hear the clank and squeal of the tank treads. No butterfly trigger, no lanyard. How do you shoot this son of a bitch? When he glanced up Rankin stood behind the breech, a round cradled in his arms.

"I watched them shoot. Not like our 105's. They use a firing pedal, down by your foot." Rankin whispered as if one of the dead Germans would hear him.

"Move out from behind the gun. Recoil will take off your head." When Rankin had hopped over a step, Salazar slid the sole of his foot across the metal plate until his boot found the pedal. He paused, checked the sight picture. The tank looked closer, almost on top of them in the scope. He could make out little dots on the tank, helmets, German infantry clinging to the hull like flies on a rotting carcass. Quickly, now. A twist of the wheel, traverse to the right. Centered. He slipped his foot over the pedal and stomped.

The carriage rocked back as the round exploded out of the barrel with a spurt of flame. The barrel recoiled back against the big buffers, leaving the familiar buzz in the artilleryman's ears. When the gun settled, Salazar jammed his eye back against the eyepiece. He blinked away the blur caused by the explosion and smoke, not believing what he saw.

Starting and stopping, the tank emerged from the smoke, slewed around. Flies were swatted away, but the tank weaved down the road, damn thing still moving. Its gun tube pivoted toward the village. Salazar pressed his eye to the sight. An old Renault clunker. Obsolete piece of French shit, but still, it kept coming.

"Top. Maybe you want an AT round?" Rankin shouted in his ear.

Salazar looked at him. "Yeah. How can you tell them apart?"

"Grandma was German, so I speak a little; read a little more." Rankin held up a shiny projectile mated to a brass case. "The first one was HE. This one ought to do the trick." He slammed the new round into the breech with the heel of his hand.

Salazar centered the oncoming tank in the sight and pounded the firing pedal. Direct hit! This time a spout of flame shot up from the tank. Salazar sensed Rankin chambering a new round. Kid might make a gunner yet. Salazar made a minute adjustment with the traversing wheel and stomped the pedal again. Another deafening report, shot away.

Downrange the tank slewed around, a broken tread flung up over the side. Smoke boiled out and merged with the mists, low against the ground. A crew member struggled up through the hatch on the top of the turret.

"HE," Salazar yelled. A pause, another round clanked onto the tray, and he fired. A yellow explosion and this time a pall of smoke enveloped the tank, shot through with dirty flames.

Salazar stood and stared down the road as fire licked up from the immobilized tank.

"See him, Top?" shouted Rankin. "Range fifty yards and closing." Rankin clanked a round on the loading tray. "AT loaded."

"Fifty? You gotta—" Then he saw. A second tank poked its front end around the corner of the last house in the village, muzzle traversing toward him. No Renault, this was a Panzer, a Mark III. Flames spat out from the machine gun mounted in the turret. Salazar barely had time to drop back behind the armor shield when bullets skipped across the cobble stones, pinged off the armor and ripped into the boxes of ammo. No time to aim, he stomped the pedal at the same time the tank fired its main gun, both almost point blank.

The eighty-eight mount exploded under him, tossing him up into the air. His world whirled around him. Blackness, blacker than the hell his priest told him he was destined for, then stars when he hit the dew-damp cobblestones and bounced across the square. His steel pot clanged on the stones, beating his head like a drum as he spun across the street. With a breathtaking thump he slammed against the low wall surrounding the angel.

Salazar tried to move. Pain shot through his body. He lay immobile on his back on the cold stones, staring up onto the dark sky. The ground shook under him. The tank rumbled, closer by the feel of the vibrations. An odd clanking sound, mixed with the screech of treads moving over idler wheels, grated in his ears. He twisted his shoulders, forced himself to roll to his stomach, levering with his arms. His couldn't feel his legs, only the pain. He wondered if he had any, but was afraid to look at them.

His carbine lay in front of his face, the sling sliced in two, upper handguard splintered. Pieces of slate from the houses crashed down, shattering all around him.

"Jake. Help me, dammit," he screamed, wondering if the kid had lived through the blast. Smoke rolled across the square, stinging his eyes. Flames shot out from the house across the street as machine gun bullets raked across the front, shattering windows and chewing though the bricks. A bullet hit his carbine. It spun like a top and clattered across the cobblestones up against the gutter.

The ground stopped vibrating. The rumbling of the tank's engine, then the clank of a turret hatch replaced the screech of the treads. The wash of engine fumes rolled over Salazar, suffocating in the heavy night air. Thin flames licked up from the rear deck. He had hit, but hadn't killed the Panzer.

Salazar clawed at the low wall, digging his fingers between the stones, and pulled his body away from the tank. Swimming in molasses, he had heard people say. Here he was in the center of a square somewhere in France, swimming in molasses, getting nowhere. He rolled his head up. He wanted to look the man who killed him in the eye. On top of the tank, a German hauled himself halfway out of the turret. Salazar almost laughed. A peaked hat gave the tanker a comic book look, an honest to God Nazi villain. But the machine pistol in his hand was dead serious.

Salazar glanced down. Legs, jump boots were still there after all. He tried to bend a knee. Slowly, his foot came up. He shoved at the wall with his boot, willing himself toward the gutter and cover. A hull mounted machine gun spat a short burst. Bullets cracked over his head, smashing stone fragments from the wall as he frantically crawled toward the gutter. Salazar looked back at the tank. The machine gun depressed, fired another burst, closer, splattering him with more dust and fragments. And scared the crap out of him. He tried to worm his way away from the tank, but could hardly move, now trapped up against the gutter. Where was Rankin? Jesus and Mary. Was that screw-up his only hope?

Across the street, a head glimmered up on the roof of the house, silver in the moonlight. Rankin, a Gammon grenade in his hand, stepped out in clear sight, hopping like a fool rabbit with his white hair, skipping across the burning timbers and the remains of the slate roof. What in the name of God was he doing?

A roof slate gave under Rankin's feet, crashing down on the front of the tank. The German tank commander looked up, paused, searching. He suddenly swung his machine pistol around toward Rankin. He triggered a long burst that splintered wood and flung bits of slate through the flames licking up from the house.

Another burst, and Rankin's head suddenly dropped from view.

The tanker turned back toward Salazar. He picked up a microphone. The tank lurched forward, sawed sideways on the remaining good tread. Salazar had seen firsthand the tendrils of the evil Nazi empire when they spread into Spain, how it murdered innocents, slaughtered prisoners. Just a kid, he had volunteered with the International Brigade where he had met the Fascists for the first time outside Madrid. In the flickering light of the lantern, he realized nothing had changed. The Nazi bastard was trying to grind him under the treads.

Salazar stretched out toward his carbine, struggling, inch by inch, along the gutter. He got his fingers around the severed sling, dragged the rifle closer.

Carbine.

Tank.

Not a fair fight, but he had never heard war was fair to anybody. True in Spain. True in France. Least it was a fight.

He looked up. The tank was almost on top of him, so close the front slope of the tank's armor hid the commander from view. The far set of treads stopped completely, seemed to be coming off the sprocket wheel. The treads closer to him ground against the gutter stones, twisting the tank so it would travel directly along the gutter, straight for him, the high pitched tread squeaks deafening as the tank rocked back and forth, edging ever closer.

He rolled up against the gutter, reached out, dug his fingertips between pavers and hauled, willed his way away from the tank. The tank engine roared. The ground vibrated and the tread clanked, almost within reach, a piece of broken tread flailing around the idler wheel slinging metal fragments and bits of stone in his face.

Salazar dragged his shattered carbine up, praying he could get one clear shot at the German before the tank treads returned him to dust. He kicked with his heels, wiggled on his shoulder blades, worming away from the crippled tank until the peaked cap came back into view, a flash of forehead. One handed, Salazar pointed the carbine toward the German. Before he could squeezed the trigger Rankin's head popped out over the roof, directly in the line of fire behind the German.

"Damn you, Rankin," Salazar shouted at the fool. "Move, so I can shoot."

Instead, Rankin leaned out over the eve and pulled the string dangling from the bottom of a Gammon grenade.

The tank lurched up over the gutter, pitched toward Salazar by fits and starts until the massive chassis blocked out the flickering lantern.

Salazar took a deep breath and closed his eyes. "Hail Mary, full of grace; the Lord is with thee—"

The world erupted with a blinding explosion.

When he was finally able to draw a breath, Salazar found himself sprawled in the ditch by the road. He struggled to his hands and knees in the mud, helmet missing, carbine gone, but so far as he could tell, he still had two arms and two legs. At least the pain to go with a complete set. He looked back toward the tank. No longer a tank, it was a smoking hulk, the turret twisted at an odd cant, an occasional flame spitting out from the engine compartment.

"Thank you, Lord," he whispered. Evil gets what evil deserves.

Salazar searched what remained of the rooftop. There, damn his eyes, stood the stupid son of a bitch. His big grin gleamed in the firelight. He looked weird, like part of his blond hair had been singed to the scalp, silver turned to ashes.

"Damn you Rankin. You're going to blow my ass off yet. Now get your sorry butt down here," he screamed.

"Coming, Top. Be right there."

Salazar crawled to his feet and staggered down the road. He stopped, bent over with a groan and retrieved his satchel from one of the ruts. He took out a round and wiped away the mud. Brass case was dinged, but the projectile looked fine, nothing dented up so bad it wouldn't chamber and fire. He waved it at Rankin like a trophy. "Hurry up. I still got the ammo. We got to find our guns. Now that we have a little practice, you and me should be able to kill a bunch of Nazis."

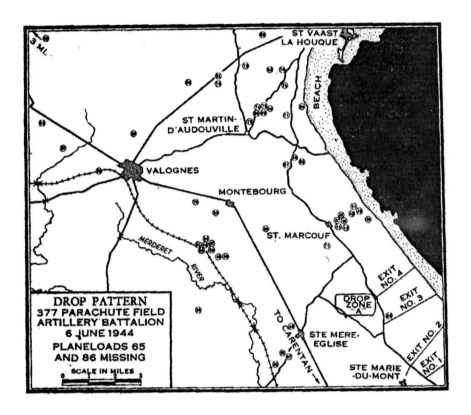

DROP PATTERN
377 PARACHUTE FIELD
ARTILLERY BATTALION
6 JUNE 1944
PLANELOADS 65
AND 86 MISSING

SCALE IN MILES

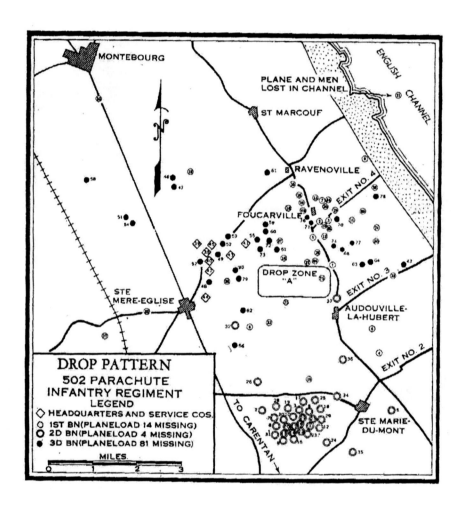

DROP PATTERN
502 PARACHUTE
INFANTRY REGIMENT
LEGEND
◇ HEADQUARTERS AND SERVICE COS.
◇ 1ST BN(PLANELOAD 14 MISSING)
○ 2D BN(PLANELOAD 4 MISSING)
● 3D BN(PLANELOAD 81 MISSING)
MILES

CHAPTER 6 - 1/502ND PRCHT INF

The stick finished their equipment check. At the jumpmaster's command, Sergeant Harry Rule started the count. "Sixteen O.K.," and slapped the man in front of him on the shoulder. The men in front of him sounded off, hanging on to their pale yellow static lines until the count reached Lieutenant Johnson, their jumpmaster. The bawdy jokes and banter up and down the stick died out as every man checked and rechecked his equipment and that of the man in front of him. Now they waited, listening to the muffled explosions, roaring engines and the scream of the wind through the open door. They had stood up and hooked up hours ago, it seemed. Rule's heart began to beat faster.

All said and done, Rule decided he'd sure as hell rather be staring down at a smoldering fire through a thousand feet of smoky sky over the Nez Perce National Forest than pushing this stick of Five-o-Duce troopers in the middle of the night.

He had been a smoke jumper for about four years before the Army drafted him straight out of the Forest Service's Missoula Smokejumper Base in Montana. At Fort Jackson the Army quickly taught him how to march and salute, then promoted him and sent him off to teach kids how to jump out of airplanes at the new Fort Benning parachute school. He figured he had more jumps under his belt than anyone else in the whole 101st Airborne Division. Jumping was his life, his entertainment, his passion. He had always shared a laugh with his fellow smoke jumpers flying high over the Rockies, diving out the door and floating to the ground. Tonight he could hardly work up a wad of spit, much less a grin.

Johnson stood in the door, leaning out into the night. By his shoulder the red light flickered like an evil eye, stared at them. Wait, wait, forever and a day, wait—then—green light. "Go, go, go," the shout went up.

Rule forced his rubbery knees to lock, his feet to shuffle forward. The stick's equipment bundles disappeared into the night, followed by Johnson, then the remainder of the stick, as fast as one man could follow the other. Tonight there would be no pause to enjoy the magnificence of the Rockies, hardly time to take a deep breath.

Rule did his job, shoving the rest of the stick toward the door. If any of the paratroopers had any hesitation, it was lost in the frantic shuffle to follow Johnson and the man in front of him as closely as possible. Not the time to think. As he neared the door, Rule felt a sudden exhilaration, a chance for redemption.

One more shuffle step and he was even with the green light, next out, last man in the stick. He grinned at the crew chief, a stubby man, barrel-like in his flak vest. The crew chief ignored Rule, intent on gathering the static lines as they streamed out into the slipstream. Rule started his turn to the door, cold darkness ahead broken by brilliant explosions and crisscrossing lines of tracers. As he leaned toward the open door, an explosion rocked the Dakota, flinging Rule back against the crew chief and filling the cabin with the rank odor of cordite. Dangling from his static line, Rule scrambled to get back on his feet, his right arm almost pulled out of socket by the heavy load strapped around his body.

The plane yawed, left, right, as ack-ack rounds exploded in the darkness. A fiery ball just off the wingtip sent shrapnel slicing and rattling through the airframe. A fragment clanged off his helmet followed by a heavy fist that slammed into his chest, knocked him back to the cabin floor, snatched his static line out of his hand and took away his breath.

Rule clawed toward the door. His exhilaration evaporated, replace by unadulterated fear as flames streamed from the engine.

The engines' pitch rose, revs built. The pilots had pulled full power. The nose of the plane pitched up, tumbling him back against the crew chief and slamming the two of them head over ass back to the rear bulkhead, pinning him to the cabin floor as the plane climbed.

Over the din of exploding antiaircraft fire, the crew chief's voice finally registered in Rule's ears. An unending string of profanity, the equal of any cowboy bar in Idaho. As a smoke jumper, a tough man in a tough man's world, Rule thought he had heard it all. He rolled forward and felt the crew chief pick him up off the floor, adding some new words to his vocabulary.

Then he was free—of the plane—of everything. The son of a bitch had thrown him out the door. A jerk and his chute opened. He oscillated around in a huge arc, bicycled his legs to spin his risers out of their tangle. Helmet finally free of the twisted risers, he looked up to check his chute. An inflated canopy floated overhead, glistening in the light of a half moon. Overhead an irregular concentration of brilliant star bursts surrounded the plane. A blinding explosion sent a blast of wind past, rocking him back and forth. Dark chunks and flaming debris fell from the sky, plummeting all around him. Black sky filled the spot where the plane had been a moment before.

Rule usually prayed before every jump. He had been too busy tonight checking on his own men to pray for himself. He closed his eyes for a moment. In that instant, high up in the sky, he prayed, wordlessly asking for the salvation and safety of his stick, the ones who had gone out before him, and the crew of the plane falling from the sky.

The cold wind in his face reminded him not to count on God to save him from his own foolish mistakes. He glanced down to prepare for landing. Below, a solid blanket of clouds stretched as far as he could see, cotton white in the moonlight. He must be two, three thousand feet above the ground, instead of the planned five hundred. As he drifted, the Channel glittered in the distance through a break in the rolling cloud bank. Suddenly, tracers arced up through the clouds, followed by a C-47 climbing out of the haze. Rule looked back up. Stars glittered in a black sky. Beyond his canopy a high-flying plane circled overhead. He prayed it was a covering Yank pilot, not some Messerschmitt about to pick him out of all this empty sky.

Rule pulled at his left front riser and turned into the wind. He was so high he would be the first American in Berlin if he didn't lose some air. He slowly turned, the Channel disappearing off to his right until all he could see was the cloud carpet and fingers of tracers rising up, arching over and vanishing back into the clouds. As he floated away from the Channel a canopy of ack-ack blossomed over the cloud bank, dirty red and orange explosions flickering like distant heat lightning. In the midst of the bursts, a plane rolled, its tail sticking up at an impossible angle, then broke apart. The pieces scattered and fell back into the clouds.

This was not the place to be sightseeing, exposed to wandering aircraft and antiaircraft fire. He pulled down hard on both his front risers, spilling air out the back of the chute. He fell faster. No longer gently swaying under the canopy, he fell dangerously fast toward the clouds and airplanes. The wind whistled through his helmet straps as he dropped toward the cloud bank. He forced the risers down as far as he could until his clutched fists pressed against his thighs.

He knifed through the clouds, plummeting down, racing after the destroyed aircraft, moon-silvered wisps of clouds streaming past until he was entombed in dampness, condensation streaming from his face like a torrent of tears. Ack-ack exploded; airplane engines screamed all around him. The noise, muffled, then amplified, beat against his ears.

An unseen plane roared below him. Rule curled his feet up like an about-to-be-born babe. A scream cut through the clouds. He wasn't sure if it was his own, the aircraft engine, or another parachutist somewhere in the sky. An instant later he dropped down into clear sky, dark, sliced into sections by rising gunfire and the narrow beam of a searchlight probing for an airplane. It settled on a C-47 below him. The plane twisted, jinked, trying to escape the light and the tracers that followed. It turned, heading directly toward him.

He released his risers. The canopy snapped overhead and the harness bit into his thighs, snatching him up short with a jolt that left him swaying. The arc peaked as the C-47 aileron sliced through the air below his feet. The searchlight beam washed over, followed by multicolored tracers, snapping through the air like a million cracks of a bull whip at the rodeo.

His helmet reverberated as a bullet ricocheted away. Bullets zipped past with loud cracks. Then tiny pops snatched at his chute. He felt tugs on the risers as bullets pierced his canopy. A "twang" and a shroud line parted, slapped him across the face. He dropped, his canopy losing air. He yanked his reserve handle, waited for the white chute to explode out of the pack strapped to his chest. Nothing. A dark blur dropped past, followed by the shredded remains of a white parachute.

The ground rushed up at him, a whirling, blurry black hole. Oh, dear God. He could feel he was spinning, his partially-deflated chute whirling him around. He crashed though unseen tree limbs. Leaves whipped across his face. A last jerk as the chute caught in the limbs, then released. His chest crashed across a large limb. He seemed to stop for a moment. Then a stomach-churning fall, his risers jerking him upright as the canopy snagged in the tree, released, and he finally slammed to the ground, flat of his back.

He lay still, unable, unwilling to move, afraid of what would fall off if he tried to get up. Overhead a body swayed from the tree limbs under a deflated canopy. Distant explosions drummed through the ground. Rule groaned and stretched out each limb in turn, left leg, right leg, right arm, then—

Pain blasted through him like a branding iron rammed against his left arm. He lay back and bit his tongue to keep from screaming. His eyes squeezed shut with the pain, lights flashed past his eyelids. He forced them open when he heard a vehicle engine, close. Brakes squealed and the engine slowed to an idle, then stopped with a cough. Rule eased his belly strap loose and reached up to release the snaps holding his reserve tight to the harness. His fingers touched a metal fragment, big as his hand, impaled in his reserve pack—shrapnel from a flak explosion, or a piece of the disintegrating airplane. Whichever, the reserve pack had probably saved his life. He let the pain wash over him as he stripped his harness free, down to the point where he could feel his .45 in its chest holster.

Was this it? He had sworn to himself that he wouldn't be a coward, not like before. If the Germans came he wouldn't run. With the back of the hand he wiped away the tears that welled in his eyes. He tried to sit up. Upright, he let the pain rake across his body, and ran his hand down his left arm. He stopped when he felt the lump. His forearm was broken, but at least the bone wasn't poking through. He pushed the pain, his frustration to the back of his mind.

He held his breath. A soft rustling in the brush. Someone crawled toward him through the damp grass. He fumbled with the snap, finally slid his pistol out and clicked the .45's hammer back.

"Hallo."

Rule winced with the pain as he whipped his head around. Inches from his face a pair of eyes stared back at him.

"Can you get up?" a woman asked in accented English.

"Think so. My arm's broken," he answered, willing to ignore all the reasons a woman shouldn't be out and about as German patrols and American paratroopers spread mayhem across the French countryside. He winced as she ran a hand down his forearm.

"Here?" she asked.

"Yes."

"Anything else hurt?" She pulled his weapons container and musette bag clear.

Shit. Everything hurt.

A barrage of shots rattled through the trees. Rule grunted as the woman shoved him down and sprawled across his chest. A German voice shouted, just feet away, and a shadowy figure ran past. Rule elbowed the woman aside and tried to sit back up, pointing the pistol in the direction of the voices.

"Don't shoot." She whispered, and pushed his .45 down to the ground. "My friends will draw the Germans away." She rose to her knees and listened. "The *Boche* go to the village." She dumped his carbine out of the weapons container and tied the canvas bag to his arm as a makeshift splint. Rule's head whirled with pain as she looped the ties around his arm and cinched it tight.

"Come." She helped him to his feet. She picked up the carbine in one hand and slung his musette bag over her other slim shoulder. "We are going to blow up the railroad. Our mission, we plan for weeks. Finally. But I will get you safe. Come."

Rule stared at her. She wasn't even five feet tall, maybe weighed seventy pounds. And she was hell bent on blowing up a railroad. Might as well tag along.

He stood, dizzy with the pain, not just his arm, his entire body felt like he had been in a rodeo run over by a bull. Head pounding with each step, he followed her along the edge of a thick hedgerow. Maybe if he talked he could get the pain out of mind. "My name is Harry. What's yours?"

Her teeth flashed in the moonlight. "Anna-Maria," she whispered. "Don't talk loud, Harry. Many *Boche* between here and the railroad." The throbbing from his arm had leveled out to a dull ache; and the rest of his body had loosened up by the time she stopped, a thin hand held up in the air.

He followed as she slipped through a narrow gap in a hedgerow and crossed a beaten path to a low wall that blocked the path. On the other side of the wall a building, larger than a house, maybe a barn, loomed. A shadowy group of men clustered around a pile of sandbags at the far corner. Rule slowly moved up beside Anna-Maria and sank to his knees beside her, so close they touched. Her body trembled. A faint scent of lavender mixed with sweat wafted from her. She motioned toward the sandbags. "Machine gun," she whispered.

Rule narrowed his eyes and stared until he could make out the barrel poking out of the sandbags. He looked back at Anna-Maria. Her eyes were full of questions. He was the soldier, should know what to do. He took a deep breath. A fire had beat him once, just because it was fast and he hadn't reacted quickly enough. Act first. Before the fire starts.

"How do we get past them?" he asked. Before Anna-Maria could answer, a voice called out behind them, from the far side of the hedgerow—in German. Rule slid his pistol back into its holster. He motioned toward the musette bag and held out his hand.

Anna-Maria carefully laid down the carbine, took out a fragmentation grenade and held it out toward him.

The voices came closer. Rule took the grenade out of her trembling fingers with his right hand, fingers closed around the spoon. "Stick a finger thought the ring and pull the pin out of the grenade."

She held his hand and the grenade in hers. Their hands, wrapped together, shook. Rule smiled. She was as scared as he was. Good. Scared made you act quickly, before you thought too much about it. She slid her finger through the ring and pulled the pin from the grenade in his hand, then took out a second grenade and pulled its pin. She held the grenade in both hands and looked up at him. "I am afraid," she said.

Rule had thought about this moment for the past three years. Jumping out of planes had always been easy, the same with fighting fires. Except for the one time. A narrow Idaho canyon on a blazing hot July. The fire had hopped the break and spread, crackling and roaring as the flames climbed to the tops of the trees, raced up the canyon floor hard on their heels. His partner, Larry, was leading them up the slope when he stepped into a depression filled with loose ash, twisted to one side, his foot caught, then tumbled to the ground. "No, go on," Larry had screamed when Rule started back. So Rule had run, the roar deafening, the heat blistering his neck. When he finally turned to look, all he saw was a blazing inferno. Despite everyone telling him he had done the right thing, in his own mind, he had been a coward ever since. When the Army brass convinced the Forestry Service to release him to the Airborne School, he had determined he would do something that would make it right for Larry, somewhere, sometime. Right here, tonight would do.

He grinned at Anna-Maria. "It's good that you are afraid. Ready?"
She nodded.
"Throw when I do."
She nodded.

He tossed his grenade over the wall toward the machine gun. Eyes big, Anna-Maria followed suit, an awkward two-handed toss. The grenade spoons clanged on the cobblestones. One of the Germans muttered something as the seconds passed. Crouched low, shoulders touching, they waited. Rule wanted to put his arm around the woman, pull her close, tell her it would be O.K. Before he could do any of that, the first grenade exploded, then the second, to screams and a sudden spray of automatic weapon fire over their heads. Bullets rattled through the hedgerow brush behind them.

In response, the soldiers behind them returned fire through the opening in the hedgerow. Bullets zinged overhead, German shooting at German. One smacked into the wall by Rule's face, fragments stinging his cheek.

Anna-Maria let out a thin moan and collapsed in a heap by the wall.

He bent close to her face. Her eyes, those dark, serious eyes, were wide open. No breath. "Anna," he whispered, ignoring the bullets snapping and cracking past. "Don't be afraid." She didn't answer.

Bastards.

He dug another grenade from the bag, mashed the ends of the pin together until he could pull it free by sticking the thumb of his left hand in the ring and pulling the serrated body of the grenade free with his right, ignoring the pain that shot up from his arm. He rose up so he could see over the wall. The pin fell from his thumb with a tiny tinkle, and the German's head turned until he had to be looking directly at him. Rule stared at him, defying him as the German ripped a burst of automatic fire against the wall. Rule opened his hand, let the butterfly handle spring open. He counted "One," for Larry, "Two," for Anna, and tossed the grenade over the wall toward the German's feet, finally dropping below the wall beside Anna-Maria's still body.

With a muffled "blam" the grenade exploded. Rule struggled to his feet and stood, .45 extended over the wall. No one moved. The machine gun barrel poked straight up out of the dark pile of burst sand bags and bodies.

A soft voice called out from behind him, on the far side of the hedgerow, then another, more gutteral. For an instant he imagined the first was Anna-Marie. He knelt down and laid her body out straight, smoothed her short hair out of her face and closed her eyes.

No more lavender.

No more running.

Rule turned back toward the sounds of the voices. He slid the .45 back in his holster and picked the carbine up by the pistol grip, leaving the wireframe butt folded up against the forestock. He mashed the carbine's safety button down with his index finger. "Thank you, Anna-Maria," he whispered and snapped off a quick shot at the dark figure slipping through the gap in the hedgerow. By the time he had emptied the magazine, the gap was piled with bodies.

He shouldered the bag of grenades and listened to the sounds of combat all around him. A quad A-A gun pounded away, tracers streaming up into the sky. He would go that direction, find Anna-Maria's railroad and finish her mission. For her and for Larry. Different battles, maybe, but good people had died in both.

A dog howled across the hedgerows, a lonely, sad sound.

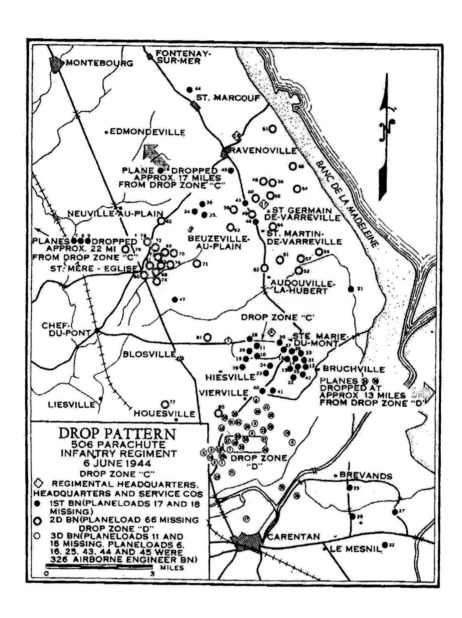

DROP PATTERN
506 PARACHUTE
INFANTRY REGIMENT
6 JUNE 1944
DROP ZONE "C"

◇ REGIMENTAL HEADQUARTERS,
HEADQUARTERS AND SERVICE COS
● 1ST BN(PLANELOADS 17 AND 18
MISSING)
◉ 2D BN(PLANELOAD 66 MISSING
DROP ZONE "D"
○ 3D BN(PLANELOADS 11 AND
15 MISSING. PLANELOADS 6.
16, 25, 43, 44 AND 45 WERE
326 AIRBORNE ENGINEER BN)

CHAPTER 7 - 2/506TH PRCHT INF

Keller fished through his musette bag until he found the opened bag of Beechnut and pulled it out. Be damned if he hadn't earned a chew. "Want a chaw?"

Stimson shook his head and walked over to the other side of the rail bed, both of them keeping to the muddy dirt to avoid the crunch of the cinders under their jump boots. Up in the low branches a disturbed bird twittered softly in the still night.

"Pssst."

Keller stopped and eased to a crouch, a long slice of Beechnut dangling from his lips. He stared ahead down the rail bed. Nothing he could see. He glanced over at Stimson.

Stimson pointed behind them. Maybe a hundred yards back a light flickered, reminding Keller of O'Shey and his map. Couldn't be O'Shey. The light vanished. Keller motioned Stimson toward the other side of the embankment as he backed into the trees behind him. He eased behind a tree trunk, waiting, peeling a splinter out of the groove in the M1's forestock that the German's bullet had gouged out. He slid down to a knee as the footsteps approached. At least two, maybe three people. He could hear murmuring voices. No sound discipline. He let them pass, almost choking as the wad of tobacco swelled in his cheek. Belatedly he realized he needed to spit something ferocious. The men passed, three of them, two bareheaded, one wearing a peaked cap. Keller slowly raised his rifle, centered the head wearing the peaked cap in his sights. He hoped Stimson was ready to fire. When he dropped the first one, the other two were sure to gallop down the far side of the track, right into Stimson's lap.

A cricket clacked from the far side of the tracks.

Keller raised his head from the rifle stock, watching the three men.

They stopped, motionless for a moment. "Who's there," one of them whispered.

Sounded American. Keller wondered about the spies they had been told about, if the Germans really did have commandos running around dressed like GIs. He pressed his cheek back against the cool wood and slowly tightened the pressure on the trigger as he tracked the cap in his sights.

"Flash."

Keller recognized Stimson's voice. Silence. Keller dropped the top of the front sight down from the cap to where the eyes should be.

"Thunder," one of the men finally answered.

Keller spit a wad of juice onto the ground. Thank God that was over with. He'd probably have choked on his wad if he had pulled the trigger. He stood and walked up the bank to the gathering. "Why don't you folks just wave a 'shoot me' sign up here, stomping along, lights, talking. For Christ's—" He stopped when he realized two of the men wore leather flight jackets and the third sported a major's leaf on his collar. Keller stifled a gag as a sip of tobacco juice slid down his throat.

"You're damn right, soldier. I been trying to tell these guys they don't know what the hell they're doing," the officer in the peaked cap said. "Which one of you guys is in charge?"

Keller glanced over at Stimson, who just grinned back at him. Well, crap. After all this, some tight-ass fly boy was going to chew his butt. "I am, sir. Corporal Keller."

"Good. Corporal, me and the Lieutenant are airplane jocks. We don't know shit about ground combat, never planned to be down here with you. Wish to hell I wasn't. The Lieutenant is stupider than usual, took a lick on the head. But Major Levine has a priority mission to blow up a radar installation somewhere along the railroad. You lead us where ever he says we need to go, and we'll follow, at least until we meet up with some more folks. Deal?"

This was about as dumb a mission he had ever heard. But it fit with the rest of the night. And it wasn't an ass-chewing, at least he didn't think so. "If you say, sir."

"And quit the 'sir' crap. You're the boss. I'm Frank." He pointed at the slender pilot with a field dressing wrapped around his head. "This is Joey, and the man with the plan is Major Levine."

Levine reached up, pulled off the major's leaf and tossed it into the trees. "Corporal, you call me Stan. And if you could help me find the radar set that's supposed to be around here somewhere, I'd appreciate it."

So he was in charge. His first thought was to tell them to forget about any damn radar. But then, what else did he have to do? Just like a herd of Herefords, all he had to do was keep them quiet and move them along. "First, let's get down off the crown of the track line. Somebody, German or American, is going to come along and shoot one of us, standing up here jawing." Once they had moved down by the tree line he listened to Major Levine—Stan—describe his target.

"It's supposed to be a modified *Würzburg-Riese-E,* a radar accurate enough to direct antiaircraft fire, and possibly including IFF, Identification, Friend or Foe, capability. The Brits raided an installation last year and got the parts for a *Freda,* the long range system. When the intel guys heard there might be a new version of the *Wurzburg* around here, somebody decided it would be worth the risk to try and find it, knock it out before the gliders came in."

"Too technical for me," Keller said. "You got any specifics about where the radar is? If we just wander all over hell and creation, we'll likely stir up a German patrol or stumble into an ambush."

"*Oi vey!*" Levine dug under his shirt and came up with a folded map, fished in a pocket and pulled out a pair of glasses and pushed them on his nose. "I forgot all about this." He unfolded the map and held it close to his face. "Too damn dark."

"Who's got a lighter?" Keller asked.

Joey pulled one out and started to snap it open.

"Not in the open." Keller grabbed the lighter out of Joey's hand. "Come here, Major Levine, Stan, whoever the hell you are." Keller pulled his poncho out of the bottom of his musette bag and squatted by a tree. Levine joined him under the poncho, unfolded the map and smoothed it out. "Right there," said Levine, pointing to a red circle barely visible in the flickering light.

"O.K. Got that part." Keller snapped off the light and pulled the poncho off his head. "Frank, come look and tell me where you think we are."

Levine walked back up to the track and Howell took his place, head under the jacket.

Keller thumbed the lighter again, and light from the yellow flame danced over the damp sheet. "Stan says the radar is supposed to be at the circle."

Howell bent closer, then coughed. "Phew." He looked up at Keller.

"Cow shit," Keller said.

"Oh. Cow shit." Howell left it at that and scanned the map for a moment, tracing the river with his finger, along to the rail line, then over to the radar site, marked about a hundred yards off the tracks, next to a cluster of buildings. "Cloud bank was so thick I'm not really sure where we came down, but I think we're still west of the radar site. Close, though. Less than half a mile away, looks to me." He tapped the map on the rail line between Carentan and Baupte with his finger. "My guess is that we're right about here."

A hand gripped Keller's shoulder.

"Keller. Lights out. Somebody's coming."

Keller doused the lighter and wadded the poncho back in the musette bag as he slid behind the tree.

A flashlight beam bobbed along the track. The light came closer, until Keller could make out two men in the reflected light.

"Joey. Get down," Howell called out in a stage whisper, desperation in his voice. "Christ, Joey!"

Keller stared along the tracks. Nothing to the right. Men and light from the left. The slender pilot stood like a cow chewing its cud in the middle of the tracks. His bandaged head gleamed in the yellow flashlight beam as the light swept across him. A befuddled look crossed his face as Joey tried to shade the light from his eyes.

The light suddenly washed up and down Joey's body, then steadied on his face. "Halt!" a voice shouted.

Keller grabbed Frank's arm as he lunged toward Joey. "Wait, Frank. Let Joey be. We'll take them." Keller looked around. Stimson had sprawled to the ground, a few feet over. Levine wasn't in sight. "Frank. You know how to shoot that shotgun?" he whispered.

"Yeah. But Joey's still half out of it. Damn Germans will get him."

"No they won't. Be patient. Like waiting for a big buck to clear the trees, just be quiet and hold still."

The two Germans came closer. Keller stared back down the track, wondering if they were alone. Was this what being in command meant? Sacrificing one of your men so the rest wouldn't get taken? Filling your pockets with dog tags?

Before Keller had time to decide, a pistol barked from the far side of the embankment, two quick reports answered by a rifle fired by one of the Germans. Then all hell broke loose, shots zinging all around as Keller raced to the top of the embankment and pulled Joey down onto the cross ties. Stimson opened up with a burst from his Thompson and Howell's shotgun boomed, racked, boomed again.

"Cease fire," Keller yelled. "God dammit, stop shooting." He rose to his knees and squinted along the glistening rails in both directions. Nothing moved. Down the track both Germans lay crumpled across the rails. The flashlight beam shone straight up into the air like a searchlight into the ground fog floating overhead. The bird stilled, not a twitter from the tree. "Stay here till I figure out what's happening," he whispered to Joey.

"Sure," the Lieutenant responded. "Just don't leave me alone again."

"Levine. Stan. You all right?" Keller called out. He picked up the flashlight and shined it along the trees on the far side of the embankment. Levine's head popped out from behind a tree, squinting into the light. Keller swept the flashlight over the tracks, paused over two Germans sprawled face down. Keller snapped off the light and stuck it in a pocket. He slowly turned his head, listening for Germans, wondering if the bird had been real, if he had all his hearing back after the C-2 explosions and flak gun trying to blow his head off, if he would ever hear real birds again like he once did.

Howell and Stimson trotted up out of the tree line, both reloading their weapons. The bird, real or imagined, apparently unperturbed by the shooting, started up again and sounded a couple of short tweets, nothing to identify the bird, just enough to announce there was life in the woods. And that he could hear. If anyone else was coming, they had stopped dead still.

Keller cocked his head, ears toward the sky. No more airplanes. The Division must all be on the ground. He sure as hell wished a few more troopers would show up around here. He sniffed the air, thick with the stench of marsh mud and frog shit. They were close to the river. He could smell it, heavy, over the lingering odor of blood, manure and gunfire.

"Are they dead?" asked a breathless Levine.

Lord. Leading soldiers was a loose bag of crap. Herding cows was so much simpler. "You're the one who started all the shooting. You go see."

"Can I have the light?"

"No, dammit. Go over and check their pulse, on the side of their neck. If they're alive, shoot them in the head. One bullet each, like you'd put down a wounded animal."

Levine stared at him. "In the head?"

Keller snatched the pistol from Levine's hand and knelt by the two bodies. One still had a faint pulse. Keller looked down at the pistol, shook his head. After all the talk, he couldn't do what he told Levine to do. Even if they were Germans, they weren't deer.

The German shuddered. His head flopped against the rail. Keller felt again. No pulse this time. Thank the Lord, he was thankful he wouldn't have to put the man down.

When he stood, everyone had gathered around him. "O.K. You dumb shits put me in command, so listen to me. No more shooting unless I tell you to." He snapped the pistol safety back on.

"But they were Germans," Levine protested.

"And what if they were the scouts for a platoon sweeping down the track?" He handed Levine the pistol. "A kraut might be putting a bullet in your big brain about now." He turned to Stimson. "You cover our asses. After all the shooting, everybody for a mile in every direction knows we're here. I don't want to be snuck up on. The rest of you, follow me, down out of the cinders. Keep an interval; keep it quiet, and no lights. And Levine, you stay behind me. If you see any sign we're close to your radar, tug on my shirt. But not another word, got it? And for lands sakes, no more shooting till I say so."

Keller spit out his wad of chewing tobacco. Didn't need any more juice tonight. A measured pop, pop, pop of outgoing mortar fire, followed by the muted explosions of their impacts stilled the lone bird's twittering. Poor bird just couldn't get the war to go away. He kind of felt the same. But somehow he had to keep this bunch together, make it through the night, back to some sense of order.

He turned to the pilots. "Frank. Can you keep a handle on Joey? I know he's out of it a bit, but he'll get us all killed if he just wanders around by himself."

Howell nodded. "If he gets to be a problem I'll collar him and hide out in the woods. But I would rather stay with you guys as long as we can."

"Sure. Just keep an eye on him."

A half mile down the railroad Keller stopped, listened as the feet stopped shuffling behind him. The muted grumble of an engine of some kind floated over the trees from the left. He stared into the darkness, sweeping his eyes side to side until he confirmed a gap in the trees. He waited; let the group close up on him. "Stan. We're getting close. You stick with me." He turned to Stimson. "You keep control of everybody else, but stay behind me and Stan. We're going up this road to see if the radar is up there. If I stop, you stop. If you lose touch or hear shooting, just get the hell out of here. Get Joey to a medic and...ah, shit, you know what to do well as I do."

Keller led them along the side of what he first thought in the dark was a road, but turned out to be a rail spur with a set of ruts running alongside. He stopped, put out a hand and pulled Levine to a halt. About a hundred yards ahead, the tiny glow of a cigarette stirred the darkness.

Levine turned to Keller, eyes wide behind his large framed glasses. Keller put his hand on Levine's shoulder and pushed him to the ground. "Stay here and warn our guys if they come up. Got to move quickly before Joey decides to walk up to some kraut and ask for a smoke. Here, take care of my rifle. And damn it, don't shoot anybody with it."

Keller slid the Fairborn knife from his boot and circled into the trees. Bent down to a low crouch, he slipped under the tree limbs and crept between a pair of tall hardwoods. A twig snapped under foot. He stopped, listening. Just another stalk. But this time not for meat on the hoof. He stepped softly, easing his toes down on the ground. He wasn't tracking a bighorn, he reminded himself. Germans shoot back.

He froze when the clouds broke for a moment and moonlight lit the forest like a billboard. Or so it seemed after the heavy darkness under the trees. In the brief moment of light he located the German, a single sentry, less than ten feet away facing the other direction, out toward the rail spur. He smelled acrid cigarette smoke drifting through the trees. Glad the wind was blowing toward him. He didn't want the kraut to think he was about to be attacked by a cow. Another step and the sentry drew on his cigarette, a red beacon glowing in the darkness. He was sitting in front of a machine gun, looking back toward where the rest of his guys hid in the darkness. His guys. Ah, the joy of command.

The kraut looked broad as a barn. Summer, so it wasn't cold. But it had been raining. Did he have on a heavy raincoat? Keller wished he hadn't lost his bayonet, or better yet, had his old skinner. He had won the Case Fairborn from a Ranger who was a crappy poker player. Poker was one skill he had honed sitting around the Ninemile smoke jumper camp on alert, after realizing the Reno casinos odds were too long for him.

Long, slim, the Fairborn's blade was perfect for stabbing, but didn't have the heft to slash though a heavy raincoat. He reversed the knife and stepped up behind the sentry. The brute sat softly humming to himself. Keller reached over, grabbed the German's helmet and pulled up, expecting the chin strap to be fastened and the German's neck to be exposed to a quick stab down.

Instead, when Keller jerked, the helmet flew off and the German roared and spun around swinging. Before Keller could blink a heavy fist crashed into the side of his head. Keller smashed the pointed steel haft into the German's temple and slashed down with the blade. The German fell on top of him, big as a grizzly; pounding his fists into Keller's ribs until Keller felt them crack, growling into his ear.

Fingers closed around his throat, squeezing. Keller twisted, bucked, got his arm free and plunged the knife into the German's back, twisted it free of the heavy coat, then stabbed again, lower this time, searching for a kidney. The German's face blurred. The grip around Keller's throat tightened. Red streaks shot across his eyes, then coal black darkness.

CHAPTER 8 - 502ND PRCHT INF

Stimson knelt down and shoved at the German. His heavy bulk barely moved. "Corporal? Keller?" Ah, shit. He didn't want to be left in command of this gaggle.

Levine knelt down beside him. "Is Corporal Keller all right?"

"Let's get the damn kraut off him and see," Stimson said. He shoved at the inert body, and with Levine's help rolled the German's massive body off Keller.

Keller, choked, sucked in a deep breath.

Stimson grinned in relief. "Keller. You hurt bad?"

Keller opened his eyes, blinked.

Stimson sniffed. Keller still stunk like cow shit. "Being with you is like working in a barnyard. Jeeze, can you get up?" he asked.

Keller rolled over to his knees, shaking his head. "Man. I took a dare once, rode a bull at a rodeo over in Arlee, Montana. The bull was nice to me compared to what that bastard did." Keller looked up, looked around them. "Did he sound the alarm?"

"Nah. Didn't get a chance with you all over him. All we heard was a bunch of thrashing and grunting. Stan, here, saved your butt."

"What? Did he fire off that .45 again?" Keller asked, the concern apparent in his voice.

"No. Stop fretting, for God's sake." Stimson said with a chuckle. "I think you 'bout bled him out first. Then Stan finished him off. Cold cocked him with your rifle."

Levine grinned. "I whapped him on the back of the head with the butt, but he was so damn heavy I couldn't move him, so I went back and got the others."

Keller stood, bones popping back in place. "Thanks, Stan," Keller said, his voice raspy. He sank back down, clutching his side, stuffing a wad of tobacco in his mouth. He chewed for a minute, then spit. "Son of a bitch cracked a couple of ribs, damn near ripped out my throat."

Stimson looked at the other three as they walked up, standing in a circle like lost puppies. In the distance a machine gun ripped through the night. Rate of fire so fast it must be a German MG-42, answered by a rapid volley of rifle fire, probably M1s. Time to bite the bullet.

"O.K., guys. Keller here is out of the fight for now. Frank, come over here. You and Joey sit down with Keller and figure out how to fire this machine gun. Anything comes up the spur, open up on them, then run like hell. Drag Keller along with you if he can't make it on his own. Stan, you and me'll go on up this track and see if that radar's up there." He looked around. "That all right with everybody?"

No one squawked. "O.K. Let's get this over so we can get to the real fight." The distant exchange of gunfire picked up again, as if to emphasize Stimson's words. He hitched his pack on his shoulders and checked the safety on his Thompson. "Come on. Let's go, then." He followed as Levine slowly walked between the rails, shortening his pace to stay on the cross ties.

Twenty yards up Levine stopped as he cleared the trees masking a bend in the rail bed. Ahead, the spur ended with a single rail car parked at the end the track. Off to the left a low building sat beside the track, a smaller shed past that. A tiny crack of light leaking around the bottom edge of a blackout curtain revealed an empty staff car parked by the shed. On the far side of the rail car an engine thrummed. They both dropped between the rails as a door to the building opened and light flashed past an emerging soldier. Stimson eased his head up to peek between the rail and the lip of his helmet. He lost the emerging man when Levine's big butt blocked his view. He rose up higher on his elbows so he could see over Levine. The soldier ambled toward an odd, crescent shape standing between the tall trees. More light rolled over the crescent and it resolved to a circular dish on a pedestal. At least one more figure sat on the rail car beside the dish.

Someone inside yelled out in German, and the door slammed shut. A thump, and the man who just left the building muttered in the darkness.

A field expedient pair of posts swayed in the dim moonlight peeking through the clouds, the posts lashed together in an "X" to support a bundle of cables draped between the rail car and the building. The stupid ass must have run into the posts in the dark, still blinded from the inside light. Or just dumb. Stimson hoped for any and all these to be true.

Stimson watched the grumbling German walk around the corner of the building, tracking him with the Thompson. After the German disappeared behind the building, Stimson crawled along the rail until he was even with Levine. "That round thing on the rail car," he whispered. "Is that the radar?"

"Yeah. See the big parabolic reflector?" Levine got up on his knees. "I need a couple of minutes at the control box to see what I can find, then time to set the charges."

Stimson pulled him back down to the rail bed. "Wait a minute, at least till the guy that just came out comes back. He probably went to check something. Or someone. There may be another machine gun out there. And see, there's at least one man on the radar, maybe more."

Levine pushed his glasses back on his nose. "Darn. I didn't notice them," he muttered. "Makes sense. A couple of men manning the set and a telephone line, or a radio, connecting them to their air defense center. The building might be the control center. We know the Germans use the *Würzburg Freda* to coordinate and direct night fighters, searchlights and flak guns. Not sure how this system is set up. Sure wish I could get a look inside." He held his arm close to his face. Tiny green smears glowed on his glasses, a reflection of his luminous watch face. "I can't wait any longer." Cinders crunched under his boots as he stood.

Stimson cussed the cinders biting into the palms of his hands, cussed his misfortune to be tangled up with some radar expert. Damn. Hooked up with too many heroes tonight. O'Shey dead already. They were moving too fast. Keller, rest of the dumb bastards will all be dead meat, himself included, before dawn. Got to slow this train down. He grabbed Levine's ankle. "Wait a minute, Stan. Too many krauts here. We'll head back to the others and then mosey on down to the rail line, link up with some more troopers. Hear all that shooting? Lots of our guys running around out there."

"Can't," Levine whispered back.

Obstinate little shit. "What do you mean, can't?" Stimson rose to a crouch beside Levine, his eyes scanning the tree line.

"First glider serial is coming in before light." Levine pulled up his sleeve and squinted at his wrist. "Supposed to be here in about half an hour. If this radar is set up especially to intercept them like the intelligence reports said they might, it'll be a turkey shoot. I'm not going to let that happen. So you do what you want, but I'm for damn sure putting this radar out of operation."

Stimson looked at Levine. "You think this radar gizmo's that important?"

"Yep."

More important than living? Stimson shook his head, remembering the terrifying flak exploding all around his plane. "All right, then. Let me lead and we'll go see how bad we can screw up their radar. But be quiet."

Stimson eased to his feet and started on a quick circle to the right around the rail car, Thompson held ready. His pack shifted on his back. Damn. He'd been carrying the EE-8 and field wire so long he forgot he had it. Not likely to be installing any phones tonight. He'd dump the pack as soon as he had a chance. He stopped, peered into the darkness, wondering where the German had gone.

Levine tugged at his sleeve. "Time's running out."

"Shush." Stimson stopped between the rail car and the woods and sniffed the air. Exhaust fumes and the cyclic rumbling confirmed a generator chugging away by the wood line. How best to shut down the radar? If he turned off the fuel, killing the generator, the troops in the building would come pouring out. Or maybe not. Techs didn't like to get dirty. They'd more likely send out some private to check the generator. "If we stop the generator, the radar doesn't work, right?" he whispered.

"Yeah." Levine stared up in the sky, lit by intermittent flashes. "The radar needs a good bit of power, more than batteries. It might be powered from the cables coming from the building and the generator is just a backup. But I don't see any permanent utility poles or wires, just those cables on the ground." He pointed to a heavy dark line leading back toward the generator.

"O.K., then. I'll shut down the generator and take out whoever comes down to fix it. You watch the radar. When you get a chance, get what you need and blow up what's left. By then the place will be crawling with Germans, so just run like hell back to Keller and the flyboys." Stimson left Levine standing beside a tree and trotted down a beaten path toward the sound of the generator. He might not be the brain that Levine was, but he knew things like generators, the bane of every signalman's life. Two years as the pole lineman and general fix-it man for the Ellerbe Telephone Company had taught him how obstinate they could be. When he saw the paratroopers training up at Camp Mackall he figured he had found how to escape fouled carburetors and fuel pumps. Instead, he had found himself doing the same thing for the Army. And he got to shoot at Germans, to boot.

He stumbled across a rut, stopped, listened. Ahead, the generator, massive up on a low slung wheeled trailer, sat parked back in the edge of the woods where the trees muted the generator noise. As Stimson got closer, the roar and rattle of the generator engine drowned out the distant shooting and the nearby crickets. He waded through a stand of ankle-high grass to a gravity feed metal fuel tank perched high up on a makeshift stand, secured by a pair of metal straps. He ran his hand over the tank. Old, rusty straps, by the feel of them.

A rickety wooden ladder leaned against the tank for access to the fill port and a big wheel valve on top of the tank. Big sucker, about four times the capacity of a single fifty-five gallon drum. He tapped the metal as far up as he could reach with his knuckles. From the thumps, the tank sounded at least half full. A hose drooped out from the bottom and led over toward the generator trailer.

Damn. Can't just stand here. Levine will take them all on with that friggin' .45. So what's easiest, Stimson wondered? He shook the ladder. Wood felt rotten as his granny's teeth.

The glow of a cigarette floated down the path. Levine didn't smoke, did he? The guy puffing on the cigarette was at least a foot taller than Levine, unless he was holding his smoke up over his head. Must be the brother to that giant Keller fought with. Stimson slipped behind the stand, laid his Thompson in the damp grass and reached down, felt his boot, whispered a curse. Trench knife was gone. Must be back at the rail car where O'Shey had bought it, flung to hell and back when the C-2 packet blew. He had been so glad to find his Thompson he hadn't even thought about the damn knife. He pulled out his TL-29 field wireman's knife—remembered the big arms on the other German—and eased the knife shut. Nope. TLs wouldn't do, not by a long shot. He let the knife drop back in a pocket.

Suddenly the fuel tank reverberated like a Chinese gong.

Looking down between the supports, Stimson saw a glint of moonlight reflected from a pair of high boots. Shiny toes stepped up on the ladder, one, two steps. The tank groaned, shifted ever so slightly on the stand. Stimson pushed against his side of the tank and it rocked back and forth. Metal clanged against the other side of the tank.

"*Was?*" muttered the German.

Stimson bent his knees, put his shoulder under the tank and shoved. A louder groan and the tank rolled off the stand, the German screaming as it fell, his shriek matched by the screech of metal straps twisting free. The tank hit the ground with a thump. The smell of gasoline filled Stimson's nose as it spewed out into the high grass. The feed hose flipped around on the ground, spitting gas like a dying snake where the hose had ripped free from the tank. Stimson blinked as the gas fumes stung his eyes.

Shit. The generator kept running.

A voice called out from the rail car.

"Crack!"

Damn. Levine and his pistol.

Stimson grabbed his Thompson and ran toward the rail car. Behind him the generator engine coughed, caught, coughed again, then went silent. Stimson vaulted up on the rail car and clambered over a tangle of electronic boxes and cables, praying he didn't find Levine like he had O'Shey.

On the far side of a big metal cabinet something clanged on the floor of the rail car.

Thompson at the ready, Stimson slid around the cabinet.

Levine grinned up at him, pulled a second belt of packets from inside his shirt and stacked them around the base of the radar. "Where's the operator?" asked Stimson.

"Gone to hell." Levine grunted as he stuffed the explosive packets around the pedestal. "Think that's enough C-2? I got more."

"Plenty, for crying out loud. Hurry up. Let's go," whispered Stimson. He slid down behind the radar pedestal and pointed his Thompson at the dark blur where he expected the building door to be. Inside, someone yelled out in German.

"Got to insert the blasting cap." Levine fished a tin box from his pants pocket. "Found them in my pocket."

"In your pocket? Jesus. You're going to blow your nuts off, Stan. Hurry up so I can get the hell away from you."

The building door swung open with a squeal.

Stimson put a burst through the doorway, then pounded the front of the building with a long sweep from the Thompson in case anyone had slipped out into the darkness. "We ain't got all night, damn it."

"The blasting cap. It's electric." Levine wailed. "The lieutenant has the wire and the blasting machine. How can I ignite the C-2?"

Stimson fired another short burst toward the building. Several muzzle blasts answered, red flashes from deep in the building. He handed the Thompson to Levine. "Point this at the door and give them a short burst every little bit. I'll take care of the C-2." He shoved Levine toward the end of the car, yanked off his pack and pulled out the roll of field wire. The clouds were beginning to break up, but the moon was dropping. Great if you didn't want to be seen, but shit if you are splicing wire to a blasting cap stuck in a string of C-2 packs. Between bursts, he heard glass crashing. "Watch out, Stan," he called out. "They're going out the back windows." He twisted on a blasting cap and jammed the cap into a block of C-2. He tied the wire around a support, fingers slick with sweat. He had developed a hatred of rail cars, just in the past few hours. Damned if he was going to let Keller collect his dog tags off this one.

"Go," he shouted to Levine. "Run down the side of the spur toward Keller. I'll be right behind you. Don't shoot until you see them come out. Maybe they won't know we're gone." Hard on Levine's heels, Stimson ran down the tracks, spooling out field wire behind him, his pack flopping from his shoulder.

A fusillade erupted from beside the building. Bullets whizzed past Stimson's ear, zinged off the rail. A searing pain raked his back and he went down, sliding across the loose cinders. The Thompson cut loose just over his head.

"You all right?" Levine asked.

"Hell, no. Sons bitches shot me in the back." Stimson squeezed his eyes shut, took a deep breath. Let the pain seep out. Just like the time he fell down a creosote soaked pole, filled his face with splinters. Just pain. Damned if he was going to die in France. Going home to do that. He slid the pack off his shoulder and pulled out the EE-8, sat it on the ground and unsnapped the canvas case so he could get to the binding posts.

Somewhere back in the trees a shotgun boomed, rattling pellets through the leaves. A man screamed, and two quick shotgun blasts answered a single rifle shot.

Levine fired another abbreviated burst, emptying the Thompson's thirty round magazine. "Oh, Lord," Levine muttered. Rifle fire from the far side of the track splattered gravel and cinders around them as the bullets ricocheted past. "We're not going to do it, are we?"

"Yes we are. I double-damn guarantee you we are going to blow up that damn radar." Stimson dug a Thompson magazine from his jacket pocket and handed it to Levine. "Here, load this and keep shooting. We ain't done yet." He fed the ends of the field wire into the binding posts and cranked the phone. He looked back at the radar. Nothing happened. Lord. Had the wire come loose from the blasting cap?

Levine jammed a magazine in the Thompson and sprayed the far side with a long burst, then bent close to see what Stimson was doing. "DC."

"What?" Pain raced around Stimson's back. He wasn't sure he had heard correctly.

"Direct Current. That's what we need for the blasting caps. Phone cranks out alternating current, AC. I don't think the phone creates enough amperage." He handed Stimson the Thompson, pulled out his .45 pistol and rose to his knees, ignoring the smattering of rifle fire cutting through the air around them.

Stimson grabbed Levine's leg, winced with the effort. "Where you going?"

Levine pulled away, waving the pistol. "Going to detonate the C-2. Stuff the barrel into a C-2 pack and pull the trigger. That should do the trick, finish the job for my family."

Before Levine could take another step a bullet clanged on the rail. Levine gasped; fell on his face beside Stimson. "Dear Lord," he whispered. "Don't let me fail Grandpa now." He started crawling toward the radar, dragging one leg behind him. Bullets whined and sparked off the rails around Stimson's head.

"Stan. Come back. Stan. Damn it."

CHAPTER 9 - 326TH PRCHT ENGR

They had droned through the night, everyone keeping to their own thoughts. Giddy from the Dramamine pill still in his system, Private Luke Dawson drew in a lung full of smoke from his Camel. Didn't help. He was still feeling drowsy, half stupid from the pill. He looked out the open door across from his seat. The glittering water below had slid off into a vast nothing. The plane off their wing tip turned and vanished into the dense clouds. Why wasn't his stick hooking up, getting ready to jump? The jumpmaster stood halfway up the aisle, talking with the crew chief. Dawson flicked his glowing cigarette out the door, his mouth suddenly dry. He could hear muffled explosions. Occasionally a line of tracers zipped past. Dawson's heart began to race. This wasn't right. They had been flying at least half an hour longer than the Major from operations had briefed, twisting and turning through a thick cloud bank.

"Sarge," he yelled out to the jumpmaster. He stood, staggered until he balanced all the gear draped and strapped around him. "Sarge," he yelled again, ignoring the frown from the man across the aisle. Dawson was a combat engineer, packed in with a bunch of infantrymen he didn't know. He couldn't even remember the jumpmaster's name. One of the men sitting halfway up the aisle waved at the jumpmaster, then pointed back at Dawson. The jumpmaster turned, stared back at him. "Sit down, trooper," the jumpmaster yelled.

Dawson shook his head, but waddled back to the end of the row of seats. He turned, facing the door, and dropped back in the metal bucket seat. He stared into the night. Something wasn't right. He felt it in his—

The nose of a plane loomed outside the door.

He stared, not believing what he saw.

Huge, heading directly for him. It was real.

Screams filled the cabin as the other jumpers saw the same image out the left side windows.

Dawson launched himself to his feet. The plane grew, monstrous. Dawson willed his feet to move, but he was unable to leap toward the open door and the oncoming plane. He watched, mesmerized, as a whirling propeller shredded their wing tip. He stared directly into the oncoming pilot's eyes, an instant of shared absolute fear, then a deafening explosion blotted out his world.

Wind screamed in his ears. He was falling, twisting, arms and legs thrashing around like noodles. He cleaved through the cloud, plunging toward the moonlit ground, tracers sparking around him. His leg bag ripped away, slapping him across the face. With an effort he gathered his right arm close to his body, straining against the centrifugal motion of his spin. Leather glove torn off by the wind, he worked his fingers to touch the cold metal of the reserve handle. Tears streamed from his eyes as the wind ripped his uniform, plucked at his skin. He strained to close his fingers around the reserve handle, and, finally, yanked the handle clear.

The reserve chute exploded out of the pack and snatched him out of free fall.

"Ahhh," he screamed as his neck snapped back and the rest of his body twisted under the white canopy. He grabbed at the shroud lines. Before he could pull himself upright, he slammed into the ground, flat on his back. His head hit so hard the webbing in his helmet liner ripped loose. Dazed, Dawson lay on the ground, breathing deeply, trying to pull air back in his deflated lungs, staring up at a single star shining through a gap in the clouds. A dark object hurtled through the sky to crash down beside him, followed by a fluttering strip of cloth that settled over his face. He snatched the cloth from his face, tasting blood. Someone else's, he hoped.

A gust of wind reinflated his chute. His shroud lines tugged at him, and before he could roll over he found himself bumping across the ground, pulled over onto his stomach by the reserve. A jerk, and suddenly his helmet banged the bridge of his nose and flopped off his head as he bounced to a stop. Dawson pulled himself to his knees, freed his waist band and unsnapped the reserve from the D-rings. Released, the ghostly white reserve chute reinflated for a moment, dragged the reserve pack across the ground, then finally settled, tangled around strands of barbed wire.

Son of a gun. If the wire hadn't grabbed his chute he'd be whistling Dixie in the middle of France by now.

The debris from the sky glittered in the moonlight, a piece of aluminum lined with rivets. He looked up. No more plane parts falling from the sky. No other parachutes that he could see. As he stared upward, the clouds closed back up, pushed by a steady breeze across his back. So dark, he could be slap in the middle of a battalion formation and wouldn't know the difference.

Free of his reserve and unused main chute and harness, he stretched his back and tried to inventory what he had left. Not much, he decided. A shoulder holster and his .45 pistol, web belt, first aid pouch and ammo pouches for the pistol and the carbine. No carbine, long gone with the leg bag. Jesus. He patted his waist. The bundles of C-2 were still wrapped under his jacket. He could blow stuff up, so he was still officially an engineer.

But more important, where was he? Where were those guys he was supposed to be supporting? Their mission was to hold some bridge, but for him to blow it if they couldn't hold against the German armor. Stop the tanks at any cost, they had been told. Knees popping, he rose to a crouch and listened to the sounds of battle. Distant machine gun fire, heavy antiaircraft guns, the faint drone of aircraft engines and the rush of surf, like he had heard on leave at Brighton. He let his head drop for a moment. Brighton, starlit nights walking along the sea side with Rebecca, teaching her to jitterbug at the dance hall. He shook his head. Not the time to think about romance. Time to think about living until sunrise. He wiped the sand from his hands and unholstered the .45, gritty with sand. Sand, not mud. He had landed by the damn beach. He slowly stood, pistol at the ready. In front of him the line of barbed wire ran along the edge of a trench line, empty as far as he could see. No battalion, not even a solitary American in sight.

Dawson touched his belt and confirmed he still had his TL-13s, pliers with wire cutters. Might as well start here. He cut though the wire, walked down the line and cut it again, pulling the tangled strands down into the German trench. Might make the life of some GI a bit easier when he came ashore at dawn.

Dawson stopped, frozen in his tracks. Voices floated though the night, in and out of the whispers from the surf. German voices. A dark mass loomed ahead. A few more steps and he reached out and touched cold concrete, gritty with damp sand. A twisted pair of commo wire, slick with the heavy moisture in the air, dangled from a post and followed the trench off into the mists blowing in from the Channel. Pliers in his left hand, pistol in his right, he snipped through the wire pair, then stopped to listen.

Dawson crouched as voices shouted, close. An airplane droned overhead, coming closer.

Suddenly, on the other side of the concrete, a gun began firing, flinging tracers up into the sky toward the sound of a plane. As quickly as it had started, the firing stopped. The droning trailed out over the Channel, fading into the night.

Heart racing, Dawson edged along the concrete wall, probably a bunker packed with krauts. He slid to the corner with his pistol trembling in his hand. The antiaircraft gun would be manned by a crew, plus spotters. Maybe support troops, more guns, inside the bunker. He eased forward another step. How dumb was this?

He peeked around the corner. Dim lantern light flicked across seven men clustered around a single-barrel forty millimeter gun in the center of an open emplacement. The lantern sat back in the narrow entrance to a bunker.

Someone yelled from inside the bunker. One of the men at the gun stood and slowly looked along the wire lines stretching from the entrance. He turned back to the bunker and shook his head. The voice inside the bunker yelled back, more insistent. The German shook his head again, but picked up a weapon, slung it over his shoulder and started toward Dawson, head tilted back as if he were tracing the phone line. The one Dawson had cut.

Dawson slid back against the concrete and dropped the pliers down into his shirt. He holstered the pistol, reached down to his ankle. His fingers closed around the gritty handle of his trench knife, sheath secured to his boot. Before the Army, he had lived his life on a farm. The only blood he had ever drawn with a knife was cleaning fish and castrating pigs. Dawson took a deep breath. Castrating boar hogs took a sharp knife, a quick hand and a determination that it was all for the best. This was all for the best.

When the German stepped around the corner, eyes still up on the dangling wire, Dawson grabbed the German's collar and snatched

106

him toward him. He always hated to listen to the pigs squeal, so he had learned to work quickly. In an instant the German's throat was cut. No whimper, no scream, just the gurgle of blood. Dawson wiped his hands on the man's jacket, then dragged him over and dropped him in the trench on top of the barbed wire.

The German's machine pistol dangled over the trench, sling snagged in the wire. Dawson worked the gun free and checked the magazine. Little nine millimeter copper-nosed bullets glimmered in a fleeting bit of moonlight. Dawson clicked the magazine back in the gun, trying to remember if German machine pistols had safeties, if he had to work the charging lever to put a round in the chamber. Not a clue, his mind was blank, as if he had never attended any of the G2 briefings on German weapons. He slid a second magazine out of the German's belt and stuck it in his baggy pant pocket.

On the horizon a plane headed directly toward him, streaming flames. The gun crew shouted, busied themselves around the gun mount. Dawson took advantage of the noise to pull the machine pistol bolt back and let it go. Nothing popped out. The chamber had been empty.

The antiaircraft gun began firing, a staccato roar, and Dawson stepped around the side of the concrete emplacement. Massive tracers spit from the gun, reaching into the sky directly on a collision course into the plane's path.

Not tonight. Not this gun. Not this plane. Dawson gripped the machine pistol by the magazine and pulled the trigger. The stream of bullets hacked across the gun crew like a ripsaw, flinging screaming men back against the concrete wall. The muzzle climbed up, spraying the rounds up over the survivors' heads. Startled by the machine pistol's action, Dawson gripped the gun tighter, elbow locked against his side and fired again, this time a short burst, holding low. Bullets thumped into walls and bodies, clanged off the metal gun mount.

The gun continued firing, tracers reaching up in the sky, wide of the plane. Dawson stepped to the side, now with a clear view of the one remaining German scrambling behind the gun mount, and held the trigger until the machine pistol stopped firing. He changed magazines and fired again. The still forms beside the gun jerked with the impacts. Ricochets spangled off the gun mount and the barrel, whining away into the darkness or splatting into the concrete walls.

The gun continued firing as the mount slowly rotated. Dawson put another burst directly into the soldier in the gunner's seat and the man tumbled to the ground. Damn gun continued to fire.

A final burst and inside the entrance to the bunker the glass globe shattered. The bare wick flickered, then went out as the gun finally ceased fire. The night suddenly fell silent after the last shell casing clanged to the ground.

He looked back over the Germans in the dim light offered by distant searchlights reflecting from the clouds. Six bodies sprawled around the gun. He had left one more with his throat cut. Who had yelled out from inside the bunker? Had he counted wrong?

The entrance was quiet and dark as a coal cellar. Sweat ran down the back of his neck, chilling. Dawson scavenged though the bodies until he had filled a leather pouch with three loaded magazines in addition to the one in the machine pistol. Then he slung the machine pistol over his shoulder and collected as many of the stick grenades as his baggy pants pockets would hold.

What now? This wasn't a scavenger hunt. He was a demolition man, so "blow something up" came to mind, starting with this damn gun. No need to waste his C-2. He stepped around the bodies and jammed the head of a potato masher into the ammo feed tray. He stuffed another grenade in beside the first, and then unscrewed the cap off the handle.

He looked around. He had blown up enough stuff that he knew he needed a safe bolt hole. He pulled one of the grenades from his pockets. Black as pitch inside. He hesitated. What if the damn place was an explosives storage area, just waiting to blow him and the C-2 around his waist straight to hell? He shivered. One way to find out.

With its lanyard still inside the handle, he tossed the grenade into the bunker entrance. The steel shell clattered on the concrete as it bounced and rolled along the floor until all he heard was a faint echo. Nobody shot back; nobody screamed. Better yet, the place didn't blow up in his face.

Time to move. Dawson yanked the porcelain button hanging from the grenade stuck in the gun ammo tray and scrambled for the bunker entrance. "One thousand," he started his count, remembering the potato mashers normally burned through a delay fuse of black powder about five seconds before ignition—unless they had been booby trapped for instantaneous explosion. He stumbled over one of the dead Germans, tumbled over the carriage and rolled over a second body. He felt the machine pistol sling jerk free and clatter away as he caught himself and scrambled through the low entrance.

"Two thousand." Inside the dark corridor he crawled on his hands and knees until his bare head banged against a wall. Up to four thousand, he dropped down flat, the pliers and belt of C-2 packets mashing against his gut. "Five," he muttered, his count stopped by a blast wave that lifted him up and slid him across the gritty floor. The over-pressure beat at his ears and filled the corridor with a suffocating cloud of grit and dust. As the reverberations died away, an odd noise, almost a howl, echoed back from deep in the darkness.

Dawson lay still for a moment, willing the stiffness out, checking to see if anything was broken. All he needed, with God knows how many more German waiting ahead somewhere in the dark. His worst pain was where the pliers had imprinted in his belly when he had been flattened by the exploding gun. He reached down in his jump jacket, pulled out the pliers and dropped them in his side pocket. One hand on the wall, he rose to a crouch, staring ahead. Total blackness. This was how he imagined a coal mine would be, buried far beneath the surface. Or maybe hell, with the fires out.

Dawson shook the thought out of his head. Whoever waited for him couldn't see any better than he could. From the echoes, he was at the beginning of a narrow corridor, probably leading to the next emplacement. With his first step he kicked something on the floor. He bent and felt around as the dust settled. His hand ran over the machine pistol, stamped metal still hot to the touch. He picked up the gun, reloaded and forged ahead, stopping every few steps to listen. He froze as a glimmer of light outlined an opening ahead. As he got closer he could see a light bulb dangling from the ceiling. As an engineer, he had to shake his head at the sloppy installation. Probably put in by slave labor. Loud voices echoed down the dark corridor.

The hair stood up along his arms when a low growl rumbled down the corridor. He raised the machine pistol, ready for a guard dog to come tearing through the dark. Suddenly the dog yelped, followed by a voice. The dog yelped again, and then squealed. Reminded

Dawson of the time his hound caught its tail in the screen door. He dropped to the floor and crawled toward the light. Carefully he slid forward until he could see around the corner.

A huge dog lunged forward against a chain, teeth bared. He ripped a shred of cloth from the pants leg of a German soldier. The soldier jumped back and slammed his helmet against the dog's nose. No love lost between the two. The dog slunk back against the wall, eyes focused on the German, tensed, ready to leap. The soldier shouted at the dog and picked up a heavy wooden staff. The dog barked at the soldier, a furious yapping. The German cracked the staff across the dog's snout. The yapping turned into a furious fang-bared snarl. The dog strained against the chain. More shouting and the soldier wound up and swung the staff in a long whistling arc. The dog jumped back, but the staff caught him across the shoulders. The dog yelped as it tumbled to the floor. It scrambled up on its feet and backed away. The soldier looked down at his leg. Blood had begun to flow, staining a rip in his pants. He screamed at the dog, threw down the staff, pulled a pistol from his holster and waved it at the dog.

Damn. Dawson decided he was on the dog's side. He slid the machine pistol from around his neck, gripping it by the pistol grip and the stick magazine. Before he could fire, a different voice yelled out from a wide corridor that branched off at right angles from the one with the chained dog.

He eased forward on his belly and inched around the corner until he could see the other men. At least two soldiers stood on a firing step, rifles on a rack against the wall. Between them sat a machine gun mounted on a tripod, pointing out an embrasure. One of the gunners laughed, the other harangued the soldier with the dog. The soldier yelled back at the two men, turned back and screamed at the dog, waving his pistol over his head. Dawson wondered if a whole damn squad waited in the embrasure.

He slid back around the corner out of sight, laid the machine pistol on the concrete and worked two potato mashers out of his pocket. Hands sweating, he unscrewed the caps off their wooden handles. He pulled the lanyard on the first one, counted, "one, two," leaned around the corner and flipped it over the first man's head and toward the two men and the machine gun. He rolled back around the corner, curled up by the wall and grabbed the machine pistol as one of the men shouted a warning.

Just as the grenade exploded, the soldier with the pistol burst around the corner. Muzzle blasts exploded over Dawson's head, filling the dark corridor with spears of flame and deafening noise. Dawson fired the machine pistol, point blank into the soldier's belly, flinging him back against the wall. Pistol dangling from his fingers, the soldier's heels slid out from under him and he slithered to the floor, leaving a trail of blood smeared down the concrete wall. Eyes open, he sat across from Dawson and stared, unseeing.

A ragged volley of bullets splatted and thudded into the concrete wall, splattering fragments into Dawson's face. He armed the last grenade; this time counted to three, and flipped it high around the corner. Another deafening explosion, then all was quiet, except for the ringing in Dawson's ears.

Then he heard the dog whimpering. Brute must be armor plated to survive the grenades and the shooting.

Dawson climbed to his knees and looked around the corner, machine pistol at the ready. He rose to his feet, ignoring the aches and pains radiating from his back. He carefully skirted the dog, now silently staring at him, and walked past the bodies to the machine gun. The machine gun port was covered with a heavy curtain, probably looked out over the beach. The gun looked intact, a belt of ammunition loaded. He lifted the gun off its mount, slung a second belt of ammunition over his shoulder and started to cross to the exit on the far side when the dog stood up on shaky legs. It looked at him, glassy-eyed from the blast. Big beast, a Shepherd, it could maul him if it got loose. Dawson laid the machine gun down and pulled out his pistol.

The shore bombardment was going to obliterate this place, and the dog. The dog whined. He knew he shouldn't worry about the German dog, started to turn and leave. The dog whined again, lifted his head, eyes fixed on Dawson's. Rebecca told him she had a dog, once, killed in an air raid, along with the rest of her family. How she missed them all. How he missed her.

Dawson held out his hand, edging closer until the back of his hand touched the dog's cold nose. One lick and Dawson knew he wasn't going to leave the dog here to die. He rubbed his hand across the dog's head, gently touching the bloody fur where the staff had broken the skin.

"You O.K., Dawg?" Dawson unsnapped the chain from a heavy studded collar, ready to fire a burst from the machine pistol if the dog lunged. Instead, the dog limped over to a puddle in the corner and lapped at the water. Dawson shifted the machine pistol to hang across his back by its leather sling, picked up the machine gun and patted his right thigh. The dog shook, a long process that worked its way from head to tail and reminded Dawson more of a horse than a dog, then limped back, toes clicking on the concrete, and leaned against Dawson's leg. He looked up, keen eyes searching Dawson's face. Damn resilient dog. Must have hated that German.

Dawson grinned down at him. He could have sworn the dog grinned back. Dawson had a blue tic hound back home. Smarter than a whip, but with her own mind. Dawg must be out of the same mold.

"Come," Dawson commanded, and the dog followed, sliding against Dawson's knee as Dawson led the dog down the narrow corridor, gradually leaving the light. "You don't like those guys? Me, neither. Let's go find some more. I'll let you bite the next one."

They reached an intersection where a second tunnel ran off to their right. Distant sounds of antiaircraft fire rumbled down the passageway. He'd had enough of that. "Come on, boy." He kept going straight.

As Dawson and his new buddy crept down the dark corridor, Dawson felt a tremor under his feet. Far down the corridor a faint light resolved into a bulb hanging from the ceiling as they got closer, pulsing with light in time with the vibrations under his feet. A generator close by, probably a larger bunker. And more Germans.

Dawg stopped, growled, a low rumbling. Smart as he was, Dawson didn't think the dog understood English. What would a German say? Screw it. Let him do his thing. Might be a good distraction if things got hairy. Around the next corner he stopped again. This time because of the smell.

Pipe tobacco. Smelled just like the brand his dad smoked. What was it? Revelation? No. Bond Street? He crept down the narrow corridor until he brushed against a wet jacket hanging from a wall hook.

He blinked. Drew back. Right there, on the sleeve for crying out loud. A Screaming Eagle patch. How the hell did a 101st jacket get in here. Another cautious step and he spotted a man in a German tunic standing in front of a radio. Dawg, leaning against his leg, tensed. Dawson felt a rumble building deep in Dawg's chest.

The radio crackled, and a German voice came out of a speaker. The soldier in the German tunic answered, also in German. Dawson eased the machine gun up so it was cradled in his left arm. He slid his hand back over the unfamiliar assembly until he found the pistol grip and trigger.

The man tossed the microphone back on the table. "Chew on that, dumb ass. Bet you didn't know the Americans had airborne tanks, did you? Up your sorry ass, kraut," the radio operator said.

In English.

Puzzled, Dawson took a step back into the darkness when the radio operator reached behind the transmitter, yanked out the antenna lead and let it drop out of sight.

Dawg tensed, a rumble building in his chest. Dawson put his hand down on the dog's head, stroked his ears.

What the hell? Sabotaging his own radio?

Dawson grinned and started to speak when a voice yelled from outside the door.

In German.

CHAPTER 10 - 1/501ST PRCHT INF

Larson sucked in a deep pull on the Lucky and let the smoke dribble out of his nostrils. His last smoke in the pack. Might be a while before he found another. Right after his first date with Betty. Behind him the machine gun bolt clanked as Meade fed a fresh belt of ammunition into the German gun. Larson wrestled with the steering wheel as the halftrack lumbered from side to side, bouncing over the tracks, steering like a pregnant whale. Either Meade's Gammon grenade had blown out something in the steering or that last machine gun nest had shot out one of the front tires. Who the hell would have thought they would end up driving off in the clunker?

Rode worse than his dad's 1934 International, which was saying a lot. The old International was great for their laundry business, but a flop when it came to dating. Strange. He never could get a girl interested in riding around in a panel truck. But he had the back fixed up swell, fresh linens, even, if only he could have gotten that far.

"Lars. This is the last belt of ammo, so be ready to jump on the gas if we get in deep shit," Meade yelled out over the grumble of the treads clanking over the railroad tracks.

Larson laughed. "What? You want to stop now? We're on a roll. Dummies let us drive right up to the last gun emplacement. Betty's keeping me safe, don't worry 'bout it. Now, if I can just keep this German bitch going long enough to get us to the shooting, all we got to do is figure out who the good guys are. Keep your eyes peeled, and I'll keep Betty close to my heart."

"Ain't worried about Betty. Worried you're going to drive us into an ambush, or worse, into a bunch of GI who are going to do to us what I did to the krauts."

Larson was flung side to side as he gunned the armored car over a spur line that veered off to the left. He turned to follow the rails toward the sound of gunfire. "Hear that? At least one Tommy gun in the mix."

The armored car engine coughed, backfired, then wheezed to a stop, steam whistling up from the radiator. "Last stop, Will, at least in this bucket of bolts until I can patch the radiator." He climbed down off the side board and wiggled his helmet on his head thinking how nice it would be to take a tiny nap. Maybe tomorrow night. His neck ached from the ammo bag and the heavy Thompson slung across his shoulders. Better close to him than lose them.

Just around the bend another Thompson barked an answer to a measured volley of rifle fire.

"Yep. Sounds like somebody could use our help," Meade said. A rattle, clank, several loud cuss words and a metallic thump, and he appeared with the machine gun dismounted from the armored car, the extra ammo belt draped over his shoulder.

Larson froze when a yellow light beam pinioned him to the side of the armored car like a treed possum, churning his stomach like a bad batch of moldy K ration pemmican biscuits. Before he could react, the light went off.

"What the shit?" Meade whispered.

A cricket clacked back in the trees. Larson eased down in a knee-popping squat.

A hoarse voice spoke, cleared his throat, and called out, louder this time. "Flash."

"Thunder," Meade answered.

A dark form materialized out of the shadows. The pale glow from a distant volley of flak explosions outlined an American helmet.

Larson lowered his Thompson. Lord, he was glad Meade had the presence of mind to answer. The flashlight had scared him so bad he damn near filled his pants.

"What's going on?" Larson asked, ducking as a stray round from the shooting up the rail track thudded into the halftrack. Damn cigarette. He threw the glowing butt down and ground it under his boot as he stood.

Around the bend the rifle fire intensified. After a final long burst, the heavy bark of the Thompson stopped. The occasional pop of a .45 pistol answered sporadic rifle fire.

The man hobbled closer, an M1 rifle cradled in his arms. He coughed, cleared his throat. "We got two guys up the track, trying to knock out a German radar. I was on my way to help them. Our plan was for me and a couple of pilots to stay here with a machine gun, but it sounds like the guys up the tracks ran into trouble. One of the pilots went back in the woods with a shotgun to keep the krauts from circling around us. The other one is goofy from a hit on the head, and I'm not much better off. Big fucking German crackled my ribs, damn near strangled me."

Meade hitched the ammo belt up higher on his shoulder. "Lars. Ready to go up with me and see what's going on?" he asked.

Damn. Meade was in his volunteering mode again. But what the hell. "Sure. Betty'll wait."

Meade turned to the man with the M1. "What's your name?"

"I'm Keller. The men out there are Stimson and Levine. Levine's some kind of a spooky civilian in army uniform with a shit pile of C-2 he's determined to set off."

"I'm Meade and this is Larson." Meade turned and pointed across the tracks. "Lars. You cross over to the trees on the far side of the spur and move up toward the shooting. I'll go with Keller to the bend, hanging close to the edge of the trees on this side. If I see a good place to set up, I'll lay down fire for you to get our guys out. We'll play it by ear from there."

Keller started off, stopped, turned and said, "Be careful. Been a lot of shooting. I don't know exactly where they are."

Meade nodded. "Got that, Lars?"

"Got it. I'm on my way." Larson crossed the track, cradling his Thompson. He popped the magazine out as he crossed the tracks and dropped down the incline. Light. He exchanged it for a full one from the bag dangling from his shoulder, wondering when they would get any more ammo. Or smokes. Wondering came easy in the dead of night, with rifle fire cracking just around the bend. He bent to a crouch, keeping his head below the level of the rails. When he rounded the bend, he spotted two dark blobs lying beside the tracks. He crept toward them, hoping the blobs were the two GIs.

One of the men raised up and blindly fired a pistol across the rails and into the woods. Single shots rang out from several different locations in answer. Yep. Our guys, in deep shit.

Why hadn't the Germans surrounded the two men? Squinting into the pale moonlight, Larson realized they had. Far down the spur, next to a dark mass, he made out a quick movement, coming toward them. Germans or GIs. Larson had no clue, but odds were Germans.

He duck-walked further to the right, almost to the edge of the trees, and pulled his Thompson up, sighting toward the moving blurs, still further away than he wanted to be before he started shooting. Too dark, too indistinct. The GIs along the tracks were too exposed. He didn't want to fire until he confirmed the men coming down the tracks were krauts and a sure kill. But sure kills work both ways. His finger tightened on the trigger.

To his left machine gun fire erupted, so unexpected Larson jerked his own trigger. A dazzling red burst of flame spat out the Thompson's muzzle. Devil's due done, Larson hit the trigger again, then a third time, paused to let his night vision recover.

A dark blob rushing toward him fell to the ground, just feet away. A second man suddenly jumped up from the edge of the trees and charged.

Larson fired, a short burst. The Thompson quit, empty.

The German kept coming, cutting loose an automatic burst of his own, bullets ripping out twice as fast as the Thompson.

Larson dove to the ground as bullets slapped and rattled through the trees. He untangled his pack and fumbled for a fresh magazine as leaves and twigs fell all around him, chopped down by the charging German's wild fire. Gas fumes stung his eyes, so acrid the hair stood up on the back of his neck as he frantically dug for a full magazine, hand shaking.

Tracer fire from the machine gun angled over and caught the German between trees, flinging him to the ground. Where the tracers raked the ground, flames leaped up around a toppled tank. The fire crackled and raced through the damp grass and climbed an evergreen, sparking and snapping as flames swept through the damp growth.

Larson shook off the twigs, snapped the magazine in and poked his head back around the tree. The German lay still, an arm's reach away, skin yellow in the firelight. Larson closed his eyes for a moment, took a deep breath, then called out, "Hey, You guys all right?"

"I'm shot. Leg. Don't think I can walk," an answer came back.

Larson could hear the pain in the soldier's voice. He scuttled over to the two men, using the rails as cover. When he peeked over the rails, a line of tracer fire swept over the trees and a low building, Meade putting down suppressing fire, he hoped.

The firing paused. "Lars. You O.K.?" Meade called out from the other side of the tracks, somewhere back by the trees.

"I'm O.K.," Larson answered. "Got wounded down here."

He crawled up to the wounded man. "Let me get an arm under you." He started to wiggle his arm under the man.

"Wait, leave me be. Levine, the radar whiz kid up the track. I think the krauts got him. He was trying to blow up the damn radar, but all I had was the phone. He said the blasting cap needed DC. Phone ringer's AC, so he was heading back to blow the C-2 with his pistol when they got him. Crank that phone again. Maybe you can get up enough amperage to cook it off."

"How about if I do something different," Larson said. He opened the canvas case. "Got a screwdriver?"

The soldier pulled out his TL-29. He snapped open the screwdriver blade with a grunt and handed it to Larson. "Long as you blow up that son of a bitching radar. I promised Levine." Pain grated through his voice.

Larson yanked the two wires clear of the binding posts and opened the battery compartment. A sudden rifle shot from the woods to his left snatched the canvas case from his hands.

Meade's machine gun erupted. Tracers ricocheted off a building and into the trees. In the silence that followed Larson could hear tracers sizzling in the damp leaves.

"Christ almighty." Flat on the rail bed, snuggled up next to the wounded soldier, Larson blinked the grit out of his eyes and felt around until he had gathered up the flashlight batteries that had spilled out of the phone. Pressed against the ground he could make out the outline of a big radar dish down at the end of the spur line, now lit up by flickering yellow and orange flames dancing along the ground and up into the trees.

The fire had left them perched on the track so lit up so anyone could see them, like dancers on a stage.

A second rifle shot barked from behind the radar. Larson felt the man next to him shudder. With a moan, he seemed to deflate, wither to an empty shell.

"God damn asshole Germans." Larson fumbled the batteries in his fingers, searching for the little tits that indicated the positive ends. "Hurry up, dammit," he whispered to himself. Just like hotwiring a car. Find the contacts and touch them together. Face pressed down to the ground, he finally arranged the batteries in one hand, the pair of wires in the other. By feel, he lined the batteries up in his fist.

Lit by the flames that by now were climbing high into a tall pine tree, a figure rose up on the railcar beside the antenna dish, a big tube to his shoulder. An instant later a rocket ignited with a bang and a flash.

Larson ducked his head even lower as the rocket whooshed over his head. Cheek pressed to a cross tie, he squeezed the bare wire strands to the opposite ends of the batteries.

The moment he made the connection a blinding flash and a deafening explosion washed over him from the radar. An instant later a blast from the opposite direction flung cinders and gravel over his head. Larson buried his face hard against the railroad tie as a red hot piece of metal sliced across his butt and something clanged against his helmet. "Done," he said in satisfaction. A limb crashed down from a nearby tree and fragments continued to patter down. When the debris stopped falling he raised his head and grabbed the soldier beside him by the arm. "Come on. Let's get out of here."

The man didn't move. Larson shook him. Nothing. Larson's hand felt wet. Suddenly the man even smelled dead. Larson slid his hand up, snapped off a dog tag and stuck it in his pocket.

Larson crawled down the track to the radar guy, Levine. "Hey, buddy," he whispered.

The man rolled his head over to look at Larson, big glasses cocked crazy on his face. "Did I do it?"

"Sure did. You blew it all to hell and back. Come on, let's get out of here." Larson caught Levine as he started to get up, then fell back with a moan. "Stay flat on the ground. I'll drag you back till we can get up."

"Where's Stimson?"

"The other guy? Fucking krauts shot him. Come on." He grabbed Levine's collar and dragged him down the slope toward the trees.

"Lars?" a voice called out. Meade appeared at the rail tracks with the machine gun at his hip.

"Down here," Larson answered.

"We cleared out the Germans. We got to go. That rocket smacked the halftrack right on the nose, tore the whole front end up. I don't think plugging the radiator's going to help."

Larson helped Levine to the wrecked halftrack, steam hissing from the engine block. The stink of burned engine oil overpowered the nauseating stench of blood he had brought with him. Three other GIs limped up. He shook his head at what he saw, at the guys, not the fool vehicle. One had a bandage around his head. Another held his ribs. The third propped up the one with the bandaged head. All of them looked like they were on the edge of death.

"There's a command car down by the building. Think you can get it going?" Meade asked. "We aren't going to get far on foot."

"Like I said, ain't nothing I can't start, if it'll run at all." And to prove his point, in minutes Larson had the vehicle, a big, long convertible, a Mercedes by the ornament on the hood, rumbling along the track, engine running smooth as glass.

"Hurry up and get in." Larson began to shiver. Too many men were dying, and his butt hurt.

Meade and his wounded choir, with a chorus of groans, climbed in the ostentatious vehicle.

When they were all settled, Larson guided the long vehicle around the curve and bounced over the rails to follow the main track, leaving the flames, wreckage and a dead GI behind them.

Larson glanced in the side mirrors at the sparks flying up from a tall tree, silhouetting armed shadows in the back seat. The pair of German machine guns waved around to his right and left.

"If we see any krauts, you guys do me a favor and don't shoot my head off, O.K.?"

Meade laughed. "You just drive this limo."

"Where to?"

"Toward the shooting."

"O.K. But if you need it, I tossed one of those German rocket launchers in the back. Took it out of a kraut's hands from back at the building. He didn't need it. He was dead."

"Good. We still got a job to finish."

What did the dead guy say, blow up that radar thing. A start. They destroyed that son of a bitch. And killed Germans. That was their job.

All but the dying.

CHAPTER 11 - 326TH PRCHT MED BN

He was lost, but he was alive—and moving with a purpose.

Captain Francois Jordain gathered up his heavy medical kit and squinted into the low mists rising from the damp fields. He grinned into the darkness. He had done it. Back in England, he had come to dread his very existence, the thought of returning to combat, the threat of not living another day, of not saving another life.

Eleven months earlier he thought he was going to die, die like a craven coward. Terrified by the flak gauntlet and the jump out into crisscrossing tracers, when he slammed into the rocky Sicilian ground he had curled up, hidden under a boulder, terrified by the haphazard gunfire, unsure who was friend and who wasn't. Since then he had been haunted, wondered what life he might have saved had he been braver, had he done a better job in those first few minutes.

Tonight was different. Instead of landing on a steep Sicilian mountain side surrounded by Germans, he had plopped down in an empty muddy field. His stick, mostly troopers from the 506th Parachute Infantry Regiment, was supposed to get the green light in the vicinity of Hiesville, close to the Division aid station's planned location. As a doc, the jumpmaster had put him at the end of the stick. Last out, delayed by his heavy bag, he had ended up alone, God knows where in France. Well, not exactly alone. A big cow had walked up to him in the darkness, scaring the living bejesus out of him.

But this time he wasn't going to hide curled up in the dirt.

Gunfire echoed off in the distance as he walked along a dark road. Faint rifle fire barked out. An occasional round cracked overhead. The gunfire seemed haphazard, coming from every direction, but the heavier reports of automatic weapons and the crump of mortars seemed to be concentrated ahead. Didn't matter. He knew men were hurt, wounded, out there, somewhere. That was the nature of airborne operations. He was a doctor, so he would find and heal, whatever the circumstances. Planks rumbled under his feet as he trudged across a long bridge, eerie in the darkness with a spider web of steel girders on each side. The clinks and groans of moored boats floated up from the river, along with the smell of old fish. No, rotten fish, caught and abandoned.

A cluster of buildings emerged from the ground fog as he walked off the bridge. Past a hanging sign announcing a tavern on the corner, a glimmer of light from one of the houses caught his eye, moving from the first floor, and then appearing again on the second. Why in the name of God were civilians still here, this close to the beaches. They had to know the Allies would eventually invade. The light re-appeared, shadows wavering across the window. This was foolish. Someone was going to get killed if they didn't cover up the windows. Or, better yet, they should get away from the coast entirely.

"Hello," he called into the door.

No response.

The shadows stopped moving. A groan came from the stairs.

"Hello. Is anyone there?" Jordain shook his head and tried to remember the smattering of French he had spoken as a kid in Quebec. "*Bonjour. Est n'importe qui a?*"

"Get help, please," a voice answered in French. A woman's voice. "A doctor."

Jordain stared at the stairs. He had paratroopers to look after, not some whining old French woman. Probably had gout, or some such nonsense, didn't want to walk away from the hell that was falling around her. But he was a doctor, God help him. He clumped to the top of the stairs and stopped, squinted against the yellow light flick-ering from an oil lamp. A woman lay propped up on a bed, in pain from the look on her face. He took a step toward the bed.

"*Halt!*"

His blood went cold at the harsh command. He slowly turned his head. A German soldier stood against the wall, his rifle pointing at Jordain. Jordain slowly pointed at his arm band with the Red Cross.

"Doctor," he said in French, repeated it in German, one of the few words of German he knew. "What is the problem?" he asked, reverting to what he hoped was understandable French.

The German motioned Jordain toward the woman.

Jordain knelt beside the bed and took off his helmet. He felt her brow. Hot, but not feverish. She groaned, took his hand and placed it on her belly. Dear lord. The last time he had been in an obstetrics ward was in residency. He rolled up his sleeves and turned to the soldier. "Get me water and clean linens." He motioned toward the window with his chin. "And close the curtain. You can see the light outside."

The soldier looked at the woman, a question on his face. She nodded; spoke to the soldier in German. He slung his rifle over his shoulder, fixed the curtain and took off down the stairs.

Apparently Jordain's French-Canadian patois was clear enough, at least for the woman.

After he came back with the water and a stack of towels, the German took the woman's hand. Not really a woman, just a girl. He spoke softly to her in German, unintelligible to Jordain. She looked healthy, pink cheeks, a bit of fat. Perhaps the benefits of being a German's girlfriend. Jordain turned off the thought. Not the time to judge. Think of the baby. And the German's rifle.

He finished washing his hands in the porcelain bowl and motioned for the lamp. The German didn't seem to understand. "Tell him to bring the lamp so I can see, and you'll have this baby in your arms before you know it," Jordain said to the woman.

She translated and the soldier moved to the foot of the bed, holding the lamp so the light flowed over Jordain's shoulder. Jordain glanced at his watch. The contractions were regular. He lifted up her knees. A bit of blood staining appeared on the sheet and the cervix dilatation appeared textbook. Thank the good Lord. He had soldiers to care for. He didn't want his day to start by losing a mother or her baby.

"Papa?" Jordain asked, nodding his head back toward the German. The girl smiled and nodded her head, then suddenly grunted, straining to meet the contraction. A bit more blood stained the sheet and Jordain could hear the German's sharp intake of breath. The girl grabbed his arm. He gently disengaged her hand. "What are your names?" he asked the girl, again in French.

Distant explosions rattled the windows. Jordain took a deep breath, pleased his hands were steady as he waited to receive the child. No curling up under a boulder tonight. He smiled at the girl, urging her on by puffing out his cheeks and blowing out his breath as he watched the dilation grow.

"I am Jeannette," she whispered. She motioned with her large eyes over Jordain's shoulder. "This is my Friedrich."

"And what is your baby's name?"

She paused, closed her eyes as a shudder shook her body. "We have not chosen a name. What is yours, doctor?"

"Francois." He smiled at her, remembering the head nurse's admonishments about good bedside behavior, never his strong suit, and the head resident's lectures about confidence. Show it even when you don't have it. "A good French name. My grandfather lives in Quebec. I spent my summers there. He insisted I speak French with them. And a great number of people in my hometown up in Maine do also. Do you understand most of what I say?" He kept up the chatter as she strained, searching his mind for the birthing procedures any good midwife should know, but he had long forgotten.

"Mostly." She puffed out a series of breaths. Jordain grasped the baby's emerging head. Thoughts of Sicily and the combat all around him were lost in his focus on bringing a new life into the world. He silently thanked the grouchy head nurse for her advice as he went through all the delivery steps, finally dangling a healthy baby boy for a slap on the butt, bringing a welcomed wail.

Once the baby was safe at his mother's breast, Jordain wiped his hands on a thin towel and turned to the German. "I must go. Others need me. You should surrender when other soldiers come, so Jeannette and the baby will be safe."

Friedrich wiped at his eyes with the sleeve of his tunic and shook his head as the new mother translated. He caressed the baby's head, ran his fingers through the thin hair. "I stay. Protect," he replied, both sides of the conversation translated by the mother.

Jeanette took the German's hand and held it to her cheek. "Friedrich has a bicycle downstairs. Go now. Take it and save your soldiers. He will keep us safe," she whispered. The baby, wrapped in a soft towel, suckled at her breast with tiny mewing sounds.

Jordain looked down at his bloodstained uniform as he repacked his medical bag. He had seen enough combat in Sicily to understand the uncertainty of life on the battlefield, for soldier and civilian alike. But he could do no more here, tonight. Perhaps tomorrow he could make a true house call.

He held out his hand to Friedrich. "Take care." Jordain wondered if he would see any of them alive again.

Outside, he looked up and down the road as he mounted an old bike, reminding himself of his promise. No hiding under a boulder. He let the bike roll down a slight slope then pedaled along the dark road toward a building crescendo of fire, perhaps several miles away. The front wheel squeaked, a rhythmic warning to anyone ahead that he was coming. He slowed as he approached a crossroad.

"*Halt!*"

Well, that was a German word he was getting familiar with. He held up his hands as a flashlight briefly swept across him. He tried to breath evenly, not hyperventilate as he stood straddle-legged over the bike frame, medical bag pulling at his shoulder, crossbar uncomfortable against his crotch. Rough hands pulled his bag off his shoulder and a face bent close. The flashlight, this time hooded by a hand, glowed between the soldier's fingers, allowing just enough light through to illuminate Jordain's face and body.

"*Parlez vous Français?*" Jordain asked.

Before the soldier with the light could answer, an arm swung out of the darkness and cracked Jordain across the jaw. He crashed to the ground, all tangled in the bicycle and his bag.

"You butcher," the German that hit him spat out in French. "All the blood. How many Germans have you killed so far?"

Jordain levered himself up on an elbow, tapped his arm band as he spat blood out of his mouth. "None. I'm a doctor. I just delivered my first baby. A boy." He wiggled his jaw. Didn't feel broken, but a couple of teeth were definitely loose. "His father was a German soldier. You better get them out of here. Pretty soon there will be more Americans here that you can count." Jordain winced when a kick snapped his head back against the handlebars.

"Where is your unit?" the kicker barked.

Jordain shook the stars from his head. "No idea. I am just looking for wounded to help, perhaps find an aid station to assist with." The German kicked him in the ribs.

A second German grabbed the kicker and pulled him back. "Are you a…" He paused, pointing up in the sky, apparently searching for the French word.

Jordain equally was at a loss for the German word. Instead he mimicked a falling parachute with his open hand.

"*Fallschirmjäger?*" the German said.

Jordain nodded his head. That sounded like the German word for paratrooper. The German tapped his chest. "*Fallschirmjäger.*"

Good lord. He had let himself be captured by a bunch of German paratroopers.

The German hauled him up off the ground with one arm, then handed him his medical bag.

"*Gehen Sie.*" The German nodded his head toward a line of tracers rising up into the sky. "*Schnell.*" He shoved Jordain up the road.

Without looking back, Jordain started up the road, waiting for a shot in the back. Rounding a curve in the road, he realized he was going to live. His knees began to shake so badly he almost fell to the ground. He shifted the bag to his other shoulder and steadied his step.

He was scared shitless, but at least he wasn't cowering under a rock. Now to find an aid station and get to work.

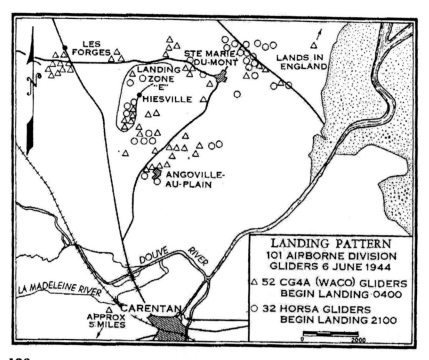

CHAPTER 12 - 434TH TRP CARRIER UNIT

Signal lights glowed below as they passed over a marker ship somewhere in the English Channel. The moon, high over the Channel, revealed the invasion fleet, reaching as far as Army Air Corps Captain Sonny Talbot could see. On each side and far ahead, long lines of aircraft and their gliders flew toward Landing Zone Easy, an empty field outside of Hiesville, almost in the center of the 101st Airborne Division parachute drop zones. It was a majestic sight, just as long as the ships steaming below him didn't shoot at them. Flying into Sicily every damn Allied ship crossing the Mediterranean Sea loosened their guns on the incoming gliders. He, like most of the glider pilots, eventually crashed in the water short of the beach. Thankfully he got his Waco close enough that everyone on board made it to shore. Many didn't that night.

He'd had all the friendly fire he could stand. At least in Burma all he had to worry about was malaria and parasites in the water and piss-ant Japs slithering around in the jungle. Made England seem like a vacation spot, even with the bombing raids. So, get Operation Chicago over with, drop this load and hitch a ride back to base. No snatching the gliders back up like they had done in Burma, at least not for now.

He nosed the Waco over, following the tug's gradual decent. As they dropped down, a silvery line of beach stretched from left to right. As they crossed the surf line intertwining arcs of tracer fire reached up toward a plane off to his left, then the fireworks display shifted toward their end of the "echelon of four to the right" formation of C-47s, each towing a Waco glider.

A single bullet twanged off a metal tube. The glider seemed to shudder. "Oh, Lord," Allen bawled. A long spruce splinter from the floor had slapped Allen's flak suit and dropped into his lap.

Someone once told Talbot that Ford made the Wacos in the same factory that manufactured Woodie station wagons, like the ones in the Hopalong Cassidy movies. He wished he had Hoppy and his trusty six-shooter along with him on this ride. Instead he had Wilber Allen, newly assigned to the Group, a raw replacement from the States. His copilot was fresh out of an abbreviated glider course in Texas. He seemed to know which end connected to the tow, but that was about it. Talbot wished he had a real hero along on this Woodie, black hat and all.

"Relax, Wilber," he yelled across the cockpit when he felt his copilot's feet vibrating on the rudder pedals. The tracers vanished as they entered a rolling cloud bank. Talbot leaned forward and squinted into the mists flowing past the windshield. Wind whistled through the Waco glider joints, adding a high keening to the bass drum beat of the doped cotton fabric beating against the frame. He ran his eyes across the five instruments on the sparse panel, something he seldom did. Seat of the pants flying was more his style.

Air speed was too fast, bouncing above 150 knots. Rate of climb had leveled out at zero. Altimeter was too high, around three thousand. Compass indicated they had veered further south than he thought was right. He tapped the glass on the middle gauge, the one that counted, the bank indicator. Despite his inner ears screaming he was about to flip upside down inside the thick clouds, the indicator promised their wings were level. For now, that's all he wanted. Once cut loose, he would deal with speed and altitude.

It did bother him that the C-47 had vanished, somewhere down at the far end of the three hundred foot tow rope, and he had lost sight of the other Wacos somewhere off to his left. A couple of times the tug had jinked off to the left or right without a peep over the intercom, forcing him to bank around harder than he liked. But to hell with the tug. He trusted in his own skills. Just a yank on the tow release lever up over his right shoulder, and he'd be in control of his baby, along with the fate of his copilot, the four men in back and the 57mm antitank gun load. The gun's Jeep and ammunition trailer rode in the next glider over, bouncing around somewhere in the clouds. But not his worry. Get his crew and passengers on the ground. Then all he had to do was get back to the beach and find a ride to England. Unlike Wilber who wasted his free time on the rifle range, soaking up infantry tactics, Talbot was a flyer; all he wanted to be. Let the heroes have at the ground combat crap.

The glider wallowed through the night, washed by the turbulence from the C-47's engines. The Dakota dragged them through the mists until they broke out of the top of the cloud bank into the moonlight where everything was grades of grey, silver to black.

"Wilber. See if you can raise the tug, see how much longer before we cut loose," he called over to his copilot. One good thing about the Waco, easy to talk to the copilot and passengers. No roaring engine to yell over. Only the sounds of the damn thing tearing itself apart. At least no mules braying in the back like they had in Burma.

A stream of yellow tracer fire reached up out of a cloud, sliding toward them, closer and closer. The line of tracers raked across a wing, splintering one of the spars. The control feel didn't change. Damn sturdy Waco. Just keep us up in the air, baby.

Germans were firing as blind as he was flying. He squinted at the instruments. The altimeter read two thousand feet. He had focused so hard on following the tug and keeping the wings level he hadn't realized they had dropped a thousand feet.

The line of tracers shifted to his left, illuminating a lone glider for an instant. Moments later a brilliant explosion lit the sky, and the glider was gone. Talbot prayed they had cut loose early, but in his heart he knew what had happened. The ammunition trailer.

The Waco's wings rocked with another nearby explosion. Too much to do here to worry about the other glider.

Allen brushed off the splinter and hailed the tug over the big microphone. He tried again, louder. "Nobody home," he yelled over to Talbot.

"See any signal lights from the astral dome?"

Allen stretched up in his seat, searching the black sky at the other end of the nylon tow rope.

"Can't see a damn thing, 'cept the exhaust."

Relax and fly. This was a cake walk. Easy to say. Hard to do. Talbot dreaded glider missions with heavy cargo. His missions into Burma included delivering a baby bulldozer into a jungle clearing. The first guy who had tried was still rotting somewhere in the jungle. A safe heavy cargo landing relied upon many things going right, to include a system of cables to yank out the safety pins and swing the nose up in the air if the cargo broke lose upon landing. In theory, the gun behind them would spit out below them while he and the copilot hung up in the air inside the hinged nose. Talbot had never seen that particular function work right. And doubted he ever would.

Suddenly a cluster of flak enveloped the front of their C-47 tug in a halo of light. Before Talbot's mind could react, his reflexes jerked him back against the seat back as the tow rope pulled them straight toward the inferno. A row of flak bursts walked across the sky from the flaming tug, rocking the Waco. A gaping hole ripped open beside his elbow. Wind funneled through the hole whipped his map away. Through the flapping fabric Talbot caught the shimmer of moonlight reflected from a broad expanse of water as the wind brought tears to his eyes. Where in hell were they? More important, where were they going? Ahead the tow rope sagged. The tug winged over in a shallow bank to the right. Talbot fought to stay aligned with the tow rope, trying to keep them from being ripping apart.

"What's he doing?" yelled Allen.

The bank sharpened. The Dakota's nose dipped down, diving down into the cloud bank. Talbot turned, following the C-47. The glider bucked in the turbulence, screaming as they gathered speed in the steepening dive.

"Tug's going down," screamed Allen.

"Cut us loose!" Talbot shouted back.

Allen reached across and yanked the big red disconnect lever, screamed at it, yanked a second time with both hands wrapped around the lever. A jolt, and the glider soared, free from the tug.

Talbot reared back on the controls at first, then jammed the wheel forward; fought to keep the nose from rising too high, flipping them upside down. He breathed a sigh of relief when the wings leveled, Gentle, gentle, he reminded himself. Don't get in a yo-yo with the nose and stall them out. Finally level, he searched below, blinking the sweat from his eyes. "Wilber. See the ground?" It was quieter now as they slowed, gliding level, the wind whistling through the shell holes in concert with the bass drum beat of the fabric.

"Can't make out anything below, Cap." Allen's voice had returned to his normal soprano.

Talbot worked the wheel back and forth to keep the glider as stable as he could, extending the glide as long as possible, or at least till he could find a safe place to park the Waco. No sign of lights, beacons, anything friendly below them. Lost as shit in the middle of the clouds.

Speed eighty knots, altitude seven hundred. Still no sign of the ground. That could be good—or bad. Talbot would like to know which.

A bright flash bloomed below and to the right, reflecting from the inside of the misted Plexiglas. "What the hell was that?" Talbot asked.

Allen stared down at the ground and shook his head. "Maybe our tug. The crew may have lost control, and they just rode it in." He sucked his head down into his flak suit as a string of green and red tracers raked across the nose. Splinters from the plywood floor flew around the tiny cabin. "Holy moly, Cap. Can you get us down?" Allen shouted over the wind, now yowling through several fist-sized holes punched up through the floor and out the Plexiglas windshield.

The cabin filled with acrid smoke from a tracer lodged in the spruce nose section directly in front of the instruments. Talbot let the nose drop. They had to come down sooner or later. Might as well have a bit of maneuvering speed where they found the ground.

The cloud bank streamed past as they dropped, thinning, now only wisps of mist. "Wilber. Help me find a clear space." Suddenly a row of trees loomed out of the darkness, a hundred feet below, rushing up toward them. Talbot fought the urge to pull up. That would just stall them, drop them tail first on the ground, break the bird wide open. "I'm taking her down. Get ready to release the drag chute when we clear those trees."

"Deploy the spoilers?"

Before Talbot had time to answer, the trees tops flashed under the nose. "Dump the chute," he yelled out. Talbot held the glider on the ragged edge between stall and dive, willing the Waco to float, holding as much altitude as he could, at least until he figured out what was under them. Out of the corner of his eye he saw Allen reach up over his head and pull the red tee handle. Almost immediately his seat belt tugged at him as the drogue parachute deployed. His feet danced on the pedals as he fought the tail's inclination to oscillate when the drogue streamed out behind the glider. They plummeted toward the ground. Where, how close, he had no idea, but slower was always better when you hit the ground. Or landed, as the instructors preferred to say.

He leaned forward, straining against the seat belt. Trees loomed dead ahead, their dark tops silhouetted against the tracers crisscrossing in front of them. "Spoilers," he yelled, struggling to hold the glider level. They flashed over another row of trees, barely skimming clear, leaving the tracers behind.

Allen yanked the spoiler lever.

Talbot felt another tug on his belt and they dropped into darkness. A jolt under his feet. The left wheel touched. The Waco bounced. Right wheel hit, then left again. Hold it level, both wheels planted. Racing across the ground, he let a grin spread across his face. Talbot stretched his toes out for the brake pedals. Then all hell broke loose.

Talbot's forehead smashed against the steering wheel and the glider seemed to disintegrate around him, roaring and ripping. He squeezed his eyes shut, waiting for the antitank gun to slam into his back. Voices screamed through the mayhem.

When they finally stopped moving, Talbot let his fingers uncurl from their death grip on the wheel. He flexed his fingers to get them moving enough to unsnap his seat belt. He glanced over at his copilot. Allen sat upright in his seat, unmoving. Too dark, too shaken to make out details, for an instant Talbot thought Allen was dead. "Wilber. You all right?"

Allen's head started nodding. "By God, we made it, Cap." Allen took a deep breath and let it out. "Lord, Almighty."

"Are you hurt?"

Allen giggled and pushed a tree limb away from his chest. "A tree branch ripped through the side, right in front of me. But it didn't puncture the flak suit."

Talbot could hear Allen patting his body and the clink of buckles unsnapping.

"I'm sore, but I don't feel like anything's broke. I think I'm just going to sit here a minute."

"Good. I'll see if anybody in the back needs help." When Talbot tried to move, he realized his legs were locked under a maze of crumpled tubing, wadded fabric and splintered wood. He stopped for a moment, his eyes stinging. He sniffed. It smelled like Christmas around the fireplace back home. Wood smoke drifted up from around his feet.

Damn glider had been reduced to a pile of kindling wood and steel fishing poles. Time to get out.

With a groan he pushed back against the seat. The metal seat frame and wooden back collapsed, sending a wave of pain through his legs. Talbot reached back over his head, got a grip on a tube and pulled. His butt slid over the seat and he dragged his legs through the tangle until his knees bumped up against the steering wheel. He pulled harder, grunting with the effort. He stretched, reaching as far back with his fingertips as he could for a better grip.

"Cap. Are we on fire?"

Damn. He had forgotten all about Allen, worrying about himself. What kind of a command pilot was he? "Tracers smoldering in the nose somewhere. Can you get out?"

Allen snapped the tree branch off, threw it back over his head. He jerked at the tubing collapsed around his shoulders. "Feels like I'm hung up in here, Cap."

With a final effort Talbot pulled himself back out of the nose section until his head bumped against the gun trails. He wiggled clear of the seat and stopped to listen. Voices from the back, but no gunfire. He climbed up, grabbed Allen under the arm pits and dragged him back out of the nose. He left Allen to untangle himself from his flak suit and climbed through the wreckage till he could stand upright in the crumpled frame. Stumbling over pieces of equipment strewed along the cabin, he felt past the gun, still lashed, thankfully, to the plywood floor. Dim light shined through a gap in the cabin fabric. The back third of the glider body had cracked open, almost like it was hinged. God bless Ford, they had made it to the ground.

He ignored the pain that shot up from his legs and crawled over the gun mount toward the tail section. He stumbled when the wood floor shifted under his feet, followed by a loud crash. He called out, "Everybody back there O.K.?"

"Fuck, no," the answer came back. "Looks like the gun chief's dead."

Talbot joined three men huddled over a fourth seated in the far end of the glider. One of the men eased an ammo box away from a soldier still strapped to the wooden bench along the side of the glider.

"Broke neck. Looks like an ammo crate came free and caught him in the head when the tail snapped around. Poor guy didn't know what hit him, most likely." The speaker looked up from the dead man. "I'm Sergeant Watson, 327th Infantry. You're the pilot, right?"

"Yep. My name's Talbot. Lieutenant Allen, getting himself clear up front, is my copilot. Guess we need to get out of here. And pretty soon. We got a fire smoldering in the nose. Anybody else hurt?"

Watson motioned across the aisle. "The guy I came with, Johnson, looks like he took a round through the floor, skewered him."

Talbot realized another soldier lay sprawled out on the bench behind him, unmoving. Damn. He shook his head, focused on the living. "We ought to get the gun out and set it up if we can. Was Johnson a gunner?"

"No sir," Watson replied. "He just transferred over from the 401st Gliders. A mechanic, like me."

Talbot turned to the remaining men. "How about you two?"

"Sparks, Signal Company, Captain." Sparks lifted up a canvas carrying case. "I'm carrying the cipher converter and key lists for the CG's radio. I'll help, though, till I get an idea where the General landed and can link up with the command group."

"You all right, soldier? You know anything about the gun?" Talbot asked the soldier kneeling in front of NCO's body, his eyes focused on the dead man's face.

The soldier slipped the dead man's dog tags off and snapped one from the chain. He replaced the chain and one tag around the dead man's neck. He turned, scrubbed a hand across his face and handed Talbot the loose tag. A couple of blinks and he gathered himself. "Yes, sir, I can shoot. I'm on Sergeant Riley's gun crew. Private Roscoe Jefferson, sir, 81st Artillery." He lifted a second ammo box away from the dead man. "Been with Riley since we sailed on the *Samaria*." He took a deep breath and hefted the box of ammo. "Guess that gun's mine now. You guys help me unload and look for a jeep?"

Allen appeared from the front of the glider. "Tried to release the nose, Cap. Darn thing didn't budge. I think we slid slap up into a tree line."

"O.K." Talbot handed Allen the dog tag, along with the one he unsnapped from Johnson. "Take these. Give them to the mortuary guys when they catch up. I suspect we'll see a lot of them before we get back to England. Just not ours, O.K." He looked around at the broken glider. "Let's get all this junk cleared and pull the gun and ammo out before everything burns up." Talbot stopped, held his hand up. An engine rumbled outside the glider, a large vehicle, coming closer by the sound. "Quiet!" Now he could hear shouts as smoke swirled around the cabin, a light, homey smell, thicker than up front.

"Germans. Everybody outside. Quick," whispered Talbot. "Scatter if you have to. Just don't get caught."

Allen tried to open the door on the side away from the voices. "Jammed."

A loud rip and Watson had sliced the doped fabric from top to bottom next to where the tubing had snapped. His knife swept across the bottom to open a large flap, big enough for them to slip through.

"Move. Scatter, boys." Watson shoved Sparks and Jefferson toward the opening.

Jefferson piled out, followed by the signals guy and Allen.

"We're with you, Sarge. Lead on." Talbot followed Watson out the opening. In Burma he had learned to listen to the noncoms on the ground. They knew how to stay alive.

Talbot slid through the opening and immediately blundered into a hard packed dirt mound. He felt around, blinking in the dim starlight filtering down through the clouds. He had stumbled into the base of a hedgerow, thick with trees along the top. That tiny bit of light went away when he slid under the right wing, folded by the trees back over the top of the glider. He moved down the hedgerow in a crouch. He paused, grimaced with the growing pain as he tried to follow the others. Both legs felt as if pokers were pressed into his thighs, searing hot pokers.

To his right a shot rang out. He veered to the left and immediately ran into the hedge. He blundered down a shallow ditch as more shots rang out, head muddled by the building pain in his legs. Now completely disoriented, he tripped and sprawled flat. He lay there, catching his breath. Gunfire rattled around him. A bullet whined past his head. A shout boomed, German, answered by several others. "God damn it," he muttered. He had sworn he would carry a rifle this mission, no pip-squeak carbine. And damn if he hadn't gone off and left the M1 strapped down in the Waco.

On his hands and knees, he crawled back to the hedge, under the wing and slipped back into the glider. A burst of automatic fire ripped through the fabric over his head. By the light of the flames flickering from the burning spruce the dead artillery sergeant sat upright on his bench, a M3 grease gun dangling from his shoulder. Talbot worked the dead man's submachine gun free and slipped an ammo pouch over the dead man's head. He slithered back out and pulled himself up beside the glider tail. Wobbly, his night vision finally kicked in, letting him get a sense of where everything lay.

A vehicle engine revved off to his right, the far side of the glider. Shots, then silence.

Talbot clicked a magazine into the grease gun.

He put one hand on the glider's busted frame and slid his feet, each step fraught with pain, around the tail. He bit off a whimper when he stumbled over the heavy strap leading back to the drogue parachute. He dragged his leg over the strap and edged forward. Not a shout. Too quiet. The only noise was a dog yowling somewhere across the hedge and the sound of vehicle engines, at least two. Where was Allen, the rest of them?

A pair of light beams swept across a large truck just a few yards across the clearing. Three Germans stood in a line by the truck. Two had long rifles; one hugged a stubby submachine pistol to his side. Talbot started to drop to a crouch, but stopped, stifling a groan when the pain shot through his legs. If he crouched he might never get up, he decided. Just grit it out.

A fourth German stood off to the side waving a flashlight across Allen and the three other Americans standing in a parallel line about ten yards across from the Germans, like they were about to play red rover. No fair, this time. The GIs had no guns.

The second vehicle's lights bounced, leveled out and drew away, apparently moving down a road. The feeble flashlight steadied on the Americans, hands held over their heads. The German with the light shouted a command and Talbot sensed a movement of the line.

Talbot brought the submachine gun up, pointed it at the line of Germans and pulled the trigger.

Nothing. The German with the light shouted a second command. The flashlight bobbed in time with his guttural inflections.

"Hey, you bastards!" Talbot shouted at the German as his mind raced through the training sessions with the noncoms. Damn. He should have spent more time with Allen. The light spun toward him and he sensed the rifles swinging his way.

He yanked the cocking lever back and pulled the trigger again, all in one rapid motion. A burst of fire spat out of the grease gun's muzzle, spraying the row of Germans with a barrage of .45 caliber slugs. Blinded by the flash, Talbot staggered forward, held the submachine gun tight to his side. A man screamed; one of the Germans staggered toward him. He emptied the magazine. The man went down. The screaming stopped. Talbot dropped to his knees, firebrands streaking up into his back, hurting so bad the gun trembled in his hands.

Allen ran over through the light flickering from the fire in the glider nose. "Damn, Cap. You sure as shit downed them krauts. Saved our asses. You all right? "

"No, dammit," Talbot answered. "Where's our other guy?"

"Before you got here their officer went off in a car and took the signal guy with him. The bastard left these guys here to shoot us like a bunch of dogs. I think he was pissed 'cause Watson shot a couple of his men before they could get the drop on us." Allen crouched beside him. "Come on. Let's get out of here before more of them shows up."

Talbot tried to stand; sank back until his hands rested on the ground. "I think my legs are broken."

Watson trotted up. "Lieutenant Allen. We got to get moving. I hear a tracked vehicle moving around; close by. Get the Captain in the truck. I'll see if me and Jefferson can pull out the A-T gun, then we'll all haul ass out of here." He tossed a wooden ammo box into the back of the truck. "Jefferson got skint up by a machine pistol hit in the side, but he's still walking." He looked toward the horizon. "Boy almighty." He waved toward a glow in the distance. "Somebody blew up something big."

"Son of a bitch!" The exclamation was followed by a crash from the glider. Jefferson had sliced a section of fabric free and was working on rolling the 57mm gun through the opening. He yanked on a rope and the gun barrel rolled halfway out. "Come help, Sarge, 'fore the fire gets to the ammo," Jefferson called out.

A series of impacts walked down the skyline. Brilliant bursts, like a press photographer at the far endzone of a football field, flared across the tops of the trees. Talbot flinched when a brighter flash illuminated the horizon, followed by a massive explosion that echoed across the fields. There was a bigger war than theirs going on out there in the bocage country.

Allen grinned down at him. "Damn, Cap. Glad to see something scares you, after all." With a grunt Allen lifted him up. "Watch for splinters in your butt." Allen slid him onto the truck bed between the ammo boxes. "Thought you were bullet proof, that's why I volunteered to fly with you. And I was right. Look at you. Calm as a cat. Saved our butts, and not a single bullet hole."

"What about my legs?"

"Legs don't count. I was there, remember. Your lack of flying skills got you your broke legs." Allen tossed an ammo box into the truck beside Talbot's head.

Just what he needed to be riding alongside, with artillery landing around them, tanks rumbling up and down the roads.

Watson and Jefferson rolled the A-T gun up to the back of the German truck. Allen jumped up on the truck out of their way as the flat clap of an outgoing tank round slammed Talbot's ear drums, rocking the truck and adding to his pain. His copilot looked down at him. "Shit, Cap. Maybe you aren't such good luck after all."

"Gun and ammo all ready to go, sir," Watson reported.

"Good. You drive, Watson." Allen reached down and pulled Jefferson up into the truck. "And get us out of here, quick like. German tanks. Sounds like a whole slew of them; must be right on the other side of the hedgerow."

The truck engine roared to life, the vibration adding to the pain stabbing through Talbot's legs. He grit his teeth as the truck lurched across a ditch and up on the road. Jefferson sprawled beside him and picked up the grease gun. "How do you shoot one of these, Cap? I can't find the damn safety."

Talbot shook his head. "Just pull the trigger. But watch out. Damn thing doesn't have a safety. It'll shoot your nuts off if you aren't careful. Point it away from me, O.K." He lay back and stared up at the sky as a handful of stars peeked through the clouds overhead.

What had he gotten himself into this time? From pilot to infantryman to artilleryman. At least the antitank gun bouncing along behind them hadn't squashed him like the bulldozer got the guy in Burma.

From the sound of the tank column, rumbling on the other side of the hedgerow, the gun might come in handy.

CHAPTER 13 - 101ST ABN SIGNAL CO

Sparks' head rang from being bounced off the bunker wall by the German. Knot was going to be bigger than the rest of his head if this jerk keeps smacking it. The kraut had a bunch of braid on his shoulder epaulets, and he sure acted mean enough to be a noncom. To make matters worse, the son of a bitch was beating him to a pulp with his own helmet.

Sparks cursed himself. He had made a big mistake not hiding the M-203 Key Converter when they crashed. Now this prissy German officer in the peaked cap was going to shoot him because he couldn't answer some stupid ass questions. That is, if the sergeant didn't beat him to death first. Shit. If he could speak German, he would read the kraut the key list, cover to cover. In another life.

He glanced down at his thigh. Blood seeped through his pants where the sergeant had prodded him with the bayonet. Sparks took a deep breath. Amazing. Leg didn't hurt yet from where the kraut stabbed him.

Back at the glider he had tried to run. But before he could clear the glider the rest of the German squad had surrounded them, gunning down that kid, Jefferson. The next thing Sparks knew he was blinded by the lights from the command car and cold cocked from behind. Damned knot on his head still hurt. Banging against the concrete bunker wall wasn't helping. God knows what had happened to Watson and the others.

But Sparks had his own troubles. They started in England when some dipshit staff officer bumped him from the plane carrying the general, paying no attention to his complaint that Watson was carrying the division commander's crypto gear. On the tarmac the harried transportation officer pointed out a glider that he said carried the Division HQ radio. By the time Sparks had scrambled on board he discovered there was no radio, just some damn gun, a motor sergeant, mechanic and a couple of artillerymen, and off they went before he could argue. Hell. He had figured they were all going to the same landing zone, so no sweat. Right.

The German sergeant dragged him up off the floor and slammed him against the wall. The officer opened the crypto box and stared at the six wheels. He asked the soldier standing beside the radio a question, pointing at the box. The operator shrugged his shoulders when the officer yelled at him, incomprehensible words mixed with a lot of arm waving. The officer snatched the radio microphone away from the operator and shouted into the microphone. The speaker hummed, but no answer came back.

Sparks narrowed his eyes, stared across the bunker at the radio. Push to talk, like the Division radio sets, but when the officer mashed the microphone talk button, the needles on the front of the radio set didn't budge. Sparks stared at the radio operator. If he was any good, he'd know something was wrong. Antenna wasn't loading. The dufus just stood there, puffing on a damn pipe like a professor or something. The dufus looked back at him. And winked! What? Was he looking for a boyfriend?

The officer yelled again, if anything louder. Again no response from the radio speaker. He threw the microphone to the table, then went through the same routine with the telephone. Apparently nothing in the whole bunker worked.

Well, that's the Army, for you, even the German one, Sparks thought. Piss on them. They might have the crypto box and the key list, but be damned if he was going to help them understand it, or even acknowledge they had to have his memorized day setting to even start it up.

The sergeant regained Sparks' full attention when he cracked his own steel pot across the top of Spark's head, followed up with a kick to his gut. The air whooshed out of his lungs and he damn near crapped in his pants. This day was really going to shit. Didn't get to jump with the headquarters troops. Had to crash land in that flimsy piece of shit glider. And now he was in a big concrete coffin with a knot on his head bigger than his pecker, being pummeled with his own helmet.

The sergeant threw down the helmet, jerked Sparks up and flung him back against the wall. Sparks tried to straighten, but it was hard to do with a bayonet pressed against his belly. Then a rifle butt caught him in the side of the head, swirling stars around the feeble light bulb hanging from the ceiling. Dufus was getting serious.

The radio operator said something to the officer in German, who shouted at the sergeant.

Breathing deep, the sergeant stepped back, glowering at Sparks.

The radio operator stuck his pipe in his pocket and squatted in front of him. Jesus. The German looked just like the professor, that old guy in G2 that taught the order of battle classes. "Sparks," the radio operator said—in English. "You know me?"

What kind of infernal trick was this?

"Mehan. Answer me, dammit," the man whispered. "I don't think any of them speak English, but say something, nothing that matters, just jabber so I can convince the Captain that you're talking. I'll make up something to tell him, keep him going until we can get the drop on the big guy. You know me. You string wire to my phone every frigging exercise." He raised his voice. "Your first name is Marion. You even slept though one of my briefings last week."

Dumbfounded, Sparks couldn't think of anything to say. The guy in the German tunic really was the professor, as the troops called him behind his back.

"Speak, dammit!" the professor shouted in his face. Then quieter. "Say something or the sergeant with the rifle will take over again."

"Crap. What do you want me to say?"

"Good." A smile briefly flashed over the professor's face. "Say anything. I'll make up the translation."

"How the hell are we going to get out of here?"

"I'll tell you just as soon as I figure it out. For now, just keep talking so they don't kill you out of spite." The professor stood and held his hand out toward the officer and said something in German. The officer paused, shook his head. The professor turned back to Sparks. "I'll make up some bull shit and feed it—"

"You need not say any more." The officer interrupted. In English.

Sparks and the professor looked up. The officer's pistol pointed directly at the professor. The sergeant glanced at the officer, stepped back away from Sparks and the professor. He swung his rifle around to point at Sparks, the muzzle as big as an elephant's ass hole.

"Your appearance and the disappearance of the other Russian was too much coincidence. I think you are an American paratrooper, a spy? And you think I am stupid." The officer leveled the pistol at the professor with one hand and waved the key lists in the other. "What do these words mean? 'Bigot Neptune?' Are these codes, for the machine?"

The professor grinned at Sparks. "Tried, buddy. Sorry." He stood and replied in German. Whatever he said, even Sparks could tell it was an insult.

His face twisted in anger, the officer fired his pistol. The professor spun against the wall, and slid down beside Sparks, leaving a smear of blood on the bunker wall.

This was it. All the talk. All the training, waiting, planning and he was going to die sprawled on his ass right here on the cold concrete. Heart pounding, Sparks measured the sergeant, wondering how far he could get before the jerk fired the rifle. Or if the kraut was quick enough to stab him with that fucking bayonet.

Before he could move, a machine gun cut loose from a dark doorway in the back of the bunker, ripping across the officer and the sergeant, deafening in the enclosed room. Ricocheting bullets and concrete chips rattled around the bunker, whizzing and zinging and slapping against the concrete. As the pall of dust settled, a paratrooper stepped from the doorway, a long black machine gun on his hip, smoke drifting from the end of the barrel. Sparks slid back against the wall. What the hell! The trooper looked like a savage out of a movie, Mohawk hair cut, smudged war paint. and a monster dog snarling at the trooper's side.

The German sergeant lay sprawled out on the floor between Sparks and the hissing radio, eyes lifeless. Sparks shook his head to clear the cobwebs, then grimaced as multicolored lights danced around behind his eyes.

Between Sparks and the door to the room leading outside, the officer, blood dripping from his face, reached out for his pistol. The Walther glinted in the light from the bulb swaying overhead, teasingly close. To both of them.

The trooper lowered the machine gun. Now Sparks was staring into the muzzle of a machine gun, directly in the trooper's line of fire. "Move," the trooper roared and fired a short burst over the officer and Sparks.

Sparks and the officer both dove for the pistol. Sparks grabbed the pistol and rolled away from the German officer. Prone on the cold floor, he brought the pistol to bear, but before he or the trooper could fire the dog leaped across the bunker with a chilling snarl and was on the screaming officer. Sparks turned his face as blood splattered and sparkled in the light.

Beside him the door to the outer room burst open. A German in a great coat yanked a machine pistol down off his shoulder and fumbled it around to point toward Sparks.

Sparks rolled on his back, raised the Walther and fired. A burst from the machine pistol spat over his head, so close hot powder stung his cheek. Sparks' bullet from the Walther splintered the door frame behind the German.

"Stay down, damn it," The trooper shouted and swept a short burst of machine gun fire over Sparks, the bullets' impacts driving the big German back into the next room and on to his back.

Sparks rolled to the doorway as a shadow dashed toward the doorway. He ignored his splitting headache, raised the pistol and fired, low, a leg shot. The shadow went down with a shriek. Sparks cringed as the machine gun fired another deafening burst right over his head and into the room.

"Yow!" he exclaimed as one of the shells scorched the back of his neck and more hot brass clattered down around him on the concrete.

The trooper stepped past Sparks and looked around the now silent room. "Anymore out here?" he asked Sparks.

Sparks waved the pistol around the room. "These four brought me back here. But there are four more that they left back at the glider. They might come back in their truck." Sparks shook his head, slowly this time, getting a handle on how much abuse he could give his throbbing head.

The paratrooper, the big dog stuck to him like glue, walked over and helped the professor, struggling to sit up. "How about you? Anymore around to worry about?"

"Couple of dead ones out on the ocean side." The professor stopped to catch his breath, and then worked one arm out of the German tunic. "Get this fucking jerry jacket off me," he whispered. "If I'm going to die, I want to be in uniform."

The trooper returned to the doorway, pulled a dripping jump jacket off a hook and brought it over as Sparks helped the professor strip off the tunic. "Sorry I couldn't shoot the son of a bitch sooner. You were in the line of fire. I was afraid if I tried to cut down the German I'd get you, too. Almost waited too long."

Pfister grimaced. "Worked out pretty good. I'm alive. For a minute I wondered." He grabbed Spark's arm and pulled himself up. "We got to haul ass. German tanks headed out way."

A red splotch spread across Pfister's shoulder.

"Wait a minute." Sparks pulled a dressing from his first aid pouch and tied it over the bullet hole in the professor's shoulder, finishing it off so it worked like a sling. "That better?" he asked as he slipped the jump jacket over the professor's shoulders. "Piece of shit bullet didn't even come out the other side. You got you a free pass back to England."

He looked at Pfister as the floor rumbled under his feet. "Tanks?"

The professor motioned toward the clock. "Nope. That's probably the Air Corps bombing. But I overheard the Captain say the tanks are coming. In about half an hour the Navy guns are going to pound this place to rubble. We got to get out of here, away from the beach before the tanks cut us off and we're stuck in the middle of the bombardment."

Sparks found his helmet, plopped it on his head, lump and all, and led them out, pistol at the ready. "They brought me here in a command car. It should still be parked outside. The rest of the guys in the glider; can we go see if we can help them?"

"Sure. You up for it?" the trooped asked the professor. "Dawg wants to eat some more Germans."

The professor picked up the machine pistol. "Let's go find some dog food."

CHAPTER 14 - 81ST ABN FA BN

Allen stared up at the break in the clouds trying to recall his navigation classes, the all too few night flights in the right seat of the Waco. "I can see the Dipper and the North Star, so it looks to me we're going north. Makes sense. Cap thought we had been flying too long by the time we punched loose, plus he said the tug was taking us south of LZ Easy." Allen dropped into the right seat beside Watson as they rumbled down the narrow road, the A-T gun in tow. A slight drizzle, really just a thick mist, floated down. Allen reached into his shirt, pulled out his lucky Dodgers cap and pulled it down over his head. There. Better than any helmet.

"So, if we head back north, a little to the west, we should be going up toward Carentan, most likely. But take it easy, Sergeant Watson. I don't want to bust into a German patrol or strongpoint."

"Don't worry, Lieutenant." Watson flipped switches until the headlights glowed on the fenders, providing just enough light through the painted slits to stay between the head-high stone walls on either side of the road. "This old truck's running pretty smooth." He drove silently for a few minutes. "That's what I do, you know."

"What's that," Allen asked, confused.

"Trucks. I know all about them. I run the motor shop in the 327 Regimental Service Company. Mostly weapons carriers and jeeps, occasional duce and a half back home. For a big truck, this one drives pretty easy. Crazy. The only reason I was on the glider was to drive a jeep towing the A-T gun. Johnson along to help me service the vehicles if there's a problem. Don't have any idea where the jeep is now. But now I got me a fancy truck. An Opel. Never thought I would get to drive an Opel. In France, no less. Scared me back there. Thought the Captain was going to shoot so many holes in it with that grease gun it'd never run again."

Allen laughed. "Glad you got your Opel. Damn glad he killed those krauts. Now get us back with the rest of the Division. I just realized those flashes on the horizon aren't artillery. Too many, too fast. That's the final bombing runs before the invasion. Let's don't go that way." He leaned forward, peering into the ground fog ahead as Watson shifted through the gears. He didn't tell Watson that the glider with his jeep was likely blown to all creation.

Water puddles glistened in the muddy road as they bounced toward the north and the rest of the 101st.

"Look out," Allen yelled. He braced himself with his arms. A smaller vehicle turned out of a side road directly in front of them, yellow cat eyes barely visible.

Watson jerked the steering wheel and the truck swerved to the right, brakes locked, careening across the rain-slick intersection as Watson aimed the truck directly at the smaller car. Allen's chest slammed against the metal panel as the Opel tilted up on one side and slid off into a ditch. Behind him Talbot's scream cut through the sounds of metal screeching against a rock wall. Allen felt himself going up, out of the seat, over the dash. He grabbed a mirror post to keep from being crushed between the truck and the wall. The truck jolted and finally stopped with Allen spread-eagle across the hood. He closed his eyes. Thank you, Lord. He had lived through another crash. Odds were getting short.

The Opel lurched with the weight of a body. The cold muzzle of a gun pressed against the back of his neck.

"Don't move, kraut," a voice screamed in his ear.

"Jesus, Sparks," Watson exclaimed. "Where the hell you been? And get your pistol out of the Lieutenant's neck, for crying out loud."

The pressure left his neck and a hand pulled Allen up. "Sorry, Lieutenant. I figured you was a German and Sarge, here, was your prisoner." He grinned at Allen. "But I doubt there's a German in France with a Dodger's cap on. We were hauling ass down the road trying to find you guys when we came around the corner. I was afraid the krauts were going to kill you guys back there. Are Jefferson and the Captain O.K.?"

"Son of a bitches were 'bout to shoot us when Cap got them first. His legs are broke and Jefferson is wounded, but we're alive. How'd you get here?" Allen asked, rubbing his neck.

"Crazy story. But I brought a couple of guys with me. The professor, Sergeant Pfister, from G2, and Dawson, a demo man from the 326 Engineers, who saved our asses."

A trooper appeared at Spark's side, his arm in a makeshift sling. "Lieutenant. Glad to see you guys. I'm Pfister." He nodded back at a man and a dog untagling thmselves from the wrecked command car. "I'm a little banged up, but Dawson's mighty handy with either grenades or a German machine gun."

"And Geronimo here has a dog that 'specially hates the Germans," Sparks added. "Ate one up back there. *Really* ate him up."

Allen stared at the soldier with the Mohawk haircut and the vicious-looking dog, wondering how literal Sparks was, then said, "You guys climb in. We need to get a move on. Tanks coming."

"We heard," said Pfister, and climbed in the back of the truck. Pfister stared at Allen, eyebrows knotted. "You look familiar. Were you ever with the 506th?"

Allen nodded. "Just made it through jump school at Benning when my application for flight training came through. Like a fool I agreed to glider school. I should have stayed with the Currahees, except I had a foolish notion that I wanted to be a pilot. I still rather jump than fly, especially when I try to land one of those crates."

A muffled explosion rumbled in the distance. Dawson's dog growled into the night, a low rumble that brought a chill to Allen.

"Buried you, you son of a bitches," muttered Sparks.

"Buried what?" asked Allen.

"The bunker where the krauts beat me up. Dawson piled together a bunch of grenades and booby-trapped them to blow the bunker and all their communications gear to kingdom come. Somebody must've tripped them." Sparks canted his head at a new noise. "What's that?"

"Quiet a minute." Allen stood up on the top of the hood. "Damn tanks are getting closer." The whine of a revving engine floated across the fields. Allen hopped back down to the truck bed. Behind them the towed gun lay tilted up on one wheel beside the ditch. "Jefferson. Can you get the gun working?" he called down.

"If we can get it upright and on the road, and someone can give me a hand," Jefferson answered. "I think we better decide pretty quick, though. See that light coming up the road?"

Allen looked up to see a single light beam slice through the mists over a hedgerow, maybe five hundred yards away. "Sergeant Watson. Pull the gun out of the ditch. ASAP."

"Done." Watson slipped the idling truck into gear. He gunned the Opel, leaving a fender hanging on the stone wall, but managed to yank the gun back out to the middle of the road. He let the truck roll, dragging the gun about twenty yards down from the intersection as Jefferson and Sparks struggled to manhandle it back upright. They both hopped clear as the gun toppled back up on its wheels.

Watson hopped down from the truck and helped Jefferson untangle the trail as Sparks sliced away the heavy drogue chute strap looped around the truck's axle as a makeshift hitch. With a grunt Watson lifted up the trail and swung it around, feet sliding in the mud. Dawson, dog at his heels, shoved the tube around until, between them, the two big men and the dog had the gun tube pointed back down the road.

Allen grinned. "They don't need my puny ass in the way," he muttered. He climbed back to the bed of the truck and lifted Talbot's head from where he had it pillowed on an ammo box. "You doing O.K., Cap?" Allen slid the box out from under Talbot and shoved it to the back of the truck.

"Doing just fine. Just keep the Japs and the bulldozer off me." Talbot's voice sounded a little dreamy.

"Cap?" Allen leaned closer to Talbot. The pilot's eyes were closed, but he was breathing easy.

Jefferson's head popped up from behind the truck. He unslung the grease gun, tossed it on to the truck bed and grabbed the ammo box. "He was hurting bad, Lieutenant. I gave him my morphine."

Allen spotted the Syrette pinned to Talbot's collar. "I thought you were the one that got shot."

Jefferson shrugged. "Yeah, but riding with you glider pilots, I'm used to getting hurt." Jefferson hurried back to the gun with the ammo.

Allen glanced back over his shoulder. The rolling rumble of bombs had stopped, replaced by irregular explosions and the whistling of massive shells. The shore bombardment had started. The tank was out of sight behind the hedgerows for the moment, but no time to waste. They had to stop that tank, then get moving. But where to? Where the hell were they, for starters?

They had crashed at a road junction. The south leg of the road ran back toward the crashed glider and the sounds of the oncoming armor. Sparks and the command car must have come from the beach. Made sense. The bunker they had blown up would have been part of the coastal defense. Visualizing the map and how the peninsular stuck up like a thumb, that would be to the east. The command car blocked the road back to the bunker, its crushed nose stuck out into the intersection. Back behind him in the direction the Opel faced, the road heading west must lead toward Carentan and the general direction of the paratrooper drop zones where they originally were supposed to land. To the north flowed the Douve River and the bridges they were tasked to hold against German reinforcements. Like the tank coming up the road. Behind the tank, who knew? More Germans, most likely.

Allen was a pilot, but he was an officer in the Army and a qualified paratrooper to boot, even if he was assigned to Troop Carrier Command. He had only met Captain Talbot back in England, at Aldermaston, the week before, and immediately felt he would be safe with a man who had survived Sicily and Burma. But the Captain was down. Time had come to take charge, straighten out this mess. "Pfister." He looked around for the G2 sergeant.

"Right here, L. T." Pfister trotted back from where he had been watching down the road to the south, a German machine pistol dangling from his good hand.

Allen pointed toward the intersection. "You and Dawson find a good place and set up the machine gun on the north side of the road, behind a wall if you can, well out of Jefferson's line of fire on the intersection. Give me a yell when you get in position so I'll know where you are. Sergeant Watson, Sparks and I'll help Jefferson set up the A-T gun. Let's get cracking." He wondered if they were doing the smart thing. Ambush a tank? Better off running, but he remembered the mission briefing, the threat of tanks to the invasion force. The distant bomb explosions reminded him what was at risk.

The gunner had Watson and Sparks each at the end of a gun trail as Jefferson stood directly behind the breech, directing the emplacement. Allen patted Talbot on the shoulder, dropped down and trotted over to Jefferson. "What else do we need to do?"

Jefferson pressed his eye to the gun sight. "This looks good. Close to the truck and the rest of the ammo. Rather be here than in the intersection. If we set up for a straight shot down the south road and a panzer runs up our ass, he'll blow us off the road before we can shoot. Coming around the corner he'll have to slow to get past the command car. We can ambush him with a side shot before he can bring his gun to bear. We got some of the Brits' armor piercing rounds, so we should be able to bust anything they send at us."

He grinned up at Allen. "If I hit it before it hits us." Jefferson looked back at the intersection. "I can't see over the wall from down here. How 'bout you get up on the truck where you can see what's coming up the road. Yell out if he tries to slip around us, and we need to re-lay the gun."

In a couple of minutes they had the trail legs split, the anchors stomped into the muddy road and a 57mm armor piercing round loaded. Jefferson sat on one of the trails and peered through the sight set into the front armor shield, his shoulder locked into the traversing rest. Sparks crouched behind the shield on the opposite side, a round cradled in his arms, and Watson stood behind them with another round ready. They watched as Jefferson demonstrated how the gun moved side to side guided by his shoulder, almost like aiming a rifle.

Allen clambered up on the truck hood. A hint of dawn glimmered in the east. Overhead the clouds streamed, thinning as the storm front moved past. No more rain, thank God.

"L. T.," Pfister called out from across the intersection, waving his gun over the wall so Allen could see where they were. "We're ready."

"Hold fire until Jefferson knocks out the tank, then take out any infantry coming up with them or tank crew that bails," Allen called back.

He dropped to a crouch when the oncoming tank's headlight beam slewed across the wrecked command car in the intersection. The tank's exhaust glow shimmered above the stone wall, almost to the intersection. The fields were quiet except for the engine rumble and the squeak and clank of the treads. His heart began pounding as exhaust fumes washed through the damp air. "Getting close," he called down to Jefferson. He dropped flat when machine gun fire from the tank tore into the front of the wrecked command car, two short bursts that ripped into the thin metal hood and sides.

The tank stopped. A German popped out of the top hatch, head and shoulders barely visible over the wall, lit by the back glow from the headlight.

Allen froze, cheek pressed against the warm hood. A rumble and the tank eased forward until its long gun poked its snout into the intersection, followed by the front end of the tank. The tank's right side tread lurched against the command car, shoving it back until it began to crumple. Metal screeched as the tank began to pivot around, the tread grinding over the front of the car.

"CRACK—BLAM!" An instant after the A-T gun fired the report and impact merged into one terrifying concussion that lifted Allen from the truck hood. Obscured for a moment by the dust kicked up by the burst, the tank lurched, enveloped by a yellow-black ball of fire. A roar of the engine and the tank tread unspooled from the idler wheels. The tank commander scrambled up in the hatch, lit by yellow flames. Smoke poured up around him.

Dawson's machine gun cut loose from a gap in the wall and the commander slumped down out of sight. A machine pistol answered from behind the tank and Dawson returned fire along the road. Ah, shit, more Germans behind the tank.

By the time Allen had taken a breath, a crackling inferno flared up over the tank. Machine gun rounds popped off inside the tank. Allen wrinkled his nose. He had never smelled such a horrible odor.

He squinted into the smoke. Pfister had climbed up on the wall and frantically waved, pointing out across to Allen's right. Allen strained to see into the darkness, peering across the field. A second tank, a vague monster in the morning mists, appeared. It wasn't following the rules. It raced directly toward them on their side of the stone wall, red and yellow exhaust plumes making its path. The tank suddenly rocked to a halt. No chance to—

Allen felt himself flying through the air, battered by metal shards and dirt clods, tossed up in the air by the exploding tank round. He whirled through the dark sky, how high he had no idea, how long he had no concept. His breath punched out of his lungs when he slammed back to the ground. He lay still for a moment until he could force a full breath of air back into his lungs. Sensation gradually returned until he sensed cold dirt and damp grass pressed against his face.

A couple of deep breaths; so painful he figured he had cracked his ribs. He finally raised his face out of the damp grass, recovered his cap from under a splintered 57mm ammo box and fixed the brim, bent straight up by the explosion. He jammed his cap back on his head, shivered. He felt as if he had been crushed under the truck, rather than thrown off. His shirt hung from his shoulders, ripped into shreds.

The tank engine roared on the other side of the wall, so close he could hear the commander yelling in German.

He looked up to see Sparks leap up on the wall, a pistol in his hand, firing toward the tank. Pfister appeared beside him, a machine pistol stuck out in front of him with his one good hand. They both screamed at the tank like banshees. Covered by the wall, Dawson and the dog sprinted toward them.

On the other side of the wall a tank machine gun cut loose. Sparks spun around and fell back, ricochets sparking off the stones.

Dawson stopped running, held his machine gun up over the wall and fired, sweeping the gun back and forth until the empty belt dropped to the ground.

Allen staggered to his feet. The tank round had blown a gap in the wall big enough for a man to clamber through. On the other side, the twisted 57mm barrel poked up over the wall. The crumpled truck hood protruded up into the air, the same hood he had been laying on when the German fired. The tank roared again, slowly spinning on its tracks in the roadway, close enough to touch. The machine gun mounted in the front of the hull pivoted around toward Dawson. As it fired over his head, Dawson, dog by his side, crawled across to Allen, bullets chewing into the remnants of the wall and whining off into the night.

"We got to get out of here," Dawson gasped.

The wall beside them began to vibrate. The tank treads ground against the rocks and a big chunk of mortar fell out. The tank main gun poked through the gap. Allen grabbed Dawson and shoved him along the wall. "You guys go. Run. I got to stop this damn tank."

Had to finish this. Cap depended on him. Allen picked up a loose 57mm round from the grass, bent low, darted under the main gun tube and on past the tank nose. He glanced down at the projectile in his hand. What the hell good was that? Maybe jam it in the treads? Got to try something.

The hull-mounted machine gun fired a burst, too late to catch him as he ran toward the intersection.

The driver gunned the engine and the treads began climbing up on the remains of the wall, bits of rocks flung out by the tanker's frantic maneuvers.

Allen sprinted to the intersection, blocked by the burning tank hulk. A second command car sat behind the hulk, bodies draped over the sides. Further down the road he could see more lights coming.

He dodged around the hulk to find the second tank had crashed halfway across through the wall and into the field, blocking his view of the truck—and Talbot—if by some miracle his pilot still lay in dreamland on the back of the truck.

Allen ran toward the rear of the tank as the driver reversed, gunned the engine, then rammed it forward again, back and forth, tank treads momentarily jammed in the A-T gun trails and the stone wall. Allen leaped up on the tank's rear deck and grabbed a tall radio antenna. The tank rocked as the engine roared beneath his feet. He fell to his knees as the driver continued to rock the tank back and forth trying to free the tank from the gun trails.

The tank commander lay sprawled across the open cupola hatch. Blood streamed down his face. He stared at Allen, but seemed unable to move.

"Allen." Dawson and the dog stood side-by-side on the truck bed, Dawson waving at him. "Here. Catch this." Dawson yelled over the roar of the straining engine and tossed Allen a stick grenade.

Allen caught the grenade and stared down at the A-T round in his other hand as the tank rocked under his feet. He ripped away a strip of his shirt and wound it around the grenade and the projectile.

The tank commander's eyes stared at him. Blinked once, twice.

Allen pulled the string dangling from the stick and stuffed the bundle down between the tank commander and the edge of the hatch. He jumped off the tank onto the road, did his best imitation of a parachute landing fall and rolled toward the truck as a muffled explosion rocked the ground. He struggled to his knees in time to see flames shoot up from the tank hatch. Then more of that sickening smell wafted down the road.

He crawled over to Watson, sitting with his back to the truck's front wheel with a dazed look in his eyes. "Can you get up?" Allen asked.

Watson shook his head and cleared his throat. "Jesus. Am I alive?" His words came out more a croak than words.

"Yeah. See if you can get this wreck going." Allen helped Watson stagger to his feet and up into the driver's seat. Allen pulled himself over the tailgate and back on to the truck bed. To his relief Talbot was still there, apparently in one piece, clutching an abandoned rifle to his chest.

"How we doing, Wilber?" Talbot asked, the morphine-induced grin still on his face. "Sure am glad this time wasn't as tough as Sicily. That was shitty, having to ditch in the Med. We lost a bunch of good men that night."

Allen pried the rifle out of Talbot's hands. "I'm glad, too, Cap. You hang tight."

The truck backfired and stumbled, then started with a roar. Allen looked up to see Dawson dump Sparks and his canvas bag beside Talbot, then jump up and stomp down the hood. Allen yelled back at Pfister as he scrambled up into the back of the truck. "Where's Jefferson?" Allen asked.

Pfister reached over and handed Allen a metal tag, shaking his head as the big dog leaped up beside Dawson.

The truck lurched, and they pulled away from the smoldering tank. He flinched when a round cooked off with a thump from inside the tank. When he looked back the hull began glowing a hot red. Then an ear-splitting explosion flung the turret up, rotating in the air, whipping the barrel around like a giant lash, followed by a tongue of fire that stabbed up toward the sky. For an instant before the flames died down, he caught a glimpse of Jefferson's body tangled in the crumpled antitank gun's armored shield.

Allen dropped Jefferson's tag in his pocket beside Riley's and Johnson's. The gunner had done his job. Sergeant Riley would be proud of him.

They all had. The remains of two tanks that wouldn't stop the guys coming in off the beaches burned behind them. He glanced at the dirty pink bank stretching low on the horizon. Pretty soon, now. He did hope he lived to see the invasion troops come ashore.

To his left he spotted more lights probing the mists. Coming directly toward them. "Gun it, Sarge," he yelled.

CHAPTER 15 - 3/501ST PRCHT INF

Private Rudy Livingston crossed a maze of hedgerows and small orchards in the pitch black night, occasionally lit by flares and a distant searchlight probing the sky and the infrequent breaks in the clouds that let silver moonlight wash over the French countryside. Several fields over a dog barked. He followed the sound and led Sergeant Barkley along a cow path to a deserted barn. He stopped at the door, the cook close behind him. A tiny sound, maybe the scurry of a mouse. No dog. If one had stayed here, it was probably scared away. Christ, he'd run if he knew where to go.

He sniffed. Something was liveried here. He recognized the stable smell from his grandpa's farm. Hay, manure, the sweat of a working horse and leather. He edged around the door, .45 held trembling out in front. The place looked empty by the bit of moonlight that shimmered through the door. "See anybody," he asked Barkley. He tried to talk in a low voice. When he whispered it came out as a lisp.

"Nobody. Nothing," was Barkley's answer. "I can hear lots of gunfire across the fields, but I don't think there's anything close. And I sure don't see shit." He pushed the door open and slipped in.

The cool air felt good as Livingston breathed through his mouth. His gums had stopped bleeding and no more teeth felt wobbly. He ran his tongue over the gap where his two top teeth had been knocked out. Small price for a crash landing in the middle of a river.

"Man, I'm whipped." Barkley's voice echoed in the empty barn. Livingston followed him in. An old wagon sat in the middle of the barn.

Barkley sat on a hay bale, pulled off one boot, held it up and let the water drain from it. "By gosh, I don't think I can walk another step." He looked around. "And I'm starving. Think there's anything to eat in here? I've already finished off my Ks. I'm ready for some real food." He pulled off his sock and wrung a stream of water out of it.

A snort from a stall and Barkley rolled to the floor.

Livingston froze, slowly swung the pistol around. A flicker caught his eye. A skinny horse stood in a stall, one ear twitching. It snorted again, eyes closed, dead asleep.

Livingston chuckled. "Quit looking at that poor horse. You're the cook, for crying out loud. Surely you can find something better. But I wouldn't start a fire. Germans probably all around us. Somewhere."

Thank goodness their pilot had pulled him into the raft. Never thought he'd be so happy to see any kind of boat again. Even though he had kept blowing into his Mae West, his chin had dipped deeper and deeper down into the murky water as his clothes become water-logged. He had never told anyone in the Army he couldn't swim a lick. Paratroopers were supposed to be able to do anything, espe- cially ones who had been fishermen. He suddenly shivered. His jacket and pants dripped and his jump boots still squished, but he was alive.

"You going to keep going?" Barkley asked.

"Sure. Sooner or later we'll find some of our guys."

"We been walking for what, an hour, and haven't seen anybody. You got that one pistol. All I got is my favorite butcher knife. I think I'm going to hunker down here until daylight and I can see who I'm running into."

"Your choice, buddy. Sure you're going to be all right, alone here?"

Barkley nodded, his head a blur in the dim light. "I'll weasel around, find me a corner and wait it out."

"Take care, then." Livingston walked back out into the night. He slipped across the farmyard to a yard fenced in by rough timbers. He crouched and stared between the timbers. A cow lay on the ground, kind of curled up, asleep. Oh, lord. Poor thing will be steaks when Barkley finds her. If his belly wasn't all ready stuffed full of horse meat.

Livingston kept walking toward the sound of firing, but by the time he got where he thought the shots sounded, everybody was gone. No Germans. No Americans. Alive ones, that is. He saw his fill of dead people, German and GI. He had his pick of weapons, though. Found a clean BAR and more ammo than he really wanted to carry to add to his .45, plus two canteens and a musette bag of grenades. Strange. After almost drowning, he had drunk a whole canteen of water, and was still thirsty. But, good and bad, he didn't see anybody to shoot at or with. Maybe Barkley had the right idea. Just hole up until some more Americans came around.

But the someone who came around could just as easily be Ger- man, so he continued walking along the side of a hedgerow. He stopped, took a drink and screwed the plastic cap back tight on the canteen, careful to keep the chain link holding the cap from tinkling against the metal canteen. He ran his tongue over the gap, and across his teeth, then fished a Pemmican bar out of his K-rations. It took a minute to figure out how to chew without the missing teeth, then munched as he listened to the sounds floating around. Seemed all the paratroop drops had long passed. A few planes just an hour or so ago, maybe the gliders coming in. But still no Americans on the ground as far as he could see or hear, just echoes of artillery and the faint stuttering of machine gun and small arm fire. He stopped chewing and listened.

Voices floated through the predawn stillness.

Two Germans, arguing by their tone, on the opposite side of a hedgerow. Livingston angled away, unsure in the night if he was about to walk into the middle of an outpost of some kind. Maybe he should have stuck with the pilot and the others from the rubber boat. Or stayed in the barn with Barkley. He probably had coffee and steaks on the fire by now.

But it just hadn't seemed right to hide with the sounds of combat all around him. Too late to worry now. He had come to fight. He turned and trotted away, boots silent except for the squish of water in his socks. Panting, he slowed after a few minutes. Cripes. No need to panic. The whole Allied armada was coming pretty soon. He stumbled as he stepped up on a road. Ahead a flash, two flashes lit the horizon. He stood stock still and counted, like he did with distant lightning flashes across the Atlantic. "One thousand, two thousand." He counted up to eleven thousand before the first explosion reached him, then continuous flashes and rumblings walked up and down the horizon.

The invasion prep.

A crunch sounded off to his left.

"You got to be a GI."

Livingston nearly jumped out of his boots.

"I can smell that crappy Pemmican bar a mile away. Got any more? I lost mine when I landed."

Livingston took a great sigh of relief when a paratrooper walked up, his left arm all wrapped together with a weapons bag. "What happened to you?" he asked. Livingston fished out a second bar and handed it to the soldier.

The soldier slipped his carbine over his shoulder and took the bar. "Broke my arm when I landed. A friend wrapped it up for me. Hurts like hell, but I'll get through the night. Where you going?"

Livingston shrugged. "Beats me. Just trying to find my unit." He glanced back behind the man, but didn't see anyone else. "Where's your friend?"

"She was a French lady, a resistance fighter." He shook his head. "Her name was Anna-Maria. Damned Germans killed her. But she had a mission, some kind of railroad bridge to blow up, so I'm looking to finish the job for her. Want to go?"

"I'm tired of lugging around all this ammo, so sure." He glanced down at the GI's sleeve. "Since you're the sergeant, where you go, I go. I'm Rudy Livingston, 3rd Battalion, 501st."

"Yeah, I remember seeing you in jump school. I'm Harry Rule, 1st of the O'Duce. Glad to see you, Livingston. Now let's go find a bridge."

Livingston followed Rule up an incline. Anxious to keep up, he bumped into Rule at the top. "Sorry, Sarge."

"Watch out and don't stumble over the tracks," Rule cautioned. "And don't bump my arm again. Hurts bad enough as it is." He started off between the rails.

Livingston stumbled along behind Rule, stretching his stride to step from one rail tie to the next.

"Whoa," Rule whispered, holding his carbine out to stop Livingston before he could get past, then easing down to a squat between the rails.

"What is it?" Livingston squatted beside Rule. Air whistled between the gaps in his teeth, but when he closed his mouth, he was breathing so hard the noise he made breathing through his nose seemed even louder. Then he realized why Rule had stopped. Someone was talking ahead. The voices sounded American.

The voices didn't get louder, nor did they move away.

"Let's check them out," Rule whispered.

The rail bed cinders softly crunched under Livingston's feet as he angled down to the tree line. He could hear Rule moving off to his left.

He stopped when a limb snapped under his foot.

A "shush" and the voices stilled.

From ahead "Flash," came out of the night, a low hoarse whisper.

"Fun.., fun...." Livingston couldn't get the reply past his tender jaw and missing teeth. In desperation he pulled out his cricket and snapped it several times.

"Flash, God dammit, before I blow your boots off." The voice was louder this time.

Livingston furiously clicked his cricket and sucked air past the gap in his teeth. "Funder, for crying out loud," he whispered. "I can't say it. But I've got my cricket."

"Thunder, you ass holes," Rule called out from behind him.

The ground crunched to his right and a GI with a Thompson limped out of the gloom.

"Jeeze, you guys get your asses over here before somebody blows them off."

Livingston followed the GI across a yard littered with wooden timbers and broken roof tiles and on into the shell of a house. All that was left was three stone walls, a dirt floor and a table. In the middle of where the fourth wall should have stood, the skeleton of a doorframe poked up in the air, all ghostly in the flickering lantern light.

Inside a medic, or at least someone with a Red Cross band around his arm, hovered over a man prone on the table. The lantern hanging from an exposed timber cast shadows out in the darkness around the ruins. Another man with a field dressing wrapped around his chest sat propped against the wall.

The waiting room. Good. Rule could get the doc to look at his arm. Livingston wondered if Joey, the pilot, was still out there somewhere, or if he had found a medic somewhere.

"You hurt?" the GI who led them in asked. He swayed on his feet as he asked.

"Broke arm," Rule answered. "But it can wait."

"I'm fine, 'cept for my teef. Knocked out when we crashed," Livingston replied. "I'll have to find a dentist when we get back to England."

"How about going back to the tracks and watching out for Germans. They been roaming all around all night, but so far they haven't come close enough to see us. I'm starting to get a little woozy." Dark blood ran down the man's arm and dripped on the ground. His pants leg was ripped open and bloody.

"I'll watch," Rule answered. "Livingston, you help the doc."

Great. Anything he liked less than cleaning fish was seeing guys bleed. He took a breath and pulled the GI into the light. Like it or not, he needed to stop the bleeding or this guy was going to croak.

"Take it easy and the doc will fix you up pretty soon. I'll put a patch on until he can get to you." He pulled the soldier's dressing out of a first aid pouch. "Come over by the light." Livingston led him across the room to stand under the lantern. Livingston glanced down at the man on the table, then quickly looked away. The doc was sewing up a bloody gash across the wounded man's gut.

The smell of burned gunpowder and scorched dirt seeped through the air. And the smell of...Livingston wasn't sure. He had been around dead fish all his life, but this smelled deader.

Rule stood on the other side of the empty doorway, his carbine laid back across his shoulder like a gunslinger in an old movie. His left arm dangled all awkward in a thick bundle. Rule motioned with his head toward the tracks. "I'll go look around, see if I can find any French resistance fighters." He disappeared into the darkness.

The guy really had a thing for French women and blowing up railroad bridges.

Livingston leaned his BAR against the wall. "You been here long?" he asked the GI.

"Christ. I got no idea. I been wandering around all night, until I ran into a machine gun nest down the road. I tossed a grenade and ran, but one of the bastard krauts got me. Shoulder. Friggin leg got hit by fragments from my own grenade, I think. Doc asked me to keep watch until he finished with the guy on the table." Blood ran down the Thompson's barrel, slowly dripping in the pale lantern light.

"What's your name?" Livingston asked. He didn't give a hoot about the man's name. He just wanted the GI to live till morning. "Why don't you set the gun down for a minute?"

The GI let the Thompson slip to the floor, swaying on his feet. Livingston helped the man take off his shirt. Blood oozed from a nasty hole in his shoulder, big as a quarter.

"Doesn't look bad," Livingston lied. "I'll patch it, then you can let it be until the doc can look at it."

"Don't waste the field dressing," the GI said.

"Not a waste, Doc's got plenty more. We need to stop the bleeding, and you'll be fine." Livingston tried to sound reassuring. He really wished he had paid more attention in the first aid classes. He figured he'd be shooting and killing, not fixing. So far all he had done was walk around.

Livingston heard a clunk. He looked up to see a blur bounce off the side wall and roll behind the GI he was helping. It spun, stopped in the middle of the dirt floor. A stick grenade.

The soldier sitting against the wall threw himself forward, grabbed the grenade and flipped it toward the door as he sprawled in the dirt. Too late. The grenade exploded in mid air, a ball of fire and then blackness.

An overpowering darkness and silence floated over Livingston. He felt that he was in the bottom of a well, unable to breath, shut out from the rest of the world. A great weight pressed against his chest. Gray light seeped into his eyes, streaked with red sparkles. He heaved his chest, struggling to breath.

"Can you hear me?"

Livingston forced his eyes open. A face looked down at him and the weight rolled away. The doc, smeared with blood, pulled him up, his eyes wild. "Germans outside," he said in a voice that matched his eyes. "I have to take care of them." The doc picked up the Thompson. When he turned Livingston could see the back of the doc's shirt had been ripped open, leaving his back pocked with black splotches.

Livingston rolled over and found his BAR on the floor. The man who had tried to throw the grenade clear turned toward him, then collapsed back on the dirt floor, face splattered with blood. The man with the wounded shoulder he had been trying to help lay in the dirt where the doc had rolled him off Livingston, looking dead as could be. A wasted bandage after all.

A crack outside and a yell, *"Sterben sie, Fallschirmjäger,"* then a long rip of automatic fire, met by the sharp thunder from the Thompson. Livingston snatched up his BAR and scrambled toward the corner of the ruined wall. He slid around the wall, BAR at the ready.

A huge German in an odd helmet charged toward the doc. A burst from the doc's Thompson stopped him before Livingston could fire. The doc rose up from behind a stone well, walked over to the German and emptied the Thompson into the body.

Livingston scurried around the wall and to the right. "Anymore of them, doc?" he asked, finger trembling on the BAR's trigger.

The doc backed away from the German. He stood for a moment looking out toward the trees. He slowly turned toward Livingston, shaking his head. "I don't see any more." He dropped the Thompson to the ground. "Come help me with the wounded. We've done enough killing."

Livingston followed the doc into the ruins. What a war. People dying all around him and he still hadn't fired a shot. Even the man he had tried to help was dead. When Livingston caught up with the doc he was on his knees beside the soldier with the shoulder wound.

"Dead." The doc shook his head, his voice trembling. "They're all dead."

"Livingston," A breathless voice called from outside. Rule stuck his head around the corner, grimacing with pain, panting for breath. "Jesus. You guys all right? I heard the shooting and ran back as fast as I could."

Livingston helped the doc to his feet. "Fucking Germans tossed a grenade in. Killed these guys."

Rule collected the three dead men's dog tags and dropped them in his pocket. "I ran into a bunch of GIs in a car down the track, our guys. They've got a couple of wounded with them. Can you and doc come help?" Rule asked.

Doc picked up his bag. "I'm not much help healing tonight, but I'll give it my best. Lead on."

CHAPTER 16 - 327TH GLIDER INF

The truck steering felt odd, like one of the wheels was out of kilter. Despite the body damage, the engine purred like a luxury car. Motor Sergeant Tony Watson was surprised the Opel's tires were still inflated, that the damn thing ran at all, that any of them were still alive. He hunched over the wheel. He had been awake for hours but the damp air and the danger had him keyed up, wide awake. Daylight would leave them exposed pretty soon. He slipped the truck in high gear and accelerated away from the mangled tanks and antitank gun. "Where to, Lieutenant?" he asked.

Allen slid down into the seat beside him. "For now, head down the road away from the damn tanks. Sounded like a whole column coming after us. We must have stopped their advance party, scouts or something." He stretched up and looked around in the darkness. "If you come to a crossroads that veers to the right, take it. Likely more Germans straight ahead. The Douve River and Carentan should be over to our right, the landing zones on the other side of that."

"So we're on the opposite side of the river from the rest of the Division? That's not good."

Allen looked back behind them. "Let's focus on getting across the river. The closer we get to the drop zones on the other side of the river and the further away from the tanks, the better."

Watson nodded. "That's where I was supposed to drive Sergeant Riley. Take the A-T gun down to one of the bridges and hold back the German armor until the 4th Infantry and the 70th Armor could get ashore, along with the rest of our guys."

Allen stood up on the floorboard, hanging on to the stub left where the mirror used to be. "Were those Tigers back there? Big damn tanks, whatever they were. I don't think they can ford the river this close to the coast. They'll need a bridge to get to our guys. Let's go find a bridge, and a way to stop them from crossing."

Watson focused on the road, shadowy in the pale predawn glow. It twisted through the fields, around the edges of the hedgerows. Ahead a curve to the right took them toward a cluster of buildings. When he slowed for the turn a rooster crowed across an orchard on the left,

another sign that dawn and the invasion were imminent. A second
rooster answered from ahead, like back home in Kansas. All he had
to do was look for the yellow brick road.

Instead of bricks, the tires thumped over cobblestones as they
approached the river and the cluster of buildings. Watson slowed,
geared down as the road turned parallel to the dark bank. A cluster of
indistinct objects bobbed in the tidal flow. Seemed everything he
saw since he landed had been indistinct, like he was going blind.
"What's that in the water?" asked Watson. "Do the Germans have
gunboats on the river?"

Allen leaned forward, staring at the shapes. "They look like little
fishing boats, dories. Too small for gun boats. O.K., now. Keep it
slow until I figure out what's ahead." He glanced toward the men in
the back. "Dawson. Got any more ammo for that machine gun?"

"Half a belt, Lieutenant. Maybe fifty rounds. I can still do some
damage."

Allen crawled back into the truck bed and motioned Dawson
forward.

Dawson climbed up beside Watson and settled the machine gun
on the battered hood. Pfister sat facing the rear with a Thompson
clutched to his side, watching their back. Sparks rolled up on an elbow, hand pressed to his neck. Dark blood seeped around his fingers.

"Hang on, Sparks. We're going to stop in a minute; see if we can
get you some help." Allen picked up a German machine pistol bouncing in the truck bed beside Talbot and Sparks. He leaned forward by
Dawson's head. "You guys watch ahead. I'll try to keep a look-see
along the river bank."

Ahead, spidery trestles extended over low stone walls along the
sides of a narrow bridge, one, two hundred feet across, hard to tell
through the mist rising up from the river. Watson grimly hung on to
the steering wheel as they bounced from side to side. A tire must be
finally going flat. No wonder, the way the German tank had shot up
everything in sight. The Opel got harder and harder to control as it
bounced over the cobblestones. He wrestled the steering wheel around
the last turn before the river and guided the truck onto the bridge.
The rumble of cobblestones turned to the rattle of floor planks as
they crossed over the river.

"Watson. You said your mission was to guard the bridge, right?" Allen asked.

"Yes, sir. Well, some bridge. Damn if I know if this is the one."

"I didn't see any fords. Think we can stop the tank column here?"

Watson looked back, scanned the road behind them and the bridge ahead of them, and nodded his head. "Yes, sir, we can do it." Oh, shit, what was he saying? They had lived through ambushing a pair of tanks, all but Jefferson. Were they going to trade another man for another tank? Hell of a price to pay.

"Bridges are damn all important," Allen said. "The river is all that stands between the German armor and the beaches."

"And us," added Watson.

"We know more tanks are coming behind us, so how can we block this bridge?"

They rumbled across the planks and Watson let the truck slow to a stop at the top of a slight slope. Ahead the road narrowed and passed between a cluster of stone houses, then ran on to disappear into the mists drifting off the dewy fields. A true fog, heavier now, rose up from the river, shimmering in the glow of the false dawn. To their right the sun still hid below the horizon, with only a glimmer off the low clouds hinting at daylight soon to come.

"We can jam the truck up between the houses. They're stone. Might at least slow them down for a few minutes. But those tanks are big fuckers. If they get a head of steam up they can crush this Opel to a pile of crap, roll right over." Watson pointed to a gap between the river and the first building, the one on the corner sporting a hanging sign. "They might even be able to get around." He glanced back over his shoulder. "Probably have a better chance of stopping them on the bridge. I didn't see a ford along the way. Pretty steep banks. We can stop them here. They get across; damn krauts can roll to Utah Beach, massacre our guys coming out of the water."

Allen nodded in agreement. "I agree. Back the truck up and lodge it in as tight as you can get it. We'll see what we can find to keep them from getting up that head of steam." He looked around at Pfister who had crawled up next to him. "Sarge, you or Dawson got any better ideas?"

Pfister shook his head. "Stopping the tanks. That's what it's all about now."

"How about this, sir. Not a better idea, but one to consider," said Dawson. "If I can rig a few charges back on the other side of the bridge, maybe we can stop one on the approach. Like Sergeant Watson said, the bridge is pretty narrow. Jam the truck across it, stop one tank, put some fire on it to keep the krauts from towing it clear, and we might be able to hold the crossing until someone else shows. Reinforcements got to come up sometime. This bridge must be on somebody's list."

"Lot of if's there. You got the makings of a mine?" Allen asked

"I'm a demo man, sir. I can make anything blow up."

"Get it ready then. And hurry."

Dawson dropped off the truck, followed by the big German Shepherd.

Watson shifted the Opel into reverse and backed until he was in the middle of the bridge. "How about here," he asked Allen.

Allen stood and nodded. "Wedge it in tight."

Watson grimaced as the frame scraped against the stone work, then cut the steering wheel sharply and rammed the front bumper against the left side of the bridge, jamming the battered Opel in tight and blocking the bridge.

Watson helped Allen slide Talbot out of the truck and carry him down the street away from the bridge. Sparks stumbled along beside them, one hand on Pfister's good shoulder, the other clutched to his neck. At the last house on the right a sliver of light shined past the edge of a blackout curtain. Pfister helped Sparks to the ground and knocked on the door. The light inside went out. This time Pfister kicked the door with his boot, then yelled out something in French.

Pfister, holding his Thompson at the ready, squared himself in front of the door. He stopped and turned to Watson, a grin on his face. "Tony. Friggin German shot me in the shoulder, and Sparks did such a nice job of patching it up for me, I don't want to bust it all loose again. Would you please kick down that door for me? I want to have a conversation with our French friends inside."

Watson nodded. Pfister really must be a professor. Such a polite guy to be a paratrooper. "Be glad to." Watson reared back and smashed his heel against the door. The latch shattered. A second kick and the door flew open to a chorus of muted screams.

Pfister jumped through the doorway, Thompson by his side.

Watson followed Pfister, the machine pistol held ready. Inside a man stood against the back wall with his arms around the shoulders of a woman and a younger girl. No wonder the family was scared. For a college professor, he looked more like a barbarian: filthy, bloody bandage around one shoulder and waving a Thompson submachine gun in his hand.

But Pfister's Thompson and soothing words soon had the family helping carry Talbot and Sparks inside and laid out on the floor, pillows and blankets spread for a bit of comfort.

Watson dug a field dressing from his belt pouch, squatted down beside Sparks and tied the bandage loose around his neck so it wouldn't choke him. "You're a lucky man, Sparks. Anybody that takes on a tank with a Walther shouldn't live to brag about it. Now hold this pressed against your neck until the bleeding stops."

"Not going to brag, Sarge. Did you get the bastards?"

"Lieutenant Allen blew them to hell. Now shut up and be still." Watson took a thin blanket the Frenchman brought from somewhere in the back and spread it over Sparks.

Pfister listened while the Frenchman spoke quietly, then knelt beside Watson and Allen as they made the wounded as comfortable as they could. "The father says there's not a doctor between here and Carentan. About four kilometers, little over three miles and a shit pile of Germans between here and there, if *père* is right."

Allen reached over, felt Talbot's forehead and nodded. "O.K. Talbot's not losing blood, but I'm worried about Sparks. We got to keep both of them warm and watch out for shock; they should be fine until a medic catches up with us. Shouldn't be long, if we can hold the bridge."

Watson stood. "Well, let's get back up there before the Germans show up." Damn. Now he was acting like a tactical genius, instead of fixing trucks. But it made sense. Too many good men dying. Got to have a reason.

"You're right," Allen agreed. "Pfister, you stay here with these two and make sure nobody sneaks up this street behind us. You take care of yourself, too, Sarge. We'll get that shoulder looked at soon as we can." He turned to Watson. "Ready?"

Watson nodded his head and started out the door. "Let's see if we can get Dawson's ideas to work, stop those damn tanks before they overrun us and screw everything up."

When they got back to the bridge Dawson was on his knees, lashing a packet of C-2 to a German stick grenade. He looked up when they trotted up.

"How can I help?" Watson asked.

Dawson handed him the explosives. "If a tank gets close, try to pitch this in its track or idler wheels. It might do some damage underneath or on top of the engine compartment, but I'm not sure. Not likely to blow the tank up. Their armor's too thick, but we might make them throw a tread. So if it stops, stay out of sight from the machine guns, and be ready for somebody to pop out one of the hatches." He dropped a similar package in a cargo pocket and hefted the machine gun. "I still got enough rounds to put a whopping on anybody who tries to come out, but be ready."

Stopping the tanks was important, but this was downright stupid. "What if the explosion doesn't stop it?"

Dawson grinned. "Don't slow down or I'll run over your ass."

Allen stood and looked across the bridge. "No time to waste, then. Let's go." He started toward the bridge.

"Whoa, L.T. Let us go across. You already got your tank back at the crossroads." Watson said. "If a tank gets by us, it'll get jammed up trying to get by the Opel, long enough for you to decide what to do. Why don't you find a good place by the tavern there, have a drink and tell the guys coming in off the beach not to shoot our asses."

"Here's a demo pack." Dawson handed Allen one of the bundles. "Just in case they get by us."

A rumble on the far side of the river stopped the conversation.

The sight of a distant light slicing through the ground fog sent a chill down Watson's back. "Come on, Dawson. Let's go before it's too late." His boots drummed over the loose planks as he crossed the bridge on a dead run. He slowed to duck under the truck bed, Dawson's jury-rigged antitank mine in one hand and the machine pistol in the other. The planks behind him rattled as Dawson with his machine gun and dog loped across the bridge, hot on his heels.

Once across the bridge, Watson cut between the river and the houses and turned to run between the river and the back of the buildings, slipping and sliding on the muddy bank. He skidded to a stop, blocked by a large boat that suddenly loomed out of the dark. Panting, he leaned against the damp wood planks of a fishing boat perched on a pair of logs, a makeshift ramp running up out of the fog, leading from the river up the bank and to the back of a large building. He crept inside the large doors past large flat work tables where the stink of old fish wrinkled his nose. The building apparently doubled as a boathouse and a fish ice house. The ice had long melted. From the smell, the fish had rotted days before.

The rumble and squawking of tank wheels got louder as he slipped through the building. He climbed over a counter and headed toward an open door. He glanced behind him. Dawson and Dawg weren't there. He stopped before he reached the door. A tank appeared on the road, almost even with him outside the window. High up, the tank commander had a microphone to his mouth. Ah, crap. The commander pointed in his direction. The tank slowed and a soldier popped up out of a front hatch.

A grenade flew through the open door. Watson heard the tank hatches slam shut as the stick grenade sailed over his head. The grenade flipped, a blur in the darkness, and landed with a thump on the other side of the counter.

The explosion rattled his teeth and rained chunks of wood down all around him. He looked out the window, the glass panes all blown out into the road. His ears rang as he spotted Dawson and his dog dash in hot pursuit after the tank.

Dawson dropped the machine gun in the roadway and leaped up on the tank's rear deck, leaving the dog to run around the tank barking furiously. Dawson knelt over the engine compartment for a moment, then leaped back off the tank. He sprawled to the road, stumbled to his knees in his haste to get away. As Dawson scrambled back to his feet, the C-2 bundle exploded with a blast that knocked the demo man down into the mud. Dawson swayed on all fours in the middle of the road, shaking his head, the dog racing around him, barking.

Smoke boiled from the engine compartment as the tank clanked to a stop. The top hatch popped back open and the commander rose up, pointed a pistol toward Dawson.

Watson stepped out of the doorway and sprayed the tank with a burst from his machine pistol, emptying the magazine, then ran for the machine gun Dawson had dropped in the road. As he snatched up the gun on the run, an irregular line of gunfire chipped at the cobblestones and chased him across the road. He glanced over his shoulder as he ran. Another damn tank coming across the field bordering the road.

Bullets zinged around his ears and cracked through the damp air. Watson scrambled across slick cobblestones and dived into the ditch as a tank lurched through the gap in the hedgerow, firing a hull-mounted machine gun in short bursts.

The second tank, ponderous as it roared through the gap in the hedgerow and turned on to the road, continued to fire, treads grinding across the ruts, digging the cobblestones out of the roadway as it pivoted.

Watson dug the C-2 and grenade from his pocket. Hot, suffocating engine exhaust washed over him as the tank straightened and started toward him. Watson rolled down into the shallow water at the bottom of the ditch, praying he was out of view of the tank vision ports and periscopes. The ground under him vibrated as the tank closed. Watson waited, hunkered down. As it drew even he pulled the igniter on the stick grenade and tossed the package, aiming for the middle of the road in front of the tank.

Damn! Too far. He had thrown the explosives too damn far. The bundle hit in the cobblestones between the ruts churned up by the first tank and bounced toward the far side of the road. Watson buried his head in the wet grass as the tank rolled over the bundle, the tread squashing it into the mud.

The bundle exploded with a muffled "whoom," flinging cobblestones and mud up in a dirty geyser up over the tank.

The tank rear end swerved toward Watson, threatening to crush him as the treads bit into the road, spewing mud and gravel into his face, engine revving and roaring. He scrambled to his feet and lumbered across the road between the two tanks. He started to turn between the buildings when he spotted the dog by the side of the road. He angled over to find Dawson sprawled face up in the mud, the dog's nose to Dawson's face.

"Dawson," Watson shouted, ears still buzzing from the grenade explosion. Fire from a machine gun ripped over his head.

No response. Dawson's jacket and pants were ripped to shreds. Watson picked him up. Behind him a second machine gun opened up. After that all he could hear was his own panting and the click of the dog's toes as they both sprinted across the cobblestones. Bullets cracked past him, chewing into the wood siding as Watson turned the corner and dashed back behind the fish house. He paused. Where to now? Voices shouted on the other side of the buildings.

Dawson, heavy in his arms, moaned. Watson staggered over to the boat. A narrow plank led up one side. He ran up the slippery plank and dropped to the deck. An open door led to a small cabin. He laid Dawson on a narrow bunk and felt for a pulse. Dawson opened his eyes.

"I brought you a new dog, honey." Dawson blinked his eyes, shook his head. "You aren't Rebecca." He shook his head. "Of course you aren't. Did we stop the tanks?"

"We put a hurting on them, buddy." Watson pushed the dog's nose to the side, enough to see blood running down Dawson's arm. Watson pulled off Dawson's belt and tightened it around the arm, as high up as he could. "We'll take care of him, boy. Don't worry."

The look in the dog's eyes confirmed it would do its part.

CHAPTER 17 - AWOL

Darrell Williamson wondered what he was going to do when he got back stateside. Maybe start a used car dealership. He could sell a few, but mostly use the business to fence hot cars. Or maybe open up a bar, run numbers. Or both. Broads loved cars and bars, at least the kind of broads he hung out with, so either one was a winner in his book. His only problem was how to get his booty home. The big feed sack over his shoulder clanked with silver platters and candle holders, a few pieces of jewelry and one fancy looking watch, anything he thought would bring a buck. He wondered if he should sell everything back in England. Or just set himself up here in France. Seemed like these Frenchies were dumber than he expected. In every farm house or barn he plundered, the valuables were stashed exactly where a good second story man like him looked, right off the get go.

He could kiss that stupid judge who told him to get his ass in the army or go to jail. This airborne duty was all right. Shiny boots, extra pay, and now dropped all by his lonesome in France, to do as he damn well pleased. Who could ask for more? Friggin jumpmaster had put him in the door; told him to wait. Never one to take orders, Williamson had picked a lull in the antiaircraft fire and jumped before the next line of tracers could get to them. And not too soon. Damn plane took a hit, blew all to hell and high water as he was floating down.

Now he was on his own; the way he liked it. He stopped and listened. The explosions up ahead had stopped, but he wasn't going to take any chances. Time to strike out across the fields. No need to get tangled up in some big fire fight. Man could get killed like that.

But ahead another cluster of houses straddled the road, all dark as Detroit jail cell. Tempting. Not a German in sight. One more house, then hunker down in the middle of one of those thick hedgerows he'd crossed.

He slipped into the first house on the right. First he'd check the pantry, then see if there was a root cellar. Nine times out of ten, the good stuff was buried in a coal bin or trash heap. Frenchies thought they were smart, but he didn't mind getting dirty. He sat the bag of loot on the floor and started going through the room. He picked up one of those fancy candle thingies. Heavy, must be solid silver. He was going to have to find another flour sack.

Footsteps, boots from the sound, clomped across the floor above. Shit. Somebody home. He slid toward the door, fumbling with his carbine. He had slung it around his neck so he could carry the loot. Smart, except now the damn sling was snagged on his helmet as he tried to pull it over his head. A dim light flickered against the far wall, revealing a staircase. The light grew brighter as the footsteps moved down the stairs. Polished boots glimmered in the light, moved down one more step.

Williamson yanked at the carbine sling. His steel pot flipped off his liner and clattered to the floor.

A German soldier came into full view, a lantern in one hand and a rifle in the other.

Williamson froze. He felt sweat pouring down his sides.

The soldier held the lantern high and leaned forward to peer into the room, sweeping the room with his rifle.

Williamson crouched, stock still. Partially hidden behind a tall chair by the fireplace, the stink of damp ashes mingled with the acrid stench of sweat filled his nose. He fought the urge to gag, eyes riveted on the German. Williamson slowly lifted his hand as the soldier took another step down, slipped it around his carbine's pistol grip and mashed the safety button down. The damn click seemed as loud as a church bell in the quiet room.

The soldier said something in German.

Williamson opened his mouth, trying to quiet his breathing.

A thin voice called from behind the German. The soldier took a step back up the stairs, paused.

Williamson took in a great breath, already planning his escape route to the front door. When the soldier's head disappeared up the stairs, Williamson bolted. One step across and he tripped over his bag. Silver pieces clattered and clanged across the dark room. Holy shit! He was losing his fortune. He focused his thoughts on the German and his rifle and kept going. Always more loot down the road.

A rifle shot rang out. Williamson dove for the floor, twisting the carbine's muzzle toward the stairs, the sling choking him, all tangled around his neck.

His helmet liner flew off and bounced across the floor. A second shot cracked down from the stairs, then the bolt worked and an empty cartridge case clattered down the stairs, one tread at the time, a tink, tink, tink, in time with his pounding heart.

He wiggled his bare head through the sling, jerked the carbine free and rolled behind a heavy table. He quick crawled on his hands and knees toward the front door, keeping as much furniture between him and the German on the stairs as possible. The open door, a dark hole in the night, lay straight ahead. He gathered his feet under him and dashed for the door. Almost out, he stepped on a loose silver piece. His feet went out from under him and he sprawled on his stomach at the foot of the stairs. A candle holder spun across the floor, glittering in the lantern light. Damn! A fancy engraved silver one, the best piece he had picked up all night. Worked hard for that one. Had to poke around in a deserted barn before he found it in under a hay bale. He reached out for the candle holder.

A shout and the shadows shifted.

Williamson looked up. The soldier crouched on a step, outlined by the lantern on the step behind him. The German fired. The bullet smacked into the stuffed chair behind Williamson. The bolt clacked, another round being fed into the chamber. The German yelled and rushed down the remaining steps.

Williamson rolled on his back and fired the carbine, frantically yanking the trigger as fast as he could, carbine out in front of him, one handed like a pistol. The carbine jerked and jumped, spraying bullets toward the German, both of them screaming. Williamson stopped pulling the trigger when he realized the carbine only clicked when he pulled the trigger. It had stopped firing, all fifteen rounds gone.

The German swayed, toppled over the banister and tumbled to the floor. He hit with a dull thump, sprawled arms and legs all cock-eyed.

Bastard. Who in the hell did he think he was, messing with Darrell Williamson?

Williamson crawled back, away from the body and stood, knees shaking. He fished a bottle of wine from his baggy pants pocket and pulled out the cork. No son of a bitching German was going to stop him. He took a long drink, the raw wine burning its way down his dry throat.

A voice called out from upstairs, so unexpected he dropped the bottle. The bottle thumped on the wooden floor and spun around, wine sloshing over his jump boots. The voice called out again, high pitched and whiney.

This was going to be a great day. A woman. Just what he needed. He picked up the bottle and held it up to the light. Still almost half full. He recorked it. My goodness. He would have to make time to enjoy it with his new friend.

He sidled past the dead German and crept up the stairs. The lantern on the top step cast a dim light over a large room. A single bed sat against the far wall. He swept the carbine around the room. No more Germans. Just the woman, hot and excited, waiting for her boyfriend in their bed. Well, the kraut lay dead downstairs, so Williamson figured he might as well take his place. Hell. So far as the woman was concerned, he'd just be another soldier to screw.

Williamson walked over to the bed, lantern held high. Cute thing laid there, sheet pulled up to her chin, cheeks all fat and rosy. Had the German just finished with her? Her eyes glowed in the light, wide, glittering with tears. He sat the lantern on a high dresser, the better to see her.

"Don't you cry, sweetie. I'll make you happier than your kraut boyfriend ever could." He slung his carbine over a wooden ladder chair back and dropped the rest of his web gear on the woven reed seat. He turned to the woman, leered at her. Tears trickled down each side of her fat face. Her rosy lips compressed together, all cute and wrinkly. He pulled out the wine bottle, yanked the cork with his teeth and spat it across the room. Scuttlebutt among the guys was French broads loved wine, and lots of other things. He might even share some wine. After the other things.

He sat the bottle on the dresser beside a photo of a German soldier, all proud in his dress up uniform. Too late for you, jerk.

Williamson turned to the woman and yanked the sheet down. He expected her to hold tight to the bed clothes, but it flew down to her feet. He expected perfume, but the alcohol smell of a hospital surprised him.

Her hands cuddled a tiny pink thing, swaddled in a thin blanket with just its wrinkled face showing. A tiny hand reached out of the blanket, minuscule fingers opening and closing. She clutched the baby closer.

"*Mon petit babe,*" she pleaded. "*Friedrich?*"

Williamson surveyed her. Shivering in a thin gown, bloody stains on the sheet, hair stringy around her face, she stared up at him, whining in some garbled language. French, he supposed.

"Well, crap." He pulled the sheet back up to her chin. What was he going to do now? The broad and her baby had drained all his enthusiasm. "Go back to sleep cutie, you and your little fritz baby." He whispered and turned out the lantern.

He sat in a chair and leaned back his head. Lord he was tired. He finished off the rest of the wine and closed his eyes for a few minutes.

He opened his eyes with a start. Christ. How long had he been there asleep? The room was dark, lantern wick smoking, almost out. Was it dawn yet? He gathered up his gear from the chair, walked over to the window and pulled the heavy blackout curtains to the side. Still night, just a hint of dawn glowed at the distant horizon. A moisture laden breeze floated in as he looked up and down the street. All clear. Well. The war must go on. He might as well scrounge up what he could downstairs and get on with his mission, getting rich as quick as he could.

A light glimmered across the street and a man stepped out the door. Oh, no. Not another damn German. Were they all conspiring to keep him from what was rightfully his? The man helped another out the door, and the two of them limped down the road until they were directly across from Williamson. They stood with their backs turned, facing a wooden rail fence. One had white wrapped around his upper body, maybe a bandage of some kind. Williamson chuckled. They were taking a piss. And unless he had stolen Williamson's pot from the room below, at least one of them was an American. Williamson stepped back from the window until the men finished and slowly gimped back into the house. Good. Time to go before it got too light to disappear.

Williamson paused.

A shadow flit across the road. A second darted past the first, then a third. Dammit. A German patrol. The Germans gathered outside the house where the GIs had gone in. Kraut bastards were about to crash in on the wounded guys. None of his business, he reminded himself.

He wondered if he knew the GIs. The tall one with the bandages looked kind of like that pissy sergeant up at division headquarters who always talked so high and mighty. Williamson felt around for his carbine. Judas priest. He hadn't changed magazines. Damn thing was empty.

One of the Germans positioned himself in front of the door.

Williamson grabbed his web gear, fumbled for a grenade. He finally pulled one out of a pouch, his fingers shaking. He peeked over the window sill. The Germans were at the door. He snatched out the pin and tossed the frag like a bowling ball through the window. It sailed into the darkness, out over the street.

He dropped to the floor. A dirty orange flash outlined the window, quickly followed by the crack of the exploding grenade. Williamson scrambled to his feet, slammed a full magazine in the carbine. He racked the bolt back and let it fly, seating a round in the chamber.

Got to go. He ran for the stairs, stopped, went back for his web gear still in a pile on the floor. He slipped an arm through the suspenders.

The baby cried out.

"Hush, child. You going to be O.K."

As he started down the stairs he heard a noise in the downstairs room. A voice called out in German. Williamson fired a wild round into the darkness, backing up the steps. At the top of the stairs he looked around, searching for an exit. Blackout curtains hung over a back window. He turned, headed for the window. Hell, he was a paratrooper. Better to blast out the window than face a bunch of Germans.

A thump on the floor behind him. He looked down. A stick grenade rolled up against his foot. He could smell black powder burning. Somewhere in the dark room the baby cried out.

Oh, Jesus.

He dropped to the floor, scooped the grenade under his belly and curled tightly around it.

"You better be a good baby," he whispered.

CHAPTER 18 - 377TH PRCHT FA

Jake Rankin led First Sergeant Salazar across the field toward the sound of scattered gunfire and the unmistakable crack of German tank cannon fire, a sound Rankin would never forget. Top had said the first tank they killed was an old French Renault, but the second was a big one, a Panzer. This one sounded like another big one to him.

More explosions, then the sounds died away. He hoped for good. He needed a drink. He was too sober. His headache was killing him. The horse's hot breath and loud farts weren't any help.

He had tried drowning himself in booze back at Camp Mackall, but that just got him in trouble with Top and the gun team. Before tonight's jump he had looked forward to combat, hoping for some relief from his pain. But killing and almost being killed hadn't helped.

The ache was still there. Lord, almighty, he missed Libby. And the child they never named, except on the tiny footstone where the baby was laid to rest with her mother. By then he had been too drunk to acknowledge the name, sobering up just enough to enlist, search out the meanest job in the Army. But the misery remained.

The low ground fog rolling over the pasture had an odd glow; a hint that sunrise was not far away. Beside him the old draft horse plodded along the narrow track as if he pulled pack howitzers to war in the old squeaking wagon every day. Rankin had worked with mules on the farm, but never a big old draft horse like the grey before he had gone to work in the textile mill. Money for the baby, he had thought at the time. The horse was better mannered, he thought, than the ornery old mules used to drag the tobacco sleds back home. Maybe that was because this horse was a gelding.

Or maybe the horse had just had the bejesus scared out of it. Rankin had found the gelding shivering in a barn stall beside a barefoot dead American GI. Beside the dead GI lay an equally dead German soldier, a butcher knife buried to the handle in his belly.

What ever happened there would have scared Rankin, for sure.

Rankin glanced back over his shoulder and slowed. Salazar had thrown away his carbine, complaining the barrel had been too badly bent to fire, and instead found a pitchfork in the barn that he used as a walking stick to help himself gimp along the ruts. The torn canvas bag swinging over his shoulder held the handful of precious 75mm HEAT, high explosive antitank rounds he had been carrying all night.

A good man, the First Sergeant. Rankin knew Salazar had tried his best to keep Rankin on the straight and narrow, telling some tall tale about losing a chunk of his ear fighting in Spain back when Rankin first joined the unit back at Fort Claiborne. Rankin wished he had been of a mind and sober enough to pay attention.

A house loomed out of the mists, the first of a row that lined a dark road that ran up a slight incline. For a moment he thought he heard voices, an American.

"Whoa, boy."

The gelding clomped to a stop, skin shivering over his bony shoulders. The grey must understand English. He snorted and pulled back against the leather reins until he had enough slack to reach the high grass, the loose collar almost slipping past his ears.

"Easy, easy," Rankin whispered, stroking the horse's thin flank. The old fellow had to strain to pull the weight of the pack howitzer they had found in a string of belly bundles scattered around the burned carcass of a Dakota a few fields back. It had taken him and Top most of the night to gather the bundles and assemble the gun in the deserted barn. They never did find the trail, but had most everything else: barrel, pneumatic tires and the cradle, but no ammo containers. Top had cussed and kicked the dirt until he remembered the bag he'd been carrying around his neck all night, grinning like the rounds were candy. Top said he'd figure out how to shoot the howitzer without the trail, anxious to get in battery.

Rankin's stomach growled. He just wanted something to eat.

In the distance a door slammed. The faint crowing of a rooster floated over the fields. Rankin dropped the reins to the ground. He slid his slung rifle from his shoulder and clicked off the safety.

First Sergeant Salazar came up on the other side of the horse, leaning on his pitchfork and breathing deeply. "Mary and Jesus, this is going to have to be my last war. But then, who would look out after young fools like you, huh?" Salazar patted the grey on his neck. "Nazis might have my ear but at least they haven't taken my nuts, yet."

He leaned forward on the pitchfork to stare off into the fog. "What do you see, Jake?"

"A road and houses ahead." Rankin sniffed the air. "And we're close to water. I thought I heard somebody whispering in English for a minute, but in this fog, maybe it was just my imagination."

Salazar pointed toward the dark outlines of the houses rising out of the mists. "Park the old grey and the gun here for the moment. Leave him hitched up and he'll be happy in the grass; won't wander far. Let's try these houses, see if we can find a Frog who speaks English. Or maybe you can keep from killing all the Germans long enough to ask one of them." He slapped Rankin on the back and propelled him along the path.

Rankin crouched when he reached a waist deep drainage ditch along side the road. Again he thought he heard the mutter of voices, but try as he could, he couldn't see anyone through the thinning fog. He slithered down the side of the ditch until he hit bottom with a muted splash. He stood, listening, as the cold water ran around his boots, sucking the heat from his toes. He dug his feet into the mud and started up the roadside bank, then stopped and eased himself down into the thick grass.

One, two; a line of Germans walked past. Jeeze, he hoped Salazar saw them and didn't blurt out another Hail Mary. Rankin slid his rifle up. Grass was too deep to see the column after they passed. Good. That meant the Germans shouldn't be able to see him. He crawled along the ditch after them until he reached a dip in the bank. He rose to his knees and elbows until he could make out the houses over the top of the ditch. Across the road a bit of light escaped a curtain, enough to see three Germans gathered in front of the house. Two more Germans hung back on his side of the road. What the dickens were they doing? Rankin eased the rifle to his cheek.

Suddenly Rankin was blinded by a flash in front of the house. He dropped, buried his face in the wet grass as fragments whistled over his bare head, one thumping into his rifle stock hard enough to vibrate the gun in his hand. The grey whinnied, and the wagon singletree rattled behind Rankin.

When he looked up, several bodies lay sprawled in the road in front of the door.

Rankin didn't hear the wagon crashing across the field behind him, so the grey must not have bolted.

The other Germans were gone.

Rankin climbed to his feet and rushed the corner of the first house. Inside a carbine chattered, followed by the muffled blast of a grenade, then silence.

Rifle at the ready, Rankin crept toward the front entrance.

A man burst out of the door, hobnailed boots clanking on the cobbles.

Rankin flattened himself against the rough stone wall as the man ran past, a blur in the darkness, so quick Rankin never figured out if he was kraut or a GI in a pair of stolen boots. As the man ran down the road a figure rose up out of the ditch and flattened him with a staff. A short scream, then nothing but the crow of a rooster still trying to get an answer. Top had figured out who the runner was.

Rankin heard a clank from inside the doorway. He crept up the low steps and looked inside. A candle lit the distinctive outline of a German helmet. The German, on his knees, held the candle in one hand and stuffed something into a bag with his other hand.

"Put your hands up," Rankin shouted in German, "or I'll shoot."

Startled, the German dropped the candle and threw the bag toward Rankin's head.

In the sudden darkness Rankin lost the German. Rankin fired wild, from the hip. The first couple of shots downed the flying bag, silver tinkling like a bell. Rankin dropped flat to the floor.

"*Hans. Wo bist du?*" the German shouted.

"Right here, you son of a bitch," Rankin muttered and fired at the sound of the voice. A scream wailed out of the darkness. "Gave you one chance, kraut," Rankin said as he emptied his clip at the sound.

"Jake," Salazar yelled from outside the door.

"Hold a minute, Top. Let me check." He crawled over to the corner where he found the German, never to share his loot with Hans.

A light flickered, grew until it outlined a set of stairs leading up to a second floor. Rankin eased up the stairs, one squeaky step at the time. One tread down from the top he stopped. A lantern, missing its globe, glowed from the top of a chest. A wavering flame reflected from the remains of a shattered mirror. One more step and he froze, blinked to make sure he wasn't having another one of his nightmares. A woman in a nightgown knelt over a shattered body. Somewhere in the room a baby whimpered.

Rankin walked over to the bed. The side rail was splintered, the mattress pocked with shouldering fragments. In the middle of the bed a wrinkled face glowed red in the flickering light. Its eyes blinked, a tiny hand waved. Dear God. Rankin blinked back a tear.

A baby. A live baby.

CHAPTER 19 - DIVISION G2

Pfister had just settled Sparks back on the threadbare couch when the explosion rocked the front of the house. Glass shattered from the street window, ripped through the blackout curtain and flung shards through the room. A short scream came from the back, the wife or the daughter. Or maybe it was him. Sparks struggled and tried to get up from the couch. Pfister pushed him back down with his one good arm. "Quit jumping around. I don't want your neck to start bleeding again."

Lord, he was tired of the killing. He had long settled his score for his family. Now Pfister just wanted this night to be over. He checked Captain Talbot, stretched out under a blanket on the floor, picked a shard of glass off Talbot's face. The captain was breathing quietly, still out of it.

"Be still Sparks. You watch Captain Talbot. I'll go see what's going on outside."

He felt around for the Thompson. The explosion had been too loud for a German potato masher. It sounded more like one of their own frag grenades. Whichever, the battle was right outside the front door. Cautiously, Pfister eased the shredded blackout curtain to the side and peeked out into the street. He ducked back when a second, muffled explosion blew the glass out of an upstairs window across the road.

The front door creaked; almost fell off its hinges when he tried to open it. Using the Thompson's barrel as a lever, he pried the door open a crack until it jammed, then gave it a good kick, grunting as the effort tore at his shoulder wound. The doorframe splintered and the door fell back against the inside wall. Across the street gunfire sounded from inside the house, then silence. He could feel warm blood oozing through the bandage.

"Sarge. What's happening?" Sparks cried out.

"You just hang tight. Don't let the Captain jump up and run out while I see what's going on."

Pfister eased out of the door. Three Germans lay on the street, one moaning; the other two still. Pfister stepped over the bodies,

Thompson held awkwardly in his left hand with the stock clutched between his elbow and his ribs. He had always prided his ability to use his off hand. He had been a pretty good switch hitter. But he wasn't holding a bat, and this wasn't a game. His head spun for a moment and he went down to a knee. Damn. He didn't think he had lost much blood, not with the half a bed sheet Sparks had wrapped him up in.

"You all right?" a voice asked. Pfister looked up. The man squatting beside him had a Red Cross on his helmet.

"Yeah. Help me up, doc. You need to go inside. Couple of our guys in there need you. Captain's out of it on morphine, got two broken legs that need splinting. Spark's been shot in the neck. I tried to make sure he didn't lose too much blood, but he keeps jumping around. Maybe you can calm him down."

The doc pulled back Pfister's makeshift bandage. "How about you?"

Pfister laughed. "Just tired and hungry, doc, like every other GI in France." He slowly climbed to his feet, using the Thompson as a crutch. "I need to check across the street and make sure all the Germans are cleared out. We got some other guys up the road trying to hold a bridgehead. After I make sure there aren't any krauts sneaking around us, I'm going up to help."

The German on the ground moaned.

A lanky kid walked up and pointed his BAR at the German. "Want me to finish off this thun of a bitch?" he lisped.

Pfister looked down at the German's face. He was even younger than the American who wanted to kill him. The German soldier could be a grown-up version of the little unthinking brats running around his old Heilbronn neighborhood yelling *"Heil Hitler."*

Or Pfister could be the one sprawled there in a German uniform if he hadn't been a Jew. He had grown up thinking he was a good German, proud of his country. Until that rainy night. Now look at the kid lying at his feet, blood seeping out onto the cobblestones. Good lord, what was this war doing to them all. He shoved the German's rifle away with his foot. "No, you don't need to—" Before Pfister could finish, the German convulsed. His helmet clanked on the cobblestones and his head lolled back, mouth agape.

The doc reached down and felt the German's throat. "He's gone." He shook his head. "Ease up, Livingston," the doc told the kid with the BAR. "We've already done too much killing tonight."

Livingston shrugged, a disappointed look on his face. "I still haven't fired my BAR."

Pfister shook his head. "Relax, kid. It's not even dawn yet. You got plenty of time to shoot people. Ones that are going to shoot back. Why don't you head on up the street—"

A gruff voice interrupted Pfister. "Hey Pfister. What the hell you doing here? Thought you'd be back at Division headquarters, where ever the hell that is. What's the situation here?"

Pfister looked around at the voice. A tall, lanky GI with a lined face in a bloody uniform, half an ear and armed with a pitchfork gimped up beside them, unmistakably, First Sergeant Salazar.

"We got two wounded inside, Top." The cluster of men all ducked as a machine gun chattered at the end of the street, sending ricochets whining around them. "A Lieutenant and a couple of men are holding the bridge. I was on my way up to help. We had a kraut armor column hot on our asses coming in here. They're going to show up at the bridge any minute. And watch out for the house across the street. Might be a sniper inside."

Salazar shook his head. "My guy Rankin's in there. Damn fool charged right in the door. But he can take care of himself." Another exchange of gunfire echoed between the houses from the direction of the bridge. "Why don't you get out of the line of fire and look out for the wounded, doc." Salazar looked across the street as the doctor took his bag inside. "BAR man, what'd you say your name was, Livingston? Go up the street and find the L.T.; tell him we'll join up toot sweet." He pointed at the sergeant with his left arm in an awkward-looking splint and a carbine dangling from his right hand. "You. What's your name?" Salazar asked.

"Harry Rule, Top."

"O.K., Rule. You help the doc. I've got to find my boy Rankin; then we'll head on up to the bridge, stop those damn tanks." He leaned his pitchfork against the side of the house. "Let me have your carbine. Damn tank ran over mine." Salazar hefted Rule's carbine. "This one still work?"

Rule nodded. "If I was a cowboy, I'd already have a couple of notches on it."

Pfister spoke up. "Top, I speak French. Let me check the house, in case there're some locals left. The family in the back said there was a pregnant woman living by herself across the street."

Salazar nodded. "O.K., do that. Just watch out for Rankin. Fool sometimes doesn't pay attention, might just shoot you for a German. He'll be the nut cake with silver hair and no helmet." He nodded to Livingston. "Come on, son. I'll go with you up to the bridge, see if we can't find you a kraut to shoot with that BAR of yours."

Pfister trotted across the street and into the house, stepping over a dead German. Like those who once he had called friend, then learned to hate. Now he was simply sickened at the sight. He started up the narrow stairway. What did the First Sergeant say the kid's name was? Couldn't remember. Maybe he was losing too much blood. "Hey, GI," he called out.

"Upstairs. Everything's all clear."

Pfister stepped around another body and stopped at the top of the stairs. By the back window a woman in a thin nightgown knelt over a mangled body. Top's nut job stood beside the bed. Top hadn't been kidding, his hair was silver, singed and smudged with soot.

Pfister squatted beside the woman. The body on the floor was a bloody GI, by what was left of his uniform, ravaged beyond recognition by an explosion. The remains of a folding stock carbine lay beside him, the wire frame bent all around in a crazy angle. "Are you hurt?" Pfister asked the woman in French.

"No," she answered. She looked over at Pfister. Tears glistened on her cheeks. "But my hero is dead."

"Your hero?"

She nodded her head. "Yes. He threw himself on the bomb so my baby and I would live. He is my hero." She worked the dead man's dog tag chain from around his neck and slipped it over her own head. She looked up at Pfister, the bloody tags clasped to her breast.

Pfister started to reach out and ask her to give him the tags, then stopped. After all, the GI on the floor was her hero, not his. If the poor guy had sacrificed his life for hers, so be it. And if he was the one who had thrown the grenade onto the street, he probably had saved Pfister's life, and the rest of the guys in the house. He gently snapped the duplicate tag from the chain and dropped it in his pocket, wiping the still-warm blood on his pants leg.

"We've got to go. Will you be all right?" he asked.

She nodded, glanced back up at Pfister. Tears rolled down her cheeks, but she looked calm, at peace. "*Oui. À la paix,*" she said, as if she had read his mind.

A loud explosion rocked the house on its foundations. The slivers of mirror hanging in the frame shook loose, fell and shattered on the dresser top. Pfister stood and looked over at—Rankin—that was the silver-headed GI's name. Rankin leaned over the bed, his body shielding the bed from the falling mirror fragments.

"Come on kid," Pfister urged. "The rest of our guys need us up at the bridge. You can come back and check on the baby when this day is all over."

Pfister wondered if Rankin would still be alive at the end of the day to come back. If any of them would be.

A Jewish refugee kid living in a Catholic neighborhood, he had never been one for a lot of praying. Today he might start.

CHAPTER 20 - 1/501ST PRCHT INF

Rule caught up with Top and the others as a tank round hit, shattered the building closest to the bridge. A hanging sign flew through the air and skittered down the dew-slick cobblestones. Brick fragments and mortar chunks pelted down around them, followed by a mantle of dust sifting through the morning fog. Rule shook the dust from his eyes and tried to ignore the pain in his arm. In front of him a truck sat sideways in the middle of the bridge. Rule wondered if this bridge was Anna-Marie's target. His thought was cut short by the appearance of a tank, inching up to the turn onto the bridge, black smoke rising up from its rear deck. Rule slid his .45 out of the holster strapped to his chest and crawled over the loose stones to the last pile of rubble before the bridge abutment. He sprawled in the dust next to Livingston and his BAR, attention torn between protecting his broken arm and ducking the machine gun fire cracking across the river.

"I got some armor piercing rounds. Will they penetrate the kraut tanks?" Livingston asked.

"Shit, man. Shoot that damn gun and find out."

Livingston fired a short burst at the tank, with no noticeable effect.

On the other side of Livingston the grey dawn outlined the First Sergeant, conferring with a GI in a muddy baseball cap wearing pilot and jump wings on a shredded shirt, but with a familiar face. Salazar grinned over at Rule as he crawled over. "I already tried taking out a tank with a carbine, Rule. Didn't work. I don't think you'll have any better luck with your .45."

"I was thinking more about the bridge, Top. How about we blow it? Anyone got any C-2?" Rule asked. He was tired of other people dying for him. And there was a bridge right in front of him. Maybe Anna-Maria's.

"Aren't you the smoke jumper from Benning?" the GI in the ball cap asked. A Lieutenant, Rule realized.

"Yep." Rule looked over the lanky soldier's face, finally remembering the cap. "Yes, sir. You were Private Allen back then, with that damn fool cap hanging out of your pocket all the time."

Allen laughed. "I used to be scared to death of you, Sarge. I went though one of the jump school's first classes before they sent me off to learn how to crash gliders. I just knew you were going to fail me for my shitty PLFs."

Before Rule could answer a tank round cracked overhead and smashed into the upper story of the house behind them. Rule buried his face in the dirt as rubble pelted down all around him, air thick with more damp dust. When he looked back up at Allen the cap was twisted so the brim stuck out cockeyed over the side of his head; the stylized blue "B," the Brooklyn Dodger emblem, smudged with dirt. "Dodgers, 3-2" inked by hand on the side of the cap barely showed in the dim light. "You know the Yankees won that series," Rule reminded the pilot.

Allen laughed, a grim hollow sound as blood seeped from a new cut on his forehead. "Yeah, but I was there, Ebbets Stadium and all, when we won the second game. Joined the Army when the Yankees took the rest of the series. Nothing left in life. Wanted to fly, get as far away from the City as I could, even volunteered to be a damn paratrooper." He worked a package from his cargo pocket. "Our demo man, Dawson, rigged a block of C-2 wired to a German potato masher. He and Tony Watson are somewhere across the river. I heard two explosions, but the tanks keep coming." His lined face turned somber. "I don't know what happened to Dawson and Watson. My turn now."

"Nope." Rule holstered his pistol and took the handmade demo package from Allen. "You stay. I'll go see what I can do with this. I made a promise this morning I'd blow up a bridge. Maybe I can at least get a tank."

Allen wiped the blood from his eyes. "Must be a damn division of krauts coming. We killed two tanks on our way here. Now there's more across the river. We got to do something or they're going to blow through us like a fart at a chili cook-off. But you? Look at your arm."

"Least I didn't get a damn-fool baseball cap knocked off my head." Rule grinned at Allen and rose to his knees.

Salazar grabbed Rule's pants leg as he started to get up. "Wait just a damn minute, fellows. No need to get all of us killed. I got a better idea. Let me go back and get Rankin and the pack howitzer."

Allen looked at him. "Where the hell are you going to find a pack howitzer?"

"Right down the road." A mud-covered satchel clanked when he hefted it. "You think I lugged these 75mm shells around all night just to throw at the krauts?" He slid the satchel back over his hip. "Rankin and I'll blow those tanks to hell and back." The First Sergeant stood and limped down the street.

Rule rolled over on his back and watched Salazar stride between the houses. "Will a seventy-five take out the tanks?" he asked Allen.

"I don't know. We took out one with a fifty-seven loaded with one of those Brit armor piercing rounds. Bigger is always better. Maybe give them enough of a headache that we can get a charge planted on them. All I really know is the Germans want to come over here, and we want them to stay over there."

A sudden burst of machine gun fire raked across the bridge. Rule rolled back and watched the tank at the far end of the bridge start and stop, moving with wounded jerks onto the bridge, something screwed up with the engine or drive train.

A soldier stood halfway out of the top hatch with a machine pistol in his hand. He pointed the gun toward them.

"Look out!" Rule shouted as bullets from the machine pistol chewed into the rubble piled behind him. He dropped back down behind the remaining wall as bullets cracked overhead.

"Top, get down," Allen screamed, then spun, went down, more blood spurting from his head.

Rule looked back to see Salazar standing in the middle of the road, turn, stare back across the bridge at the tank. Dirt kicked up around him and he seemed to fold, then finally stagger to the side of a house.

Rule hugged the ground as the machine gun mounted in the tank hull traversed back and forth, sweeping the street. Beside him Livingston fired several bursts from the BAR. "I got him; I got him," screamed Livingston just as the tank main gun fired again. The concussion pounded Rule into the rubble-strewn ground. He spat dust out of his mouth. Beside him Allen lay still, eyes blinking, blood seeping from his face.

If he stayed here it would be just as cowardly as running, Rule thought. He still owed Anna-Marie a bridge. And Larry his life.

Rule struggled to his knees, wondering how he could stop the tank. Across the bridge the tank turret sawed back and forth to bring the coax machine gun to bear across the bridge. A body hung from the open hatch on top, Livingston's kill. A bloom of smoke and fire spat out of the main gun barrel with a massive blast, the round screaming down the middle of the road to explode in some poor farmer's field out past the town.

This was his chance, while the main gun was reloading. Rule climbed to his feet and sprinted for the bridge. The tank's engine roared, spewing black exhaust that shot up to mix with remnants of mist floating up from the river. He ducked under the truck jammed in the middle of the bridge and raced for the tank, angling to the right out of the line of fire from the two machine guns. The main barrel depressed and fired into the truck behind Rule. The concussion spun Rule around and bounced him off the metal girders. Dazed, he stumbled, tripped over a loose plank and sprawled on his broken arm. He gasped as pain sizzled through him like he had clutched a burning pine bough to his naked chest.

The explosives rolled from his hand and lay in front of him, the white button dangling from the end of the potato masher lashed to the brown C-2 brick. He dragged himself to the package, picked it up in his left hand, sticking out from the end of the weapon container. He pushed himself to his knees, on up to a crouch, took one step, staggered, another. He stumbled over the loose boards toward the tank. His ears felt funny, as if they were bleeding. Behind him the BAR barked, a faint tinny sound, drowned out by the rattle of the coax firing past his ear, so close he could feel the bullets snapping through the air. Rounds from the BAR zinged over his head and twanged off the tank turret and bow, tiny sparks flying where the armor piercing bullets hit the rolled steel armor. He finally reached the tank and leaned against the heavy armor, gasping with pain.

The tank lurched forward, almost dragging him under the treads.

He grabbed a handhold on a section of replacement track draped over the front of the tank and dragged himself up on to the front of the tank, demolition charge clutched in his left hand, screaming with pain.

A hatch flipped open right in front of his face and a bald head popped up. Rule sucked the porcelain button between his teeth and yanked. He felt a tooth break and smelled the burning sulfur as the black powder ignited in the fuse train. He flopped his broken arm across the sloping deck and stuffed the package down the hatch beside the German crewman. "Anna-Maria sent this for you, you Nazi bastard," he screamed.

Eyes wild, the German dropped down into the tank and came up with the C-2 demo package clutched between both hands.

Rule hauled his right arm back, praying this was the best brawl punch he had ever thrown. He slugged the German with every bit of power left in his body.

The German flopped back against the hatch lip, shaking his head. The C-2 dropped out of sight down into the innards of the tank.

Maybe not a bridge, Anna-Maria, but at least one tank. For you. For Larry. For the First Sergeant lying back on the cobblestones. For the Lieutenant and his Dodgers.

CHAPTER 21 - 3/501ST PRCHT INF

Livingston cautiously raised his head back up when the debris from the truck stopped falling, blown to high heaven by the last tank round. Where the truck once blocked the bridge, only scattered bits of wreckage remained. An engine block rolled to a stop at the end of the bridge, smoldering in the middle of the roadway, steam spewing up to join the mists rising out of the river. Now all that was between the tank column and their side of the bridge was him and Rule, and he had lost sight of Rule when the tank round disintegrated the truck. He had wanted a fight, but not one where everyone was killed.

There he was. Rule. Livingston didn't know whether to shout with joy or dismay. Rule had crawled up on the front of the German tank. "Get down!" Livingston screamed. Too far away to help, Livingston emptied the remaining rounds in the BAR magazine at a handful of German soldiers running toward Rule and the bridge, knocking a couple down in the road, but at least three made it to the tank. Livingston swore in frustration, slammed a full magazine in the BAR.

Suddenly, a tremendous explosion tossed Rule up and over the bridge rail. A ball of flame engulfed the tank and the soldiers who had taken cover behind it. A quick series of explosions built, the last one flipping the turret up and off the tank body.

Livingston peppered a second tank that nosed up behind the exploded hulk at the bridge, forcing the commander to slam down the hatch. The second tank reversed back out of sight. Firing stopped as smoke and flames boiled up in the sky, blotting out the pale glow that signaled the coming dawn.

Livingston stood, mesmerized by the spectacle, until he remembered Rule flying over the bridge rail. Livingston looked around. Allen was unconscious. Top was down. Rule in the river. He searched the far bank for Germans as he stumbled over the remains of the wall, all that was left of the tavern on the corner. He dashed to the bank of the Douve and stared down at the water flowing out toward the English Channel. He had been in the water once already tonight, in over his ass and damned near drowned.

He spotted Rule in the middle of the channel. Damn if he wasn't floating face up, surrounded by bits and pieces of paratrooper gear drifting downstream and new debris from the bridge. A canteen, shattered bridge timbers, then a full parachute pack floated past. Livingston relaxed. Rule would be O.K. without him. Then he saw Rule raise his arm, and his face slipped under the water. The waving weapons container was the only sign of Rule left on the surface. Damnation! Livingston threw down the BAR, went over edge and slid down the bank, a sandy, silty clay, slick as greased shit.

"Thank goodness!" he muttered when he hit the edge of the water. Only knee deep, the water was cold. He never though he would miss the warm Gulf Stream so much. He waded out toward Rule, slowly floating out toward the English Channel, head bobbing in and out of the water. Had to hurry, catch Rule before he stayed under.

Tide was almost full low at the beaches. Maybe a half hour or so before it tuned this far up the channel. The water stretched about fifty feet from one bank to the other. A grey line on the bank indicated the high tide mark, maybe six or seven feet higher than where the water level was now. Must have a bitching tidal flow. He reached out. A couple of yards more. Livingston's foot slipped as the bottom sharply dropped, and he found himself chin deep. One more yard, just out of reach of a stretched fingertip reach. Livingston lunged when Rule's head sank back underwater. He grabbed Rule's jacket and pushed it toward the surface as his own head went under, choking on a mouthful of water.

He let himself sink until his feet hit bottom, and kicked up. When he broke the surface he gulped in a wet breath, his senses screaming for him to let Rule go. Instead, he held Rule up with one arm as he flailed at the water with the other. He gasped when his face went back under water, his mouth full of salty, gritty, nasty, water; tasting of mud and oil and dead fish—and dead men. Back down he went. When his feet hit the bottom he kicked up again. This time he was too deep. He looked up. A faint glimmer teased, a hint that the surface was up there, but far away. He kicked his feet frantically like he thought a swimmer would kick. Instead of moving toward the surface, he sank, his jump boots dragging him back down to the bottom.

Suddenly Rule's jacket was snatched from his grasp.

194

When he hit bottom he let his body sink until he could bend his knees and kicked, hard toward the surface. He shot up, then slowed, his lungs screaming for air. He stretched his arm up, felt his fingers break the surface. He started sinking, back down toward the bottom.

Pop was right.

A hand grabbed his. He locked his fingers around the hand. German? He didn't care, just as long as he could breathe again. The hand dragged him up and through the water, finally to drop him on the bank where he breathed, mud flat air that had never tasted so good. Livingston dug his fingers into the pebbles and silt and crawled, coughing and spluttering, up the sloping bank. Halfway up he collapsed flat on his belly, shaking the water and gritty mud from his eyes.

"Come on, kid. Haul your ass up out of there. Damn Germans close by on the bridge. We got to get out of sight."

Livingston clawed through the mud to the top of the bank.

"Lord haff mercy!" he coughed out. Suddenly he was nose to nose with a giant dog, long teeth glistening in the growing light. A sharp whistle and the dog backed away and leaped over the rail of a fishing boat that had been hauled up out of the river on a make-shift way made from a pair of big logs. Recent hull patches still smelled of fresh tar. Livingston staggered up a plank propped against the side of the boat and plopped down on the narrow deck, water draining from his burr hair cut and soaked clothes.

The man who had dragged him ashore, a burly tech sergeant, dropped Rule facedown inside a minuscule cabin. He lifted Rule up and down by his belt, pumping and cussing. Nasty water gushed from Rule's mouth with each pump. Rule choked, spat more water and moaned. Alive.

A second soldier propped against the bulkhead grinned at Livingston, smoke curling up from a cigarette stuck in the side of his mouth, the big dog's head across his legs. He was a mess, clothes half shredded, more bloody skin showing than cloth. He tried to speak, but was incoherent. He gave up trying to talk, leaned his head back against the bulkhead and drew on the cigarette. A morphine Syrette hung from his collar.

Rule coughed again, blinked his eyes. The sergeant turned to Livingston. "Check outside. At least three tanks on the road the other side of the buildings. Bastards are probably going to come around here to try and take the bridge. Why the hell did you jump in?"

"Sergeant Rule here blew up one of the tanks trying to cross the bridge, but the explosion threw him in the river. Damn. I thought he was going to drown, wondered if he was still alive. I left a Lieutenant on the bank. He looked dead. I was maybe the last guy left on the other side." Livingston spit dirty water and blood over the side and shrugged his shoulders. "Just couldn't let Rule drown." He slid across the deck and peeked over the rail. He could see a flurry of activity down by the bridge. One man started across from the German side to be met with the rattle of a BAR. Livingston grinned, the chill air stinging his raw gums. He wiggled a tooth with his tongue, popped it out to the taste of fresh blood. Damn. He spit the tooth into his hand, probed around with his tongue. Damned if one more didn't feel loose. Soup tonight.

"Somebody is still over there, holding the bridge. Lieutenant Allen must be still alive, or somebody else has my BAR." He staggered to his feet. "Got any weapons? I need to get back up there."

"Nothing but a pair of pliers in my pocket." The sergeant grinned at Livingston. "Can jerk some nuts off if they get too close." He continued to pump Rule up and down on the deck.

Rule coughed, spat and tried to roll over.

The sergeant released Rule's belt and helped him up, propping him up next to the man with the dog. "Guy must have swallowed fifty gallons. Look. I don't think your chances of getting back up to the bridge are any too good. Allen and the other guys, looks like they got the krauts stopped for the moment. Did you see a way to get these two out of here before the Germans come down and pluck us all. I don't want to see the inside of a POW camp, and I ain't going to leave these guys up for grabs."

Livingston could hear shouting. In German. And the roar of a tank close by, on the other side of the building. He ran his tongue over the gap in his gums. "O.K. Sarge, get these guys thettled and I'll slide the boat down the way, take her out to the Channel, motor as far away from the Germans as I can get her."

"Can you do that?"

"If she's whole and the engine runs." Livingston looked fore and aft. Everything looked clear. He hoped the Frenchman who owned this boat was as meticulous as his pop, and the boat hadn't been out of the water so long the seams had opened. Be a bitch to sink in the middle of the river.

"You know boats?" The soldier sounded skeptical. "You looked like you were drowning out there."

Livingston shook his head, spit the last loose tooth over the rail. "I can't thwim. But I grew up working boats, till my pop drowned. That'th when I joined the Army, to get away from fithing boaths." He hopped over the rail. "Hang on," he called out.

The boat was held up out of the water by a heavy beam set in a pair of notches cut in the logs. Livingston kicked at the beam with his foot. The shouting grew louder as he kicked again. Stuck. He looked up to see a large timber propped against the side of the boat house. A thwack with the timber and the beam popped free. The boat rocked, but that was all. Livingston ran to the bow, put his shoulder against the boat and pushed. With a groan, as much from the boat as from Livingston, the fishing boat moved, stopped. Another shove and it slid a couple more feet, then slowly slid down the mud-slick logs toward the river, gathering momentum, suddenly moving faster, pulling Livingston off his feet.

Livingston grabbed a bow line and hauled himself over the rail, praying the narrow channel still had enough water left to maneuver the boat. He'd settle for just enough to float. He held on for the lurch and short ride, then breathed a sigh of relief as the boat splashed into the water and bobbed, enough to let him know they were afloat.

Overhead a gull screamed at him, swooping past looking for bait fish. "Neth trip, gull," Livingston yelled up at the birds, already a small flock wheeling around the boat.

He pulled at the starter rope. The engine sputtered. "Oh, crap."

"Get out of the way." The sergeant shoved Livingston aside. "This I can do." Crouched over the engine compartment, he bent over the engine, tinkered with the carburetor and yanked the starter rope. One more sputter and the engine thumped like it was happy.

Livingston spun the spoked wheel, the tiny engine clattering behind him as they puttered down the river channel, heading toward the rising sun and out to join the massive armada coming to liberate France. Get him another BAR and he'd be back.

Back to sea. Pop would be proud.

CHAPTER 22 - 1/501ST PRCHT INF

Meade flinched when a tank fired somewhere to their front, the round cutting through the air directly over the Mercedes to explode in the tree line across the field. He shook the sleep out of his eyes. Amazing. He had dozed off as Larson drove them through the night in the sleek convertible. What kind of a squad leader was he? He stood up in the front seat and scanned the area as Larson slowed to a stop, then focused on the road in front of them.

No Germans in sight, but that last round had to have come from somewhere. Ahead the road sloped slightly up and snaked between a cluster of houses. He could hear a machine gun, German from the rate of fire, and a BAR barking back. He'd join the fight, except for a slight problem in front of them.

A real problem, not a dream as he had first thought.

"What the hell is this all about?" Larson asked.

A helmetless GI blocked the narrow road, an unruly shock of silver hair glinting in the thin beams from the car's cat eyes. His heels dug in, he leaned back and pulled at a skinny horse. On the other end of the reins the horse, eyes wide and foaming at the bit, twisted and turned, struggling to pull a rickety farm wagon out of a ditch. The soldier screamed and lashed out at the horse with the end of the reins.

Meade hopped out and walked up to the GI, hands out, palms down in a calming gesture.

The GI glanced over, then heaved at the reins. "Help me get this wagon across, hurry."

"What's your panic, man? Take it easy." Meade urged. "No need to kill the poor horse." A bulky cargo, too dark to distinguish, weighted down the wagon and the frantic horse lunging against the traces.

"German tanks coming across the bridge ahead. Doc's got wounded in one of the houses we can't move. A woman and her baby are across the street." The soldier stopped and turned to Meade, tears running down his face. "And my First Sergeant's dying beside the damn road. Krauts shot him while he was coming to get this damn gun in position. We gotta stop them."

Meade stared, for just a tiny moment, blinked. Not a dream, not a problem. A damn nightmare, even if he was wide awake. "O.K., buddy. Cut the horse loose and get it out of the road. We'll help." He turned to Larson. "Move the car past so we can drag the wagon up the street." He looked back at the soldier. "What's your name?"

"Jake Rankin." The kid pulled his bayonet and with a quick slash severed the leather traces from the singletree. He slapped the old grey on the rump and the horse struggled out of the ditch, dragging the leather traces behind it. It ambled over to the other side of the road where it put its head down and began grazing as if nothing was ever as important as another blade of grass.

Meade waved Larson and the Mercedes past the stuck wagon. "Rankin. Are you a gunner? You know how to shoot whatever it is you're hauling?"

"Sweet Mary and Jesus, Corporal. I can shoot anything that will throw a projectile down range. Just help me get this gun up the road, off the wagon and in battery."

"Frank," Meade called out as the car eased past. "Rankin here says a doctor's in one of the houses. Why don't you get Joey and Stan inside?"

The car stopped in front of the wagon and Frank helped Joey and Levine out of the car. "Doc's in the first house on the left," Rankin called out as he lashed the wagon singletree to the back bumper of the car. "The house missing a door."

"Wait." Levine stopped and pulled out a musette bag. "Can't leave the radar tubes behind."

"Just get your ass out of way, Stan. Come on, Frank. Move the rest of these guys under cover."

Frank nodded and led the others to the house as Larson eased the car in gear. "Where to, boss?" Larson asked.

Meade ducked as another cannon round whistled over his head. Damn. Two minutes ago he was asleep and now the world was falling apart around him.

The grey finally decided enough was enough and cantered off into the field. Smarter than the rest of them.

Rankin hopped up on the front of the wagon and motioned up the street. "Can you get us up to that alley?" he shouted, pointing between two houses where a GI sat propped up against a wall. "Top wanted the gun 'bout where he's sitting." Tears rolled down Rankin's cheeks. "He told me he had lived through the siege of Madrid with the International Brigade. Said the German's couldn't kill him with Saint Michael watching over. Now look at him."

"Is he dead?" Meade asked.

"I don't know. He told me to get this gun in battery and that's what I'm going to do."

"Keller. Go get the doc and see if the First Sergeant's alive. Then go up to the top of the rise and figure out what the hell's going on. Lars, follow Rankin's directions and let's see if we can get this gun set up. Fast as you can without getting us killed."

Larson gunned the motor and the Mercedes dragged the wagon up the road. The wagon weaved back and forth with Rankin using his feet on the singletree to steer the wagon's front wheels, trying to follow the car as it swept in a wide turn into the alley.

Keller and a doc ran past and stopped where the First Sergeant sat with his back against the wall, silent, but his eyes following every move. Meade thought he caught a glimmer of a grin. He grinned back as they guided the gun past.

"We'll stop it, Top," yelled Rankin. "Don't you worry, Top. We'll kill the son of a bitch!"

Halfway in the alley, the wagon hung, the right rear wheel jammed up against a low stone wall enclosing a tiny flower garden. Larson gunned the engine, tires spinning, and Rankin manhandled the wagon's front wheels until the wagon started the turn, front wheels scraping between the houses. Meade joined Rankin at the rear of the wagon and they pushed, pulled and cussed until the spokes in the right rear wagon wheel snapped and the wheel collapsed. With a crash the load slid down the wagon bed and into the garden as Meade jumped to the side.

Rankin stared down at the gun, then up the road toward the bridge and the shooting. "That'll work." He stopped for a moment and dug through the remains of the wagon. "God dammit." He stopped and ran back to where the doc was helping the First Sergeant across the street, then dashed back, panting.

"Now what?" asked Meade.

Rankin held up a canvas bag. "Found the AT rounds. Top still had them." His silver hair glistened with sweat and black soot. "Now all I got to do is set up the gun. Pretty soon that tank's going to come across, right down the road in front of us. Then I'll blow it to hell. Top and I been doing it all night. Got two tanks already."

An instant after the crack of a tank gun fired from the bridge, the upper story of the house across the street exploded. Meade flinched and ducked back into the alley. "Shit!" The house with the doc and the wounded.

Someone inside screamed as the front wall collapsed back into the house, belching a huge cloud of dust. A mixture of heavy machine gun bursts and the pops of smaller caliber weapons came from the direction of the bridge. More chilling were the squeak and clank of tank treads, getting louder, echoing off the remaining walls.

Meade poked the German machine gun around the corner and spotted a GI sprinting down the street, hobbling, but running like his pants were on fire. Meade fired a short burst up the road to cover him, mindful he only had a handful of rounds left in the ammo belt. He ducked back when return machine gun fire pinged off the cobblestones and shattered the few windows left in the house across the street. Meade poked the gun out and fired again as the GI rolled to the ground and burrowed down into the rubble. Bastards were going to overrun them.

"Rankin," Meade yelled. "We don't have time to mess around."

"Then help me," Rankin shouted back.

Meade fired his last round, threw down the German machine gun and shoved at the howitzer. Meade's desperation equaling Rankin's desire, together they got it upright. "What now?" Meade shouted over the rattle of machine gun fire raking the street.

"This." With a grunt, Rankin single-handedly lifted the jammed gun carriage wheel around, leaving the back end of the carriage resting against the low garden wall. He cranked the barrel down so it pointed straight toward the bridge and the German tank grinding through and over the remains of a destroyed vehicle partially blocking the bridge. Rankin dug a round out of the canvas bag draped around his neck, rammed it home and slammed the breech.

Machine gun fire from the tank pocked the buildings across the street, swept over the cobblestones toward them.

"Kill it, dammit!" Meade screamed.

Rankin yanked the lanyard just as the tank rolled up on a large chunk of debris, exposing its underbelly to the seventy-five millimeter HEAT round.

Meade fell back against the wall at the explosion, the range so short the gun report and the hit merged into one deafening explosion.

When the dust kicked up by the shot had dissipated, the tank had ground to a halt, smoke spewing from the hatches. A BAR barked from across the street when a figure appeared out of the top hatch. Keller hobbled up and joined in with his machine gun, spraying the tank and the German soldiers who appeared beside it on the bridge.

Black exhaust tinged with red flames spewed into the sky as the tank driver revved the engine trying to get it free.

Meade pulled out the .45 and fired at the tank in frustration. "Rankin, can you hit it again?" He looked back and realized what a stupid question that was. Lacking its trail, recoil had flipped the pack howitzer over onto Rankin. Meade stuck the .45 back in his belt and heaved at the tire.

Rankin wormed out from under the gun, his pain apparent in his face. Meade eased the tire back down to the ground

"Did we kill the tank?" Rankin asked.

"Stopped it, but it's just dying, not dead. Can you shoot again?"

Rankin struggled to his knees. The gun was lodged between the wagon and the house wall. One wheel was bent so badly that even if they got it turned over, Meade didn't think they would ever be able to fire it.

Rankin stopped, looked at Meade, determination stamped across his face. "Quick as I can, but not right now. Minutes, maybe."

"Hurry. We ain't got many."

Frank Howell, his aviator's cap crushed down over his head, appeared in the alley, shotgun in hand. Of all things, a pilot with a shotgun was the last thing they needed now.

Meade motioned toward the collapsed wall. "Doc and the wounded?" he asked.

"We got them all out the back before the ceiling collapsed. Doc's with them out in the field. Sounded like you might need some help."

"Thank God for that. Now we got to get to that tank, finish it off."

"Levine had this left over from the radar." Howell pulled several bundles of C-2 linked together with a length of detonating cord from a canvas bag. "This stuff will drop the whole bridge if I set it right. Tank's no good if it can't get across the river. Nor the ones behind it."

Meade nodded his head. Maybe Howell had something. "Sounds like a plan. Larson, you help Rankin with the gun. See if you can get it back working. Come on, Cap. Bring that shotgun and follow me."

CHAPTER 23 - 435TH TP CARRIER GP

Captain Frank Howell zipped up his leather jacket and followed Corporal Meade past the Mercedes, down the alley and behind the houses, circling to approach the bridge and the smoking Tiger from the flank. On the other side of the river, flames from a burning tank missing its entire turret and main gun lit up a gaggle of Germans huddled between the hulk and a third tank half-hidden behind a building. Vague outlines behind that one hinted at even more armor waiting on the road.

Smoke floated up from the tank on the near end of the bridge, but he could still hear an engine revving. The Germans must be trying to pull the wounded tank free, clear the bridge and force another tank across.

Howell looked down at his Remington. Great in a bar fight, but not so hot against a Tiger. In front of him Meade led the way with his .45 drawn. What the hell were they doing, two men, a shotgun and a pistol? Well, he had gotten Joey into this mess. Now to get him out.

Meade leaped over the top of the bank and Howell followed, sliding and slithering down the slick mud to the slow moving water and under the bridge before the Germans, intent on freeing the tank, could react.

"You know where to place the charges?" asked Meade.

Howell didn't. He wished it were morning so he could see better. A stray round slapped the mud beside him, and he changed his mind, prayed it would stay dark a bit longer.

The bridge stretched at least a hundred feet across to the far bank. From what he could see, rusty iron girders seemed to be the main structural element. The main girders angled down into stone and masonry abutments set into each bank, stinking with the smell of old mud and dead fish, mixed with the stench of burning rubber and oil from the damaged tanks. More crisscrossed rusty steel stretched from bank to bank, supporting plank flooring. A low brick wall protected the girders from vehicle traffic, and more importantly, hid them from the Germans working around the tank.

He slid further under the bridge and stumbled through the mud until he reached the abutment. A row of massive bolts connected the girders angling down from the bridge to the steel stubs set into the abutment.

"There," he decided. "Blast away those old rusty bolts and the whole thing will crash down, especially with that tank sitting up top."

"Blow it, then." Meade snapped a shot off from his pistol and scurried deeper under the bridge as rifle shots splattered into the water. "In a damn hurry, before the Germans get that tank thumping around over our heads going again."

"Blow it all down on top us, you mean." Howell packed the C-2 bricks into the joint. His hands trembled. Just tired, he thought. Long flight, long row, long walk. Damn long night. He thought about Joey, waiting down the road. Couldn't let the Germans get across.

"If that's what it takes," Meade answered. "But better if not."

Howell silently agreed. He stared at the C-2 as he molded it around the bolts in the joint, remembering how Larson had told them how he had used blasting caps and batteries to blow up the radar. He felt all around the packets. No batteries. No ignition caps. How the hell was he supposed to set it off?

C-2 in place, Howell waved his Remington pump at Meade. "Will that crap explode if I shoot it with this?"

Meade shook his head. "Not likely. Unless you want to stand right next to it and poke the muzzle into the C-2. That's not what I would recommend, but keep it in mind if you don't figure out something soon."

They scurried further back under the bridge as a German fired at them from the far bank. The rifle bullet pinged off a girder and splattered in the shallow water. The click and clack of a bolt action rifle echoed off the stone pilings.

Howell took out a handful of double-ought-buck shotgun shells from his map case. "How 'bout if I stick a couple of these in the C-2 and shoot them."

"It's damn dark under here. Think you can hit the primers?"

Howell shrugged his shoulders. "Got a better idea?"

"Nope."

"Then you get out of here. When you're clear, I'll pop the C-2. But if I go down, you got to find the shotgun and finish it off. O.K.?"

Meade grinned at him and laughed. "Sure thing." Meade gave him a pat on the shoulder, slid down to the water and slowly crept downstream and out from under the protection of the bridge.

Overhead the shooting had intensified on both sides of the river. Maybe some more GIs, reinforcements, had finally shown up. About time. Water dripped from the underside of the bridge down to his cap. He cringed when a ricocheting bullet pinged off the girder and thudded into the mud next to his face, narrowly missing him and the C-2 as he packed it around the girder joint.

Howell worked two shotgun shells deep into the wad of C-2, leaving their brass ends exposed. How big a blast would this stuff make? Enough to kill him? You bet. He slithered back until the brass cases were barely visible in the light from the burning tank fuel that had begun dripping between the planks, tendrils of flame reaching down like he was in the very center of hell.

A shout, then a beam of yellow light from the other side of the river raked across the jetsam floating down the river. The light dropped lower, then up, reflecting off the planks overhead as the holder of the light entered the water, the flashlight bobbing across the water's surface.

Howell spotted Meade, his head and shoulders showing in the reflected light, waiting for him just clear of the bridge. Idiot should run like hell. If this worked, the explosion would drop the bridge on top of them. If it didn't get them, the Germans would.

The shotgun suddenly felt too light in Howell's hands. How many shells had he fired at the radar station? How many were left in the gun? How many in the bag? The light was almost to the middle of the stream. Bastard should have drowned by now. Too late to worry the details. Meade's .45 fired. The light wavered.

Howell sighted down the sawed-off shotgun barrel at the brass cases stuck in the C-2. Here goes. He fired. The shotgun blast reverberated under the bridge. Howell forced his eyes back open.

Damned bridge. Damned war. Howell had to stop himself from running back up to the C-2 and plunging the muzzle of the shotgun deep inside the explosive. Joey, the other guys might could damn well use some help when this was done. So do it and stay alive. Now!

The light flashed over the underside of the bridge, the bearer just feet away in the darkness, his light joined by an array of beams criss-crossing across the water from the German side.

Howell racked another shell into the chamber and snapped off a quick shot toward the flashlight moving toward him. The light beam drooped down in the water and dimmed to nothing. From the far bank a barrage of muzzle flashes reached out in the darkness from up and down the river, all coming toward him, bullets pocking the mud around him. Suddenly he went down, a sledgehammer blow to his leg. He rolled across the mud back toward the abutment. He had lost track of the exact location of the C-2, blinded by the gunfire.

He ran his tongue around his mouth, feeling where he had bitten it during the crash landing. One last try. He pointed the shotgun into the darkness, praying he was on target, and fired.

The explosion lifted him out of the mud and threw him into the river with a numbing splash. He came to a stop, then felt himself sliding across the mud, pulled by his jacket collar. Vibrations through the water shook his teeth, followed by a loud grumble and a sharp creak. He could hear footsteps running across the planks overhead, yells.

A massive rumble began, so strong he felt it through the mud under his butt. The voices on the bridge turned to screams. Rocks dislodged from the abutments and tumbled down into the water, splashing spray into his eyes and pelting his head with bits of masonry and grit.

Howell wiped the mud and water from his face in time to look up and see the near girder slowly twist, then more quickly the side supports ripped free. With a grinding crash the entire span collapsed, metal screeching as it twisted and ripped apart. Howell stared up, watching the burning tank slide down the collapsing bridge, then stop with a shriek of twisted iron, jammed sideways in the girders.

"Come on, Frank. No time to sightsee."

Howell realized Meade was pulling him through the shallows. He slipped on the silty mud, slick, almost like grease. He clawed his way up the bank and finally scrambled over the top. A beautiful sight. The bridge had collapsed, taking the wounded tank down with it.

When he looked back, a German tank still sat on the other side of the river. When he shook his fist at it, the tank lurched forward toward the collapsed bridge. Howell dived toward a pile of rubble as the tank turret rotated and the machine gun fired a burst across the wrecked bridge.

Son of a bitch! What was it going to take to stop these bastards?

CHAPTER 24 - 3/506TH PRCHT INF

Pfister sprayed a short burst from the Thompson at the Germans gathered on the far end of the bridge, then ducked behind the rubble as return fire twanged overhead. "Did you see that, Lieutenant? They dropped the bridge." He crawled to the side and peeked through a gap in the remains of the low wall as Allen fired a burst from a BAR.

Two men, covered in mud, scrambled toward them. "Watch out," Pfister warned as Allen raised the BAR. "I think that's two of our guys." Pfister wondered about the pilot's marksmanship with all the blood running down his temple. "Give them some cover, but careful." Allen joined in as Pfister fired over the two men, putting down cover fire as they crawled across the open ground between the wall and the river bank.

Pfister fired in short bursts, aware they were low on ammunition, only firing when he spotted a German head. "L. T., I'll be glad when the rest of our guys get here. Been a long night. I need a drink, and from the smell of things, I think this was a tavern before that damn German tank blew down the walls," he said during a lull.

Allen sniffed the air and grinned over at Pfister. "I believe you're right. I smelled it, too. I didn't say anything. I thought I had just pissed in my pants." He held up a magazine. "My last," and slapped it in the BAR. "You can have the wine. I want me a good old canteen cup of K-rat instant coffee."

"We need more than coffee. We did good, but without ammo, this isn't going to last much longer. Krauts will figure out a way to swarm over. Sooner or later, they're going to find a bridge, ford up at some shallow place, swim across or something; or worse, put some artillery down on us. I don't know what the Germans are thinking, not bringing up their artillery. He cocked his head to the side. A hum of aircraft buzzed somewhere out of sight. "Our planes might have something to do with that," Pfister said. "Listen."

"Might be too late for us," Allen replied. "We got troubles coming. We're going to have to run for it pretty soon, find some help. Just look across. More German helmets across the way than before."

Pfister looked across. "I agree. I can see another tank nosing around the corner. Can't cross, but can sure put a hurting on us. Once we get these two back, let's run for it."

Pfister pushed himself up on his knees, ready to make a final dash down the street, when a rocket spurted out from their flank and struck the oncoming German tank with a crack.

"Jeeze!" Allen exclaimed.

The volume of friendly gunfire picked up as GIs surged into the ruins all around Pfister.

"Here they are, Captain." Joey squatted down beside Pfister, followed by Keller and a new guy. "You guys seen my dad?" Joey threw down an empty Panzerfaust launcher.

Face streaked with soot and dirt, jump jacket ripped, mud caked on his helmet, the new guy looked like he had gone through hell.

"I'm Captain Forester, 506th. The fly boy says y'all from a bunch of different units. Who's in charge here?" he asked.

Pfister nodded toward the two men crawling toward them. "The man in the stupid looking pilot's cap and flight jacket is our ranking man, Captain Howell, C-47 pilot. The man in the loser ball cap next to me with the BAR is Lieutenant Allen, Waco pilot. I'm Pfister, G2, probably the ranking NCO who can still walk." He looked up and down the line of men sprawled in the rubble. "I don't think we got any two men from the same unit." Pfister looked at Joey and laughed. "Frank's your dad? Jeeze, Joey. Help the old man out of the line of fire before he gets his butt shot off, for Christ's sake," and fired the last of his magazine at a head bobbing along the far bank.

Forester shook his head. "How many of you?"

"Still walking?" Pfister thought a minute. "Six last count. Four more of our guys got trapped over on the other side of the river. I heard a boat start up, so they're probably out helping the Navy find their way ashore by now. Before they left they slowed down the tanks across the way, set one on fire and blew the turret off another. The two crawling in the dirt blew the bridge. We got some wounded back with a doc in the field; where you and Joey should be, Keller."

Keller spat in the dirt, slid a new looking M1 over the wall and fired a couple of shots toward the bobbing helmets across the way. "Shit. How 'bout you Sarge, still up here on the line with one wing.

For me, I got tired of helping the doc. A medic showed up, doing a hell of a better job."

"Hey. Did you guys see the grey-haired kid back down the street wrestling the seventy-five? He popped that tank sitting ass-crooked in the river. Did he get the gun set back up?" Meade asked as he tumbled over the berm. "We need to get some fire on the other side."

"The kid that brought the gun in the wagon? Yeah. I saw a couple of guys back there helping him get his gun right side up. Looked like he was getting it ready to shoot. Real ramrod, hollering at the other guys like he was a sergeant or something, real fired up."

Pfister flinched when Joey suddenly screamed in his ear, "Pop! Get your ass over here. Are you bleeding? Son of a bitch."

Howell looked like he had stopped to rest in the gap between the river and the wall. Joey jumped over the wall, grabbed Howell and dragged him back over the rubble. The two tumbled to the ground.

Howell rolled to his back, face covered with mud. "Did you see that, son? I blew down that bridge with my shotgun." He looked down at his leg, blood staining a ripped pants leg.

"And with a shit-pile of luck," Meade added as bullets whizzed overhead.

"I ought to shoot you myself for acting so crazy. Mom will kill me if I don't get you back in one piece." Joey ripped open Howell's pants and wrapped a field dressing around the wound.

Pfister squinted down the river toward the Channel as the edge of the sun broke the horizon and sliced through the haze. "We all needed a little luck to make it through the night. But morning's here. We're alive, over here, and the German tanks are still over there."

"And guys off the landing craft are coming in from the beach, damn near unopposed." Forester added. "Thank God you guys held off the tanks. You did one hell of a job."

An American fighter buzzed overhead, swooped around and fired a salvo of rockets at an unseen target.

"Hot damn. Just what we need." Pfister pulled out his pipe and stuffed it with his last bit of Bond Street, ignoring the bullets cracking overhead. "We paid a steep price, but we did the job. And we'll keep at it, until the Nazi bastards are done."

That's what Papa would want.

EPILOGUE
MISSING STICKS CHARACTERS
and where they might have been in 1960
in order of appearance

Tech Sergeant Alex Pfister, Division G2 Intelligence Analyst; originally from Heilbronn, Germany, now from Newark, Delaware and Dean of Students at a prestigious college;

Corporal William "Will" Meade, 1/501st Parachute Infantry Regiment; Squad Leader, from Los Angeles, California, is now president of a local bank in Burbank;

Private First Class "Lars" Larsen, 1/501st Parachute Infantry Regiment; Infantryman from Middleburg, Tennessee, owner of a automobile dealership in Knoxville and married to Betty Greyson;

Captain Frank Howell, 435th Troop Carrier Group; C-47 pilot from Key West, moved his float plane charter service from Key West to Anchorage to be close to his grandchildren and visit his son, Joey;

Lieutenant Joey Howell, 435th Troop Carrier Group; C-47 copilot from Key West, Florida, Colonel, USAF is a staff officer with the Alaskan Air Command Headquarters stationed in Elmendorf, Alaska. He never flew after WWII due to his head injury;

Private Rudy Livingston, 3/501st Parachute Infantry Regiment; Infantryman, Myrtle Beach, South Carolina, is now the owner of Livingston Seafoods and a fleet of fishing boats;

Sergeant Barkley, 3/501st Parachute Infantry Regiment; Mess Sergeant, died 6 June, 1944 from wounds suffered in combat;

Stanley (Stan) Levine, technician for Western Electric; heads a classified electronics research team for the US Government;

Corporal Louis (Lou) Keller, 2/506th Parachute Infantry Regiment; Infantryman from El Paso, Texas, now ranch foreman in central Texas;

MISSING STICKS

Lieutenant O'Shey, 3/505ᵗʰ Parachute Infantry Regiment; 82d Airborne, Mobile, Alabama, died of wounds 6 June 1944;

Private Stimson, Regimental Communications Platoon, 502ⁿᵈ Parachute Infantry Regiment; signalman from Ellerbe, North Carolina, died of wounds 6 Jun 1944;

First Sergeant Juan Salazar, 377ⁿᵈ Parachute Artillery Regiment; Battery first sergeant, born in San Juan, Puerto Rico, joined the International Brigade and wounded in 1936 in Madrid, Spain fighting the Fascists, returned to the United Sates and enlisted in the US Army in 1937, now retired in New York City with a medical disability from his wounds;

Private Jake Rankin, 377ⁿᵈ Parachute Infantry Regiment; artilleryman, farmer from Lumberton, NC, now manager of the Lumberton Tobacco Market, found Jeannette Guignard in France in 1947, married her and became the adoptive father of Francois Guignard, Jeannette's son;

Sergeant Harry Rule, 1/502ⁿᵈ Parachute Infantry Regiment; Squad Leader, recruited from the US Forestry Service Smokejumper facility at Ninemile Camp at Missoula, Montana, died of wounds on 24 December, 1944 at Bastogne, saving the life of a fellow trooper;

Anna-Maria Billard of the French Resistance; died of wounds on 6 June 1944;

Private Luke Dawson, 326ᵗʰ Airborne Engineer Battalion; demolition specialist, smuggled Dawg back to England on an LST, married Rebecca back in Brighton between D-Day and Market Garden, decided to leave the farm after a year back from the war, became a veterinarian and now lives in northern Virginia;

Captain Francois Jordain, 326ᵗʰ Airborne Medical Battalion; Combat Surgeon, born in Maine, now maintains a family practice in Portland, Maine;

EPILOGUE

Jeannette Guignard; born in a French village on the Douve River between Carentan and the English Channel, originally used Darrell Williamson's dog tag unsuccessfully trying to convince the US Consulate that Williamson was the father of her son. Married Jake Rankin.

Francois Guignard; son of Jeannette Guignard and Obergefreiter Friedrich Braun, now lives in Raleigh, North Carolina as a US citizen and the adopted son of Jake Rankin.

Captain Sonny Talbot, 434th Troop Carrier Unit; Waco Glider pilot, now owner of a construction company in Denver;

Lieutenant Wilber Allen, 434th Troop Carrier Unit; Waco Glider copilot, now Brigadier General in the US Army at Fort Bragg;

Tech Sergeant Tony Watson, 327th Glider Infantry Regiment Motor Sergeant, now manages the Kansas City hub for a major trucking company;

Private Roscoe Jefferson, A Battery, 81st Airborne Field Artillery Battalion; (57mm A-T Gunner), died of wounds 6 June, 1944;

Sergeant Riley, A Battery, 81st Airborne Field Artillery Battalion; (57mm A-T Gun Chief), died of injuries suffered in a glider crash 6 June, 1944;

Private Johnson, 327th Glider Infantry; mechanic, recently assigned from the 401st GIR, died from wounds suffered in the glider assault on 6 June 1944;

Private Marion (Sparks) Mahan, 101st Airborne Signal Company; radio operator, attended Georgia Tech and is now the operations manager for a television station in Atlanta;

Private Darrell Williamson; died 6 June 1944 sacrificing himself to smother an enemy grenade and saving the lives of Jeannette Guignard and her newborn son.

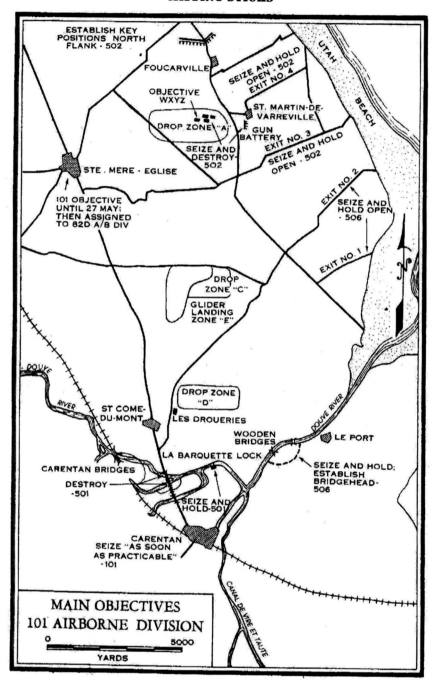

ESTABLISH KEY POSITIONS NORTH FLANK - 502

FOUCARVILLE

SEIZE AND HOLD OPEN - 502 EXIT NO. 4

UTAH BEACH

OBJECTIVE WXYZ

ST. MARTIN-DE-VARREVILLE

DROP ZONE "A"

GUN BATTERY

EXIT NO. 3

SEIZE AND DESTROY - 502

SEIZE AND HOLD OPEN - 502

STE. MERE - EGLISE

EXIT NO. 2

SEIZE AND HOLD OPEN - 506

101 OBJECTIVE UNTIL 27 MAY; THEN ASSIGNED TO 82D A/B DIV

EXIT NO. 1

DROP ZONE "C"

GLIDER LANDING ZONE "E"

DOUVE RIVER

DROP ZONE "D"

ST COME-DU-MONT

LES DROUERIES

DOUVE RIVER

WOODEN BRIDGES

LE PORT

LA BARQUETTE LOCK

SEIZE AND HOLD: ESTABLISH BRIDGEHEAD - 506

CARENTAN BRIDGES

DESTROY - 501

SEIZE AND HOLD - 501

CARENTAN SEIZE "AS SOON AS PRACTICABLE" - 101

CANAL DE VIRE ET TAUTE

MAIN OBJECTIVES
101 AIRBORNE DIVISION

0   5000
YARDS

N

EPILOGUE
THE FACTS

A few facts, as I have found them in my research, always subject to correction:

The Mission:

The 101st Airborne Division first saw combat during the Normandy invasion—6 June 1944. The division, as part of the VII Corps assault, jumped in the dark morning before H-Hour to seize positions west of Utah Beach. Given the mission of anchoring the corps' southern flank, the division was also to eliminate the German's secondary beach defenses, allowing the seaborne forces of the 4th Infantry Division, once ashore, to continue inland. The SCREAMING EAGLES were to capture the causeway bridges that ran behind the beach between St. Martin-de-Varreville and Pouppeville. In the division's southern sector, it was to seize the la Barquette lock and destroy a highway bridge northwest of the town of Carentan and a railroad bridge further west. At the same time elements of the division were to establish two bridgeheads on the Douve River at le Port, northeast of Carentan.

Critical to this plan was the isolation of the beaches from the German Armored forces positioned inland and under the direct control of Hitler.

The one—albeit critical—fact altered in the story is Hitler's release of the armored forces during the early morning of 6 June. Had he done so in reality, those missing men could have been critical to safeguarding the troops coming ashore, as portrayed in this novel.

Extracts from the book *UTAH BEACH TO CHERBOURG (6 June-27 June 1944)* found on the US Army Center of Military History web site at <u>http://www.history.army.mil/books/wwii/utah/utah2.htm</u> summarize the six hours of death and destruction between midnight and dawn:

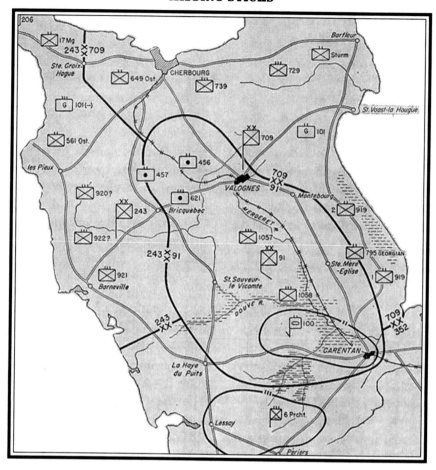

"At 2215 on D minus 1, 432 C-47's began taking off from 7 departure airdromes in England, with 6,600 paratroops of the 101st Airborne Division. They were scheduled to begin dropping at H minus 6 hours. *(H-hour was set for 0630 British Double Standard Time – jmt)* At dawn (H minus 2 hours) they were to be reinforced by approximately 150 glider troops from 51 gliders, and at dusk (H plus 15 hours) by an additional 165 in 32 gliders. Preceding the main echelons of paratroops by half an hour were 20 pathfinder aircraft which had the mission of marking six drop zones (for both divisions) and one landing zone. Marking of the zones was not entirely successful, but all of the pathfinder teams carried out at least part of their missions.

218

EPILOGUE

Paratroop echelons approached the Cotentin from the west and made their landfall in the vicinity of les Pieux. Formations were tight until reaching the coast, but from the coast to the Merderet cloud banks loosened the formations, and east of the Merderet flak scattered them further. In general the Division did not have a good drop, although better than that of the 82d Airborne Division. About 1,500 troops were either killed or captured and approximately 60 percent of the equipment dropped was lost when the bundles fell into swamps or into fields covered by enemy fire. Only a fraction of the division's organized strength could initially be employed on the planned missions, and many of the missions carried out were undertaken by mixed groups which did not correspond with original assignments."

And later:

"The plan of the 101st Airborne Division called for the seizure of the four inland exits-the western ends of causeways-from the inundated area west of Utah Beach between St. Martin-de-Varreville and Pouppeville. *In the southern part of the division's sector two bridges across the Douve River, on the main highway northwest of Carentan and the railroad bridge to the west, were to be destroyed. In addition, the division was to seize and hold the la Barquette lock and establish two bridgeheads over the Douve at le Port northeast of Carentan. (emphasis added - jmt).* The sum of these missions thus provided for the clearing of the enemy's secondary beach defenses and the organization of the Corps' southern flank for defense and further exploitation. After being relieved in the beachhead area by the 4th Division, the 101st was to seize Carentan and establish contact with V Corps, fusing the Utah and Omaha beachheads. Thereafter the 101st Airborne Division was ordered to protect the southern flank of VII Corps east of the Merderet River. The division would be reinforced by the attachment of a company of tanks of the 70th Tank Battalion, the 65th Armored Field Artillery Battalion and a troop of the 4th Cavalry Reconnaissance Squadron when these were landed by sea."

The Sixteen Missing Sticks:

The missing planes are listed by planeload (stick/chalk) number and unit, as indicated on the maps in *Rendezvous with Destiny*. The unit designation on the left indicates the principal unit, but often paratroopers from other units, especially combat support and combat service support, were mixed in, especially communications, medical and engineers:

501st PIR	502nd PIR	506th PIR
Stick – Unit	Stick – Unit	Stick – Unit
13 – 1/501	14 – 1/502	17 – 1/506
29 – 1/501	4 – 2/502	18 – 1/506
30 – 1/501	81 – 3/502	66 – 2/506
31 – 1/501		11 – 3/506
33 – 1/501		11 – 3/506
18 – 3/501		11 – 3/506
54 – 2/501		
32 – 3/501		

5 – 506 Pathfinders with stick leader Lt. Gordon C. Rothwell, objective DZ "C," crash landed in the English Channel. All were saved.

The premise for the crash landing in the English Channel in *Chapter 1 - Pathfiners* was taken from First Sergeant O'Malley's account, quoted in *D-Day with the Screaming Eagles*. O'Malley was a member of Rothwell's stick. Their plane was hit by ground fire and crash landed in Channel where all survived.

Glider Mission Chicago:

Fifty-four Waco CG4-A Gliders departed from Aldermaston in England flown by the 434th Transportation Command. The Wacos carried 155 men including elements from two batteries of the 81st AA Bn, 326th Engineers, 327th Glider Infantry Regiment (Anti-tank Platoon and Headquarters Company), 101st Signal, 326th Medical and Division staff, plus one bulldozer, sixteen 57mm A-T guns and twenty-five vehicles.

REFERENCES

In addition to the many tales, memoirs and scholarly articles found on the Internet, I used the following references as a source for much of the background in *Missing Sticks*:

BOOKS:

Beyond Band of Brothers, Major Dick Winters, 2006;

D-Day with the Screaming Eagles, George E. Koskimaki, 2006;

June 6, 1944, D-Day, the Climatic Battle of World War II, Stephen E. Ambrose, 1994;

Rendezvous with Destiny, a History of the 101ˢᵗ Airborne Division, Rapport and Northwood, 1948.

WEB SITES (many of which supported my research with answers to specific questions):

D-Day: **http://www.6juin1944.com**

Silent Wings Museum: **http://silentwings.ci.lubbock.tx.us**

The DC-3 Aviation Museum: **http://www.centercomp.com**

The Dwight D. Eisenhower Presidential Library and
   Museum Website:
      http://www.eisenhower.archives.gov

US Army Center of Military History:
      http://www.history.army.mil

Waco CG-4A Combat Glider:
      http://www.aircraftresourcecenter.com

World War II Airborne Demonstration Team Foundation:
      http://www.wwiiadt.org

World War II by the Book: **http://www.wwiibythebook.com**

Airborne in Normandy:
      http://www.airborneinnormandy.com

The US Airborne World War II:
      http://www.ww2-airborne.us.

THE AUTHOR

J. M. Taylor is the author of the award-winning south Florida thriller, **FLASH OF EMERALD**, and the international thriller, **BEHIND THE GREEN WATER**. Combining his experiences as a paratrooper, nuclear weapons specialist and operations research analyst with travels in the Far and Middle East, Europe and the States, he packs a ton of adventure into action-filled page-turners. First Place winner in the Mystery/Thriller (Unpublished) category of the Florida Writers Association 2007 Royal Palm Literary Awards Contest, **GULF WINDS**, expected out in Spring, 2009, introduces Homosassa fishing guide and Iraq combat veteran Uly Grant to bribery, terrorism and romance, right here on Florida's Gulf coast.

Read more about Taylor and his books at http://johnmtaylor.com.

2796203

Made in the USA

Faces streaked with soot or burnt cork, over six thousand paratroopers and glidermen of the 101st Airborne Division Screaming Eagles jumped or crashed into the swamps, canals, hedgerows and villages of the Cotentin Peninsula of France sometime after midnight on D-Day.

Over four hundred C-47 Dakotas carried the Screaming Eagles through the darkness and into a thick cloud bank that night. One load of pathfinders crashed into the English Channel. Planes were seen to explode in midair. Others crashed and burned past all recognition. Just before dawn, the initial glider serial slammed between the hedgerows, into trees and each other.

Come dawn, eighteen planes, each carrying a stick of paratroopers, were missing.

Eighteen Missing Sticks.

What could, what would the missing men have done if these sticks had made it safely to the ground? Not every man is brave in combat. Not every man is a hero. Everyone makes mistakes. However, in the fire of battle, a handful of heroes is forged as bravery overwhelms the fear that naturally keeps soldiers from harm. Would these men have been the heroes if they had entered the battle?

This is a novel about those missing Screaming Eagles, their buddies and the friends and enemies they met on the ground on June 6th, 1944. Every character, every incident, is fictional, hopefully representative of the diverse men who flew into darkness and danger that fateful night, but never came back. This is a novel to honor their memory.

J. M. Taylor served with the 101st Airborne Division Screaming Eagles as a platoon leader and battalion commander. Airborne and air assault qualified, a scuba diver and trained as a system engineer, he also designed military command and control systems in civilian life. Using his background in nuclear weapons and extensive travel in the Far and Middle East, Europe and across the States, he packs a ton of adventure into an action-filled page-turner.

Read more about Taylor
and his works at
http://johnmtaylor.com.

ISBN 978-1879043008

9 781879 043008